SAXON HEROINES

WOMEN OF DETERMINATION AND COURAGE

Saxon Heroines: A Northumbrian Novel/Sandra Wagner-Wright.–1st Edition

ISBN 978-1-7354132-0-4 (Paperback)
ISBN 978-0-9963845-9-9 (eBook)

SAXON HEROINES

WOMEN OF DETERMINATION AND COURAGE

Sandra Wagner-Wright

WAGNER
WRIGHT
ENTERPRISES

"Blessed are the peacemakers:
For they shall be called
the Children of God."
— Matthew 5:9

Contents

PART 3: ELFLEDA

Anno Domini 670 — *Anno Domini* 706

Cast Of Primary Characters

In Order of Appearance

Part 1: Ethelberga

Hildeburg, Princess of Northumbria (Later, Abbess of Streoneshalh)

Hereswid, Princess of Northumbria, Hildeburg's sister

Breguswid, Mother of Hildeburg and Hereswid

Edwin, King of Northumbria

Ethelberga of Kent, Queen of Northumbria (Later, Abbess of Lyminge)

Bishop Paulinus (Later, Archbishop of York, Archbishop of Rochester)

Enfleda, Princess of Northumbria (Later, Queen of Northumbria)

Coifi, High Priest of Woden

Penda, King of Mercia

Part 2: Enfleda

Hildeburg, Princess of Northumbria (Later, Abbess of Streoneshalh)

Ethelberga, Abbess of Lyminge

Enfleda, Princess of Northumbria (Later, Queen of Northumbria)

Oswy, King of Northumbria

Alhfrith, Prince of Northumbria (Later, sub-king of Deira)

Aidan, Abbot of Lindisfarne

Egfrid, Prince of Northumbria (Later, King of Northumbria)

Wilfrid, Student (Later, Bishop of York)

Elfleda, Princess of Northumbria (Later, Abbess of Streoneshalh)

Ermenburg, Prince Egfrid's Companion (Later, Queen of Northumbria)

Etheldreda of East Anglia, Prince Egfrid's Consort (Later, Queen of Northumbria, Abbess of Ely)

Cadmon, First English Poet

Colman, Abbot of Lindisfarne

Part 3: Elfleda

Hildeburg, Abbess of Streoneshalh

Elfleda, Princess of Northumbria (Later, Abbess of Streoneshalh)

Egfrid, King of Northumbria

Wilfrid, Bishop of York

Enfleda, Dowager Queen of Northumbria, Co-Abbess of Streoneshalh

Etheldreda, Queen of Northumbria (Later, Abbess of Ely)

Ebbe, Abbess of Coldingham

Ermenburg, Queen of Northumbria

Cuthbert, Abbot of Lindisfarne (Later, Bishop of Lindisfarne)

Wilfrid, Bishop of York

Trumwine, Bishop of Albercorn

Aldfrid, King of Northumbria

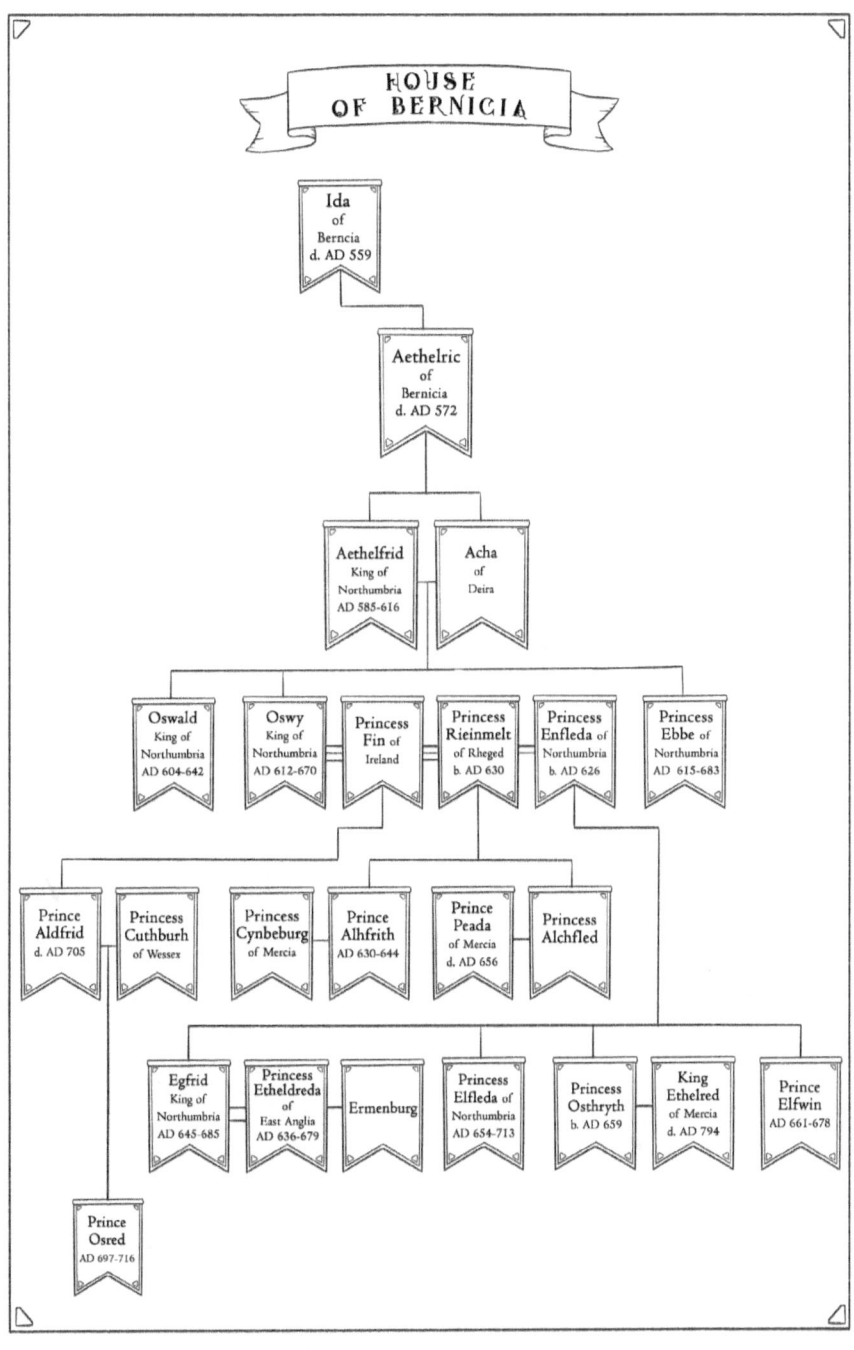

HOUSE OF BERNICIA

Ida of Bernica d. AD 559

Aethelric of Bernicia d. AD 572

Aethelfrid King of Northumbria AD 585-616

Acha of Deira

Oswald King of Northumbria AD 604-642

Oswy King of Northumbria AD 612-670

Princess Fin of Ireland

Princess Rieinmelt of Rheged b. AD 630

Princess Enfleda of Northumbria b. AD 626

Princess Ebbe of Northumbria AD 615-683

Prince Aldfrid d. AD 705

Princess Cuthburh of Wessex

Princess Cynbeburg of Mercia

Prince Alhfrith AD 630-644

Prince Peada of Mercia d. AD 656

Princess Alchfled

Egfrid King of Northumbria AD 645-685

Princess Etheldreda of East Anglia AD 636-679

Ermenburg

Princess Elfleda of Northumbria AD 654-713

Princess Osthryth b. AD 659

King Ethelred of Mercia d. AD 794

Prince Elfwin AD 661-678

Prince Osred AD 697-716

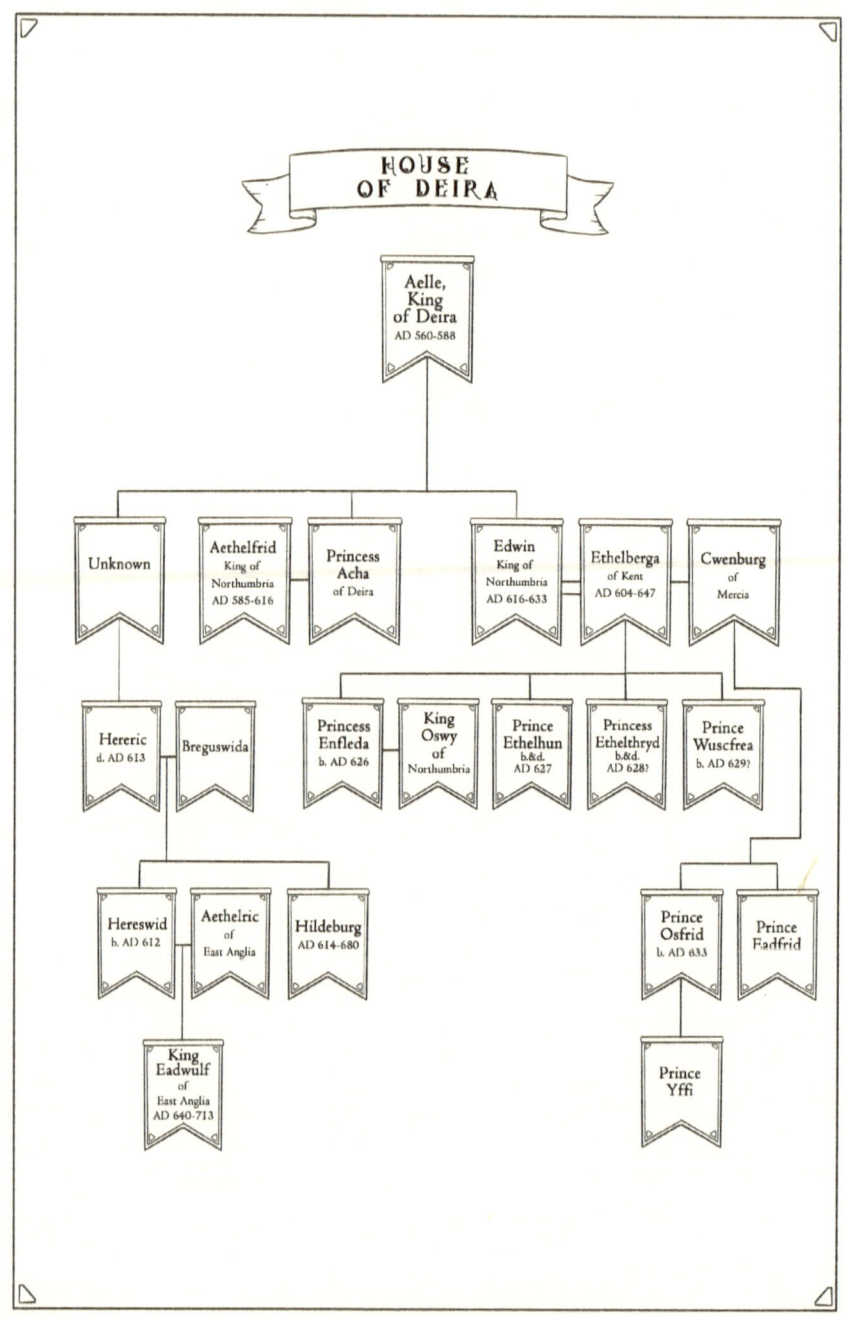

HOUSE OF DEIRA

Aelle, King of Deira
AD 560-588

Unknown

Aethelfrid
King of
Northumbria
AD 585-616

Princess Acha
of Deira

Edwin
King of
Northumbria
AD 616-633

Ethelberga
of Kent
AD 604-647

Cwenburg
of
Mercia

Hereric
d. AD 613

Breguswida

Princess Enfleda
b. AD 626

King Oswy
of
Northumbria

Prince Ethelhun
b.&d.
AD 627

Princess Ethelthryd
b.&d.
AD 628?

Prince Wuscfrea
b. AD 629?

Hereswid
b. AD 612

Aethelric
of
East Anglia

Hildeburg
AD 614-680

Prince Osfrid
b. AD 633

Prince Eadfrid

King Eadwulf
of
East Anglia
AD 640-713

Prince Yffi

Dunnichen

Firth of Forth

Coldingham
Lindisfarne
Farne Islands
Yeavering
Coquet Island
BERNICIA
Bamburg
Heretu
Streoneshalch
Carlisle
Hexham
Catterick
RHEGED
DEIRA
Ripon
Driffield
York
Goodmanham
Sancton
Hatfield
Chase
River Humber
Villa by River
Derwent
LINDSEY
MERCIA
GWYNEDD
EAST
ANGLIA
ESSEX
River Thames
Rochester
KENT
Reculver
WESSEX
SUSSEX
Lyminge

Chapter 1

Anno Domini 624 – The Year Princess Ethelberga of Kent Marries King Edwin of Northumbria

Hildeburg, Princess of Northumbria
July

I'm not supposed to be here, but I can't tear myself away. I'm mesmerized, watching the red deer graze with her fawn close beside her. The smaller creature balances on spindly legs and tries to nurse. The hind ignores it and continues tearing into the grass. Tiny insects buzz near my eyes and land on my neck, but I don't slap them. The doe lifts her head. Bits of grass cling to her mouth. *Does she smell me?* I hold my breath. *Don't run away.* After a moment, the hind returns to her meal. I can't hold my breath anymore. My exhale makes a small whooshing sound, but the doe doesn't notice.

I shouldn't be here. I'm supposed to be in the Queen's Hall helping my mother. I roll onto my back and squint at the sun until clouds move in front of it.

Someone calls me. The voice gets louder as it nears my hiding place. The doe lifts her head again, whirls, and leaps into the brush, her fawn trying to keep up.

"Hill-*day*!" the voice shrieks.

I push myself up, brush off my clothes, and turn around. I see that it's one of the shepherd boys. He's tall for his age, with light, matted hair. His voice hasn't cracked yet.

"If you're going to call for me, you should say my name properly. It's *Hildeburg*, as you well know."

"I wouldn't have to say it at all if you didn't run off so often. Your sister's looking for you."

I jump up and tweak the boy's cap. He straightens it, exasperated. "I've enough to do without running after you," he whines. "What were you doing?"

I glance back at the open grass. "Watching."

"Aren't you a bit old for that?"

I pout. "What would you know about it? All you do is take the sheep out." I stamp my foot. The lad gives me a quizzical look and starts walking. "You can't walk ahead of me," I stammer. "I'm a *princess*."

"Then stop acting like a dairymaid. I must see to my dogs. I have to go back to the pasture tomorrow, and my lead dog has a limp."

"If you're so busy, why did you come for me?"

"Hereswid sent me."

I smile. The boy is afraid of my sister. When I catch up to him, he hands me a sprig of rosemary—the aromatic herb of remembrance and death.

Despite the bright sunshine, the Queen's Hall is dim. Smoke swirls around the cauldron, lingering over the central fire before wending its way out through the roof. I spot Hereswid; she is fingering her amber beads in the far corner.

"Where's Mother?"

My sister raises her head. "More to the point, where were *you*? Lying in the grass again?"

"What makes you say that?"

"It's all over your sleeves. You could at least brush it off before you come in."

I look down at the bits of soil and grass still clustered at my elbows and wrists. I brushed my tunic but forgot my sleeves.

"Did you want me for something?"

Hereswid shakes her head in disgust. "I have important news. Our uncle, the king, has given us a great honor."

"How can he give us honor when *he* has none?" I wince as the words fly out of my mouth. *When will I learn to hold my tongue?*

Hereswid looks toward the doorway. "Keep your voice down," she hisses. "How can you say such a thing? He brought us out of exile and made us part of his court."

I shrug. "Only because Queen Cwenburg reminded him. Now that she's dead, I'm surprised he thinks of us at all."

"You'll get us both in trouble for saying such things. The king's new wife arrives in a few days. Now isn't the time to moan over the past."

I'll never forget Queen Cwenburg. She clothed us, fed us at her table, and made us members of her court. Now she's dead, and everyone acts like she never existed. "Cwenburg gave King Edwin two strong sons. Surely he could wait before marrying again. Aren't there raids for him to lead?"

My sister's lips move as if separate from her face. "You mustn't do, say, or even *think* anything disloyal to our uncle," she says. "Especially now, when he honors our father by giving us both a role in the King's Hall."

I glance at the doorway and whisper, "What do you mean?"

"When Princess Ethelberga arrives, our mother will serve in place of the king's lady, and we will be among the serving maids. Everyone will watch us. Everyone will know Edwin the King sponsors us."

I think about the warriors, the cup-bearing, the drinking horns. I ponder the music and boasting.

"What pleases you so about being on display?" I ask.

"Don't ask such stupid questions. The new queen will respect us, and the king will make good marriages for us. We'll attain the position our mother should have had." Hereswid wears a satisfied smile, before quickly frowning again. "And you won't embarrass us, or give them any reason to think we don't know how to behave. Do you understand me? *Do* you?" Hereswid squeezes my ear.

"Yes," I manage to gasp out, pushing her hand away. My fingers are sticky from the rosemary, and its earthy fragrance clings to my skin.

Hereswid wrinkles her nose and says, "For goodness sake, go wash. Then go to the Queen's Hall."

Queen's Hall, indeed. I kick up dirt as I walk across the compound to Queen Cwenburg's Hall. *I won't accept a new queen.* Slaves and servants hurry past me carrying wall hangings. Others sweep old rushes out through the doorways. The weaving looms stand outside, their weights and spindles strangely still. I don't know how we'll ever untangle the threads. *Why did Mother allow such waste?* I step aside as two servants drag out a bench.

Inside, the fire releases aromatic herbs, and I smell rosemary again. Mother stands where the queen's chair belongs.

"Hildeburg." She gestures for me to come forward. I step around the workers and greet her with a kiss.

"I see your sister found you. I could have used your help earlier."

"May I take you outside, Lady Mother? It's too warm in here. Why did you light a high fire on such a hot day? And why are the looms outside?"

Mother takes inventory of the activities and accepts my arm. I start to take her to the queen's chair, now sitting outside in the shade. She redirects me to a stool beside it. A slave hands us cups of ale.

"What happened to your ear?"

I shrug. "Hereswid and I had a disagreement."

Mother takes off my cap and moves my hair to the side. "You'll have a bruise. Too bad it won't be green to match the grass stains on your sleeves." She winks, then puts on her serious face. "Hildeburg, you must make amends with your sister. You're not a child anymore. This is your tenth summer."

I hang my head. "I'm sorry, Lady Mother, but truly, I've no amends to make. Hereswid acts like Queen Cwenburg never existed. Mother, she was a good wife to the king and a good friend to us. But Hereswid, well, she acts like the queen no longer matters." I push my foot into the dirt.

Mother detaches her comb from her kirtle and begins looking for lice in my hair. "I see you keep your cap on, as I advised." Her fingers work in tandem with the comb. She parts the follicles and peers at my scalp. Then she looks away, deep in thought. "Hildeburg, have I told you about the dream I had before you were born?"

"About the necklace?"

"It was a terrible time. Your father was dead, and I thought your sister and I would be next. I didn't know who to trust, and I couldn't flee with you in my belly. I ate so little the midwife warned me you would die. I prayed to Goddess Freya for your survival and sent gifts to her shrine. I didn't expect to survive your birth—and then what would have happened? To you? To Hereswid?

"My serving woman brought me a birthing draught. I pushed her hand away. She told me you were taking too long, that I had to rest because you had a right to be born. I was so tired, I took the drink. That's when I dreamed." Mother falls silent. She halfheartedly picks up the comb again.

"But what about the necklace?"

"Ah, yes. The necklace. In my dream, I wandered in a dark forest and stopped to rest under a tree. Something rubbed my belly, but I couldn't feel anything. Finally, I lifted my tunic and saw a necklace so dazzling it lit the darkness. And then I was awake and crying and pushing, and you were born."

"What did you do with the necklace?"

"It wasn't real." Mother laughs. "It was a sign from Freya that you would be a treasure of great value. You're not like other girls, or even boys. Do you understand? Freya chose you for some great purpose."

I clench my eyes closed and concentrate on my future. I'm the daughter of a dead prince. The king can't use me for an alliance, so he'll probably give me to one of his thanes as a reward.

I look at my mother. "I don't think I have a useful purpose."

Mother laughs again and hands me my cap. "Perhaps not. But you'll never find any purpose if you can't accept reality. A new queen is coming, and we'll support the king and make her welcome. Can you do that for me?"

I nod. "But . . ."

"There is no *but*. We belong to King Edwin. As long as he rules, we are safe. And the alliance with Kent makes us strong."

"Yes, Mother."

"And one more thing: Princess Ethelberga didn't choose to come to Northumbria. It is her fate. She'll be a good wife, and we'll support her. Your sister is right. You mustn't speak of Queen Cwenburg again."

"I won't forget her," I say, setting my jaw.

"You are a good, loyal girl. But you're also stubborn." Mother taps my chest. "You can remember the last queen, but you may not speak of her. She's gone from us forever." Mother rises, kisses my forehead. "Survival depends on acceptance."

My uncle, the king, gave a tapestry from his hall to decorate the new queen's chamber. I wonder if she'll notice that the silk fabric—with its exotic, circular designs—has silver threads woven through it. The king took it from a merchant whose boat ran aground, and placed it behind his *giefstol*. Now the king gives it to his bride. She may not regard it as anything special, but it's the most beautiful hanging I've ever seen. Yesterday, Mother placed it behind the queen's chair, and I couldn't tear my eyes away.

This morning, the entire compound fills with horses and carts. The most important thanes mount up to join the king. We follow in the carts. Mother, Hereswid, and I share a cart with our maidservants. The new queen's wagon is twice the size of ours and filled with furs and cushions. And she'll have horses—not oxen, like we do.

The king raises his arm and leads the cavalcade. He's in good spirits, and there's lots of friendly jostling and shoving among his men. The queen will be much pleased with her husband. Men have come from all over Briton to fight with him against Rheged and Mercia. The scops sing of his bravery, of his relentlessness in the thick of battle, willing his men to victory. The new queen must be proud, and perhaps fearful, of her good fortune.

When we arrive at the campsite, fresh venison is already roasting on spits. I jump off the wagon and run to the shore to see if the new queen is near, but I only see endless water. I ask one of the stewards if anyone has seen the queen's boat.

He leers at me. "Why? Are you hoping to join her household?"

I take a step back. "You can't speak to me that way. I'm Hildeburg, the king's niece."

"Then, for the safety of us all, go back to your mother. There are too many men about, drinking their weight in mead. They won't stop to ask for an introduction."

I drop my head, clutching my skirts. "But the queen … ?"

"Her boat will arrive soon, but she won't come ashore until morning." He motions to a slave. "Gunnar will take you back. Now, be away with you."

Gunnar is apparently in no hurry to return to work, so we take our time. He's clean-shaven like the Britons and looks older than most of the slaves. I wonder if our thanes captured him in a battle against Rheged. He doesn't speak. When the wagons come into sight, he gestures for me to go forward, turns back around, and is soon gone.

The venison is black now. The thanes are singing and gambling, having drunk rounds of mead. I give them a wide berth and approach the queen's wagon, where my mother stands directing the servants.

Eventually, we return to our wagon, and I settle in with my sister and the maidservants. I listen to the scop strum his harp and sing about King Edwin's battles until I fall asleep.

"Hildeburg, wake up." Hereswid shakes me. "We have to be at the shore for daybreak." She hands me a beaker of sheep's milk. "Come quickly."

"The sun isn't up yet," I grumble, and reach for my shift.

"Hurry. We have to be there before the queen's boat arrives."

Everyone wears their best clothing. The king and his thanes, dressed in their finest tunics and coats, mount their horses. Beside them, a groom leads a packhorse laden with gifts for the bride. The rest of us assemble according to rank. We walk to the shore in the predawn darkness. The horses whinny softly, as if surprised to be moving. At the shoreline, the king and his thanes ride to the edge of the water and wait. Just as the sun peeks over the horizon, we see the queen's three long ships appear, their carved prows proclaiming their importance. It's so still; I hear the oars striking the water in perfect unison.

When the ships are well into the estuary, our men row out to meet them. The king's thanes reach up to lift the queen's ladies into the boats, but leave her escorts to climb down into the bobbing vessels. It takes three trips to bring the queen's household ashore. The queen arrives last. King Edwin rushes to help her out of the vessel, but her own man, clad entirely in black, steps ashore first and gives her his hand. When the queen steps ashore, everyone but the king falls to one knee. She bows deeply to my uncle, and then stands silently with her hands folded.

My uncle speaks with her man, marches away from the shore, and motions the man to follow. The man turns to the queen and escorts her to her place, facing the king. Then he stands between them. The king removes his gloves and clasps the new queen's hands. I watch the man wrap fabric around their wrists and pray loudly in a language we can't understand. Finally, he gestures above the couple and turns them to face us. King Edwin smiles, and we cheer.

Ethelberga, Queen of Northumbria

My new husband places a thick gold torc around my neck and gives me bracelets for my arms and wrists. I incline my head and allow him to draw my arm into his. We lead the assembly back to a clearing. A woman introduces herself as the king's sister-in-law, Breguswid. She prepared a sumptuous wagon for me, and looks disappointed when I don't invite her to join me for the journey to the king's villa at Sancton. I'm not in the mood for pleasantries. I gesture for my ladies, my scop, and Bishop Paulinus to join me.

My husband and his men mount their horses and thunder ahead of us. I don't expect to see him again until the celebrations begin. The scop begins a song, and Paulinus, with his small dark eyes and pronounced nose, turns to speak with me. I've had enough of his self-importance.

"My lady—"

I raise my hand. "Stop there, my lord bishop. I am now Queen of Northumbria. You may address me as Your Majesty, or Your Grace, but never again as your *lady*."

Paulinus inhales sharply. "You forget yourself. I'm the one who made you queen."

"Spin your tales for someone else. King Edwin needs the alliance with Kent, and my brother, King Eadbald, needs help against the Saxons. You merely facilitate my brother's intentions."

The priest disdainfully looks down his nose at me.

"Your, ah, Grace," he says. "Your duty to God is far greater than any duty to kings. The pope gave you a task as great as that given to your mother, the Frankish princess."

"And I shall have the same result. My husband wants to be a great king. To do that, he needs what I bring—an alliance, more heirs, and the pope's blessing. He does not, however, need *you*. If necessary, another priest can be pressed into service. You are here to serve me and to serve the king. And if you serve us well, I'm sure your reward will be great in heaven and on earth."

Paulinus drops his jaw, closes his mouth, and swallows several times. I've never seen him look so surprised. For once, he's at a loss for words. I allow myself a small smile that doesn't reach my eyes.

"Are we allies, Bishop?" I ask. "Or shall I ask my brother to send another priest?"

Paulinus clenches his fists, but otherwise regains his usual self-control. "We are perfectly aligned," he says smoothly.

"Scop," I call, "sing a new song in the hall tonight. Sing about my wedding to the strongest king in the land."

The lad nods and begins composing a song for tonight's celebration.

When we arrive at the king's villa at Sancton, I can hardly believe my eyes. The courtyard is awash with mud and there are no recognizable pathways between buildings. Men and animals trample over the soggy ground, creating small puddles in their wake. Surely this is a way station.

Edwin and his thanes dismount. *No! This cannot be!* Edwin stands before me, reaching up to lift me down from the wagon. I have no choice but to place my hands on his broad shoulders. He leers at me as he swings me to the ground.

"What do you think, wife? Will you be happy here?" Edwin looks at me expectantly.

My eyes tear up. "I am overcome, my lord. You do me great honor."

Edwin places my hand on his arm. With his thanes acting as escorts for my ladies, we make our way to the Queen's Hall. Our boots make soft, sucking sounds in the mud. A servant holds open the door, and we enter the timbered structure with slivers of light shining between the wall planks.

I clutch my throat in horror. Edwin looks at me, and I realize I should say something. "My lord, I didn't expect so much beauty this far north."

He laughs heartily. "I leave you to your ladies' activities."

I bow, and he leads his men away to their entertainments. My ladies and I stare at each other, shocked by our fate.

The sister-in-law is here again. "May I show you the hall, Your Majesty? We didn't weave new tapestries, because we didn't know what designs you prefer."

"I *prefer* that the walls are covered from the drafts," I say. "Fortunately, I brought tapestries from Kent. Tell me your name again."

"It is Breguswid, Your Majesty. My late husband was the king's brother."

"Well, Breguswid, why haven't you ordered the central fire to be lit?"

"We were away, Your Majesty, and we knew that today everyone would be in the King's Hall. The fire will be ready tomorrow."

I scowl.

Breguswid's eyes dart away from my face. "Your Majesty, may I show you the king's wedding gift to you? It hangs behind your chair."

My ladies and I follow the woman to the dais. The chair has a back, and there are stools for my ladies. The gift is a tapestry with a few silver threads shot through the geometric design, but it's nothing special. Two nervous girls stand below the dais.

"Your Majesty, may I present my daughters, the Princess Hereswid and the Princess Hildeburg."

I'm glad I didn't ask if they were my chambermaids. Unlike their mother, who has dark hair and eyes, these girls both have light eyes and hair that looks like wheat. "You must join my household," I say. The taller girl smiles broadly, but the younger one looks at the floor. "Which of you is Hereswid?"

"I am, Your Majesty." The girl bobs her head.

"Princess Hildeburg." I call the other girl back from her reverie. "Escort me to my chamber."

"It's the next building. I can take you," Hereswid says.

"I didn't ask you. I asked your sister. Hildeburg, I'm waiting."

The child leads us across the mud to a chamber that is smaller than any of my mother's chambers in Kent. There are chinks in the timbered walls, and the central fire smokes. I wave the smoke away. A maidservant cowers in the corner.

"You there!" I shout for emphasis. "Get someone to fix the chimney immediately. I will not greet my husband in a smoke house."

The girl scuttles away.

"Hildeburg, bring torches and servants to clean every corner of this chamber. Tell someone to bring the tapestries in my baggage. And bring furs and clean straw for the bed."

"But Your Majesty, we changed the straw, and cleaned everything for you already."

"Then you didn't do a very good job. Tell your mother it all has to be done again."

Under my eye, Breguswid summons every servant and slave to clean my chamber. They take every piece of furniture outside, sweep out the floor rushes and lay new ones, and refresh the straw in my bed with sweet-smelling herbs. My ladies attach tapestries to the walls, blocking out the drafts and the pinpoints of light that come through chinks between the wall planks. When everything is put back, the aromas of rosemary and lavender replace that of smoke from the fire.

At dusk, the king's men arrive to escort my ladies and me to the King's Hall. I order them to wait while I finish dressing. I'm wearing my costliest tunic with its heavy embroidery, the king's golden gifts, and a headdress my mother brought with her from Frankland. Breguswid is suitably impressed and holds out the household keys for me to hang from my belt. I snatch them from her hand. The woman winces and drops her eyes.

The King's Hall is twice the size of mine, built of planked timber, and has a fire pit running the length of the building. The flames create an interesting shadow play on the walls. I focus on the shapes as I prepare my entrance. The men are well into their mead, but still respectful. I briefly close my eyes, take a deep breath, and then nod for my escorts to enter through the upper door while I wait outside the center door until the hall becomes quiet. As I pass through, my ladies fan out behind me.

The king rises from his giefstol at the head of the hall. With the firelight on his ruddy cheeks, I realize he is quite handsome. He approaches me. I'm mesmerized watching his long stride and feel a flutter in my belly. My husband winks as he raises my hand and presents me to his thanes. They cheer and bang the tables, but I don't hear them. I'm too engrossed in my husband's touch, and the realization that though his gesture is gentle, his hands are rough from swinging his sword. I shiver to think of them touching my skin. I incline my head to accept the thanes' admiration. The king releases my hand and returns to his seat.

I accept a chalice from the seneschal and follow my husband so I may present him with the first formal cup of the evening.

"My lord." I incline my head. "Please accept this cup with my best wishes and regard. I bid you drink joyfully as you serve your people."

My husband drains the beaker and returns it to me. I begin serving his court, the cupbearers at my elbow to keep the drinking horn full. My eyes spy Paulinus sitting alone at the lower end of the court. I lock my eyes on his so he knows I am the one who controls his status.

"My lord bishop," I say loudly with a commanding voice. "I enjoin you to be one with my husband's court."

A warrior glances at Paulinus and turns away, unimpressed by a foreign priest. Paulinus glares at me before nodding his head. "Your Grace," he mutters. I send him a glittering smile before passing on to the warriors below the court and the younger men below them.

Everyone responds to me with bows and broad smiles. Their acceptance gives me confidence that I will be their true queen, not just a womb to produce princes. When I return to my seat, I glance at the king, who lifts his beaker to me. He seems pleased by my reception. I hope he realizes I can make his court as respected as the court at Kent or even Frankland. My scop recounts the joining of Kent and Northumbria, concluding with jests about the handsome princes who will soon crowd the trestle tables. I'm pleased with his songs.

Servants light the torches and begin serving the meal. It is a sumptuous feast, and I wonder how many heads of cattle were slaughtered. The men sup their mead and use their daggers to separate meat from the roasted haunch. Many slices dispense blood onto the floor and furniture. I feel slightly nauseous and content myself with bread and cheese. There is no wine, so I drink ale. My ladies don't share my scruples and eat heartily.

My husband's face is red, with grease from the meat running down his chin. He gestures with his beaker in his hand before slamming the container on the table. Like his men, the king uses both hands to tear meat off the bones before tossing them to the dogs below the table. The hounds growl and snap. My head begins to pound.

Finally, everyone is sated. Servants place dishes of honey cakes on the table. I nibble the dry pastry and listen to the wedding toasts, which become increasingly graphic. The king laughs heartily and sends me meaningful looks. I drop my eyes, embarrassed by his lewd attention. When my tipsy ladies draw me away from the noisy revelry, I'm both relieved and terrified.

In my chamber, I shiver by the fire and watch my women place tapers into the wall slits. The light grows to give the room a shadowy glow.

"Your Majesty?" Breguswid hands me a beaker. "Drink this. It will make the night ahead easier." *Easier?* I swallow the liquid without stopping until the beaker is empty. "Stand up," Breguswid says.

Breguswid lifts off my headdress and frees my hair. My ladies slide off my armbands and remove my torc. Each time an item leaves my person, my heart thumps louder in my chest. The women lay aside my tunic and tell me to sit. They remove my boots and stockings. Only my shift is left to protect me from the air. I shiver, but refuse to enter the fur-covered bed.

"Do you know what you have to do?" Breguswid asks. I look at her, speechless. "Never mind," she says, and pats my hand.

I hear masculine scuffling and laughter outside. My husband arrives with his closest thanes, who crowd inside my chamber with their torches. They stare at me, momentarily silent. The heat is unbearable.

"Wife" is all the king says, but the word portends our marital consummation.

Paulinus pushes himself in front of the men and begins making the sign of the cross over the bed. Breguswid and her women pray for Goddess Freya to grant the king and me many sons.

While they mumble, the king strips down to his tunic and confers with Woden's priest—a man called Coifi. Finally, the prayers stop, and everyone departs. Paulinus is the last to leave, a look of mild concern on his face.

"Wife," the king says again, and joins me atop the furs.

I lick my lips. My husband looks at me, then gets up to pour me a beaker of ale. "Drink this," he says. "You look like a scared rabbit."

I watch him as I drink. "That's better," he says. "You have a bit of color now." He takes back the empty beaker. "What do you think?" he asks softly. "Shall we make a prince?" He puts his hands on my shoulders and pulls me forward. His breath smells sour from the mead. I turn my face away as he suddenly and quickly makes me his wife. I'm horrified. My husband ends his activity with a great shout, and begins snoring.

When I'm sure Edwin sleeps, I struggle out from under his body and pour myself more ale. Thankfully, I see that Breguswid left me a clean shift. I wash and change out of my bloody one. It will be better next time. I'll know what to expect.

Hildeburg, Princess of Northumbria

Queen Ethelberga isn't anything like my mother or the first queen. She orders her slaves to build what she calls a "chapel," and puts a wooden table in it. She puts a white cloth over the table and a gold image she calls a "cross" in the center. Every morning she makes the entire household go there. The queen and her people kneel on cushions on the floor. The rest of us stand and watch. The priest makes fragrant smoke come out of a covered cup and prepares what the queen calls a "special meal" she takes with her god.

Then she goes to her hall and reads something called a book. I don't understand the words, but I love listening to her soft, musical voice while I spin wool with the other girls. Spinning wool is boring, but the words make the time pass quickly.

"You," the queen calls. "Tell me your name."

I look around to see who she's talking to. My mother looks in my direction and nods toward the queen.

"Y-you want to speak to me?" I stammer.

"Yes. What's your name?"

"I'm Hildeburg, Your Grace. The king's niece."

"Yes. I remember now. You escorted me to my chamber when I arrived. Come forward."

I feel everyone's eyes on me as I walk the length of the hall. The queen waves her lady away and motions for me to sit next to her.

"Would you like to see the book?" she asks.

"Yes, please, Your Grace."

"Come sit beside me, and I'll show you how I read."

The book is beautiful. It's bound in leather with golden designs on the cover. The pages inside are thick with black marks on them, and there are beautiful drawings with colors.

"Would you like to hold it?"

"Yes," I breathe.

She places it in my lap and lets me turn the pages. They feel like thin leather.

"It's from Frankland," she says. "Now I'll show you how I read."

The queen places the book on her lap and uses a silver pin to show me each word she speaks. I don't understand what she says, but it's beautiful to watch the pin cross the page.

"Would you like to read?" the queen asks.

I hang my head. "I don't know what the designs mean."

"We don't have symbols for the words we speak. These designs are words from the Latin language, and once you know how to speak Latin, you can learn how to read and write it. Would you like that?"

"I don't know," I mumble.

"Then trust me. Everyone in my household must read and write, so you will learn. Bishop Paulinus will teach you, your sister, and even your mother. What do you think, Breguswid? Are you willing to learn with your daughters?"

My mother hesitates. "If you wish it," she finally replies.

"I do. In fact," the queen declares, "all my ladies will learn." The queen graces us with a self-satisfied smile. "My court," she whispers to herself, "will outshine Kent."

Ethelberga, Queen of Northumbria
August

I've been sick every morning for weeks. Breguswid persuades me to send for the wise woman, a wizened hag. Her ragged clothing and lined face make me uncomfortable, until her tranquil eyes smile. With a gentle touch, the woman looks in my eyes and mouth, pats my belly, and asks when I last laid with the king.

"And when did you last bleed, Your Majesty?"

"Not since I married the king."

The old woman grins a nearly toothless smile. "Send an offering to Goddess Freya. She blessed you with a child."

Praise God! I hardly dared to hope for His favor so soon.

"Are you sure?" I ask, tentatively. "I thought it might be the food."

"I'm sure, Your Grace. If all goes well, your child will be born in the spring."

"May God be praised." I drop to my knees in thanksgiving.

⚭⚭⚭

Every night, Edwin's thanes escort him to my chamber and clap him on the back before returning to their own pursuits. My husband leaves his shield by the door and his sword an arm's length away from the straw mattress. We share a beaker of ale by the fire before he takes me to bed. This evening will be different. I bow before him and lead him to the bench. He looks at me curiously. "You don't seem ready for me," he says.

"Come, Your Majesty, let us enjoy a drink together. I have something to tell you."

Edwin turns to look at my face and raises his eyebrows. "Is something amiss?"

I drop my eyes. "My lord, something happened that changes everything. My lord—"

"Spit it out! You know I can't abide women's concerns. Are you sick? Have I come when you're bleeding?" Edwin stands.

"No, no, Your Majesty. Pray, sit down again. I have wonderful news. I'm—" I tremble and force myself to go on. "I carry a prince, my lord." I can't read his face. *Is he pleased?*

"You're sure?"

"Yes. The wise woman was here today. She said the prince arrives in the spring."

My husband chuckles. "Who would have thought it?" he says to himself. "And so quickly." Edwin turns to me and smiles. "You please me, wife." He pulls a gold ring off his finger and hands it to me. "You please me very much." Edwin pats my shoulder and stands. "I'll not trouble you again until it's time to make another prince." He gives me a warning look. "Don't do anything foolish to harm my son."

Edwin picks up his sword and shield and walks into the night, his laughter echoing into the distance.

⚮

After chapel the next morning, I invite Paulinus into my hall. "God blesses me," I say.

Paulinus puts down his beaker of ale. "How so, Your Grace?"

"I carry a prince, the first of many," I say smugly. "Once he's born, my position will be secure."

Paulinus's face lights up. "Your Grace, God smiles upon our work. We'll baptize the child as soon as he's born. The king will see how God blesses him."

"Suppose the king thinks Coifi's prayers made me pregnant?" I needle Paulinus.

"Never say such a thing, or even think it! The prince is God's holy work."

I nod my head while Paulinus praises God. My husband believes he has the prowess of a bull. My priest thinks his prayers filled my womb. And I am happiest of all. Not only will I give the king a son, but he'll bestow his favors elsewhere for the foreseeable future.

Chapter 2

Anno Domini 624 – The Year Pope Boniface Sends Gifts to King Edwin

---

Ethelberga, Queen of Northumbria
August

We're at Yeavering, the king's most recent acquisition. The people are sullen, the provisions fewer than they should be, but we are here so the king can show himself to both his subjects and his enemies. Whenever possible, King Edwin conquers by sheer intimidation. The king expects a proper villa when he returns from Carlisle.

After chapel this morning, my ladies and I walk through the timber buildings observing their dilapidated condition. I send for the seneschal to meet me in my chamber. When I arrive, both he and Paulinus are awaiting me. Paulinus isn't adjusting well, because the king and his warriors have no time for him. This morning he has an expectant look on his face, so perhaps he won't have a new complaint. I take my seat, pick up my embroidery, and nod for my servant to admit the bishop. He clutches a parcel under his arm and strides forward.

"Your Grace." He stops and kneels. "His Holiness sends you this letter and gifts. There's another letter for the king."

I keep my face neutral and hold out my hand, but I feel a flutter of anticipation. It's not every day I receive a letter from the pope.

Pope Boniface encouraged my marriage as a means to convert my husband to Christianity. So far, I've failed. But what does he expect? It's hardly been two months. Edwin claims to be Woden's true descendant. His thanes come to him because he has luck in battle and plunder. Why would he toss that aside on the word of a woman and a skinny priest?

His Holiness writes of my mystical cleansing and regeneration when God touched my mind. He applauds my unshakeable labor to spread the Christian faith. I wince, remembering my occasional quiet prayer to Goddess Freya to protect my child.

After praising my conviction, His Holiness gets to his point: King Edwin still follows idols, which means I failed in the true purpose of my marriage. He is wrong. The king will keep me, my dowry, and my brother's loyalty, whether he becomes a Christian or not.

I imagine the pope droning on as he dictates his letter. He writes that I must "melt my husband's heart by teaching him about the Holy Ghost," because my only purpose is to convert my husband. And so he sends me blessings from St. Peter and gifts.

"Bishop Paulinus … His Holiness says he sent me a mirror and a comb made from gold and ivory. Do you have them?"

My bishop holds out the parcel. Inside, the mirror and comb lie nestled in soft wool. With a wide smile, I show them to my household. "See what His Holiness the Pope sends me from Rome." I turn the articles to catch the light, and my ladies press forward. The news will soon spread. I beckon for Paulinus to sit near me on the dais where our conversation can't be heard.

"Bishop," I say softly, "I hope His Holiness also honors the king."

Paulinus's eyes light up. "Your Grace, he too has a letter and wonderful gifts."

"Will they impress the King's Hall as well as the king?" I ask pointedly.

The bishop's excitement fades. "I hope so, Your Grace."

"And will you read the letter aloud to the assembly?"

"I thought to read the letter after I present the gifts. The king will know great esteem once he puts away his idols."

"Do you happen to have a copy of the king's letter, as I'm sure you do of mine? It might be best if I read it first to ensure it will be well received." I smile encouragingly. "You wouldn't want the king to take offense."

Paulinus looks shocked, though I'm not convinced he is. "Your Grace, it is a private letter from the pope to King Edwin. It is for their eyes alone."

"Yet the scribe has already seen it, and no doubt the pope's secretary. I'm sure, without a doubt, you have a copy, for what secrets could the pope have from you? Show me the letter, so we can be sure it will please the king. If you read the letter aloud, and insult the king and his warriors, how do you expect to complete your mission to baptize the king? Your pride could easily jeopardize the entire purpose of your presence. I advise you to show me the letter."

Paulinus stiffens and protectively holds his sleeve close to his arm. "It is a private letter, Your Grace."

"Nothing at court is private," I admonish. "If you value the success of your mission, show me the letter."

At last he reaches into his sleeve and hands me the document, a scribe's copy of the letter. Pope Boniface writes well, but abruptly. He reminds my husband of God's creation of the world and His placement of man above all other creatures so he can obtain eternal life. The pope remarks that all of humanity recognizes God.

I pause in my reading. *If that were so, conversion would be unnecessary— but I keep my thoughts to myself.* When I read on, I learn that the pope cites my brother, Eadbald, as an example of a Christian king. I don't think it a good comparison. Edwin is stronger than my brother and won't like being told that he is in any way inferior to the King of Kent.

"Renounce idol worship," Pope Boniface writes. "Reject the mummery of shrines and the deceitful flattery of omens. Believe in God the Father Almighty; in His son, Jesus Christ; and in the Holy Ghost."

I hand the letter back to Paulinus and pick up my embroidery. "The king doesn't listen to me or to you. Why would he be changed by a letter from a stranger who has no power here?"

"But the gifts will bind him, Your Grace," Paulinus says with some desperation. "If he accepts the gifts, he's in the pope's debt."

"How far is Frankland from here?" I inquire, not bothering to look up from my stitching. "How many days' journey? Might it be a week—or even two by sea?"

"Yes, Your Grace."

"How many days from Frankland to Rome? Crossing mountains and avoiding robbers? Might it be a month?"

"Yes, Your Grace."

"And, on such an arduous journey, wouldn't men need to stop and rest?"

"Perhaps, Your Grace," Paulinus says with a trace of impatience.

"And is it true the pope has no warriors worth mentioning? No way to force anyone to do his bidding?"

"He has the power of the Keys of St. Peter, Your Grace. He can send sinners to hell," Paulinus says with all the authority of his office.

"Even if that be true, why should my husband, the king, have any fear of the pope? The gifts are a mere tribute to the king's position. If you want to convert the king, you'll have to make use of opportunities as they present themselves. And if you want to stay in his company, you'll have to be useful."

"Your Grace, I do God's work."

"I suggest you also do the king's work. Do you know how many hides of land connect with Yeavering? Can you tell the king how much his people should render for his use, and whether they have done so? If you can, the king will have use for you. Otherwise, he merely suffers you on my account. You're the only literate man in the king's court—make use of your skills, and the king may find your advice advantageous, if you take my meaning." I give the cowering bishop a long look, only continuing once I'm sure I've made my point. Paulinus's stony expression confirms as much.

"As to the pope's letter," I go on, rethreading my needle, "you've no choice but to present it. But not in the King's Hall, where all and sundry can hear what they don't understand. I suggest you read the letter to the king in his chamber, with only his closest thanes present to hear the pope's misguided advice."

Two weeks later, I order a feast in the King's Hall to welcome my husband back to Yeavering, and I invite people from the countryside to join in their own celebration. The hall has new hangings, which will travel with us to all the villas. Everything emphasizes my husband's power. To my surprise, Bishop Paulinus completes a regional inventory and is ready to present it to the king—after he tells him about the pope's letter.

Edwin is in a good mood. He picks a new favorite to serve as his companion and spends a few hours with her before joining his men in the hall. I hope she doesn't expect advancement. No doubt Edwin will leave her here with a new tunic when the court moves on. When the king arrives, the thanes cheer while the scop tunes his harp before singing about tribute collected from our enemies and the bravery of men on the hunt. After the toasts, Paulinus offers the king greetings from the pope in Rome. My husband nods to me in appreciation, and grants Paulinus permission to bring the pope's letter to him later.

"Your Majesty," Paulinus says, "Pope Boniface sends you blessings and protection from St. Peter, and these humble gifts, which you may find pleasing."

Paulinus motions for a servant to lay the gifts at the king's feet, and leans over to lift them up for my husband's inspection. A second servant assists in opening the parcel, and the two hold up a tunic of Byzantine silk shot through with gold embroidery. Edwin stands to inspect it more closely. I can see it is finer than anything at my brother's court.

Edwin puts the tunic on, admiring the sleeves. Light from the fire dances on the golden threads. Paulinus holds out a gold medallion that hangs to the middle of the king's chest. Paulinus snaps his fingers, and the servants display a thick silken cloak. The warriors send up a mighty cheer. A king with so much wealth will have to share some of it with them.

"Your Majesty," Paulinus says, "I hope these gifts demonstrate the love His Holiness has for you. And they are nothing compared to the message he sends. These are treasures for this world, but His Holiness invites you to build up even greater treasure in heaven."

I don't think the king is listening. He appears fascinated by the tunic with its intricate workmanship. Paulinus stands before the king, waiting to be acknowledged or dismissed. Eventually, the excitement dies down. The king steps forward with a dagger in his hand. He holds it so all can see the sharpness of the blade, the gold on its hilt.

He hands the blade to Paulinus.

"Tell the pope I'm pleased with his gift. I'm also pleased with you. I don't know how much use a dagger will be to you, since you carry no weapon, but I present it as a sign of my pleasure. Welcome to my court."

The warriors cheer, and Paulinus takes a seat near the king. I wonder how many golden tunics the pope presents and if they always have this effect. Paulinus is elevated, his status raised from a member of my household to a man in the king's court.

The next afternoon, my husband invites me to his chamber. Paulinus is there. So are Osfrid and Eadfrid, my husband's sons by Cwenburg. I stroke my belly. My son will be king, not these callow youths.

It's an informal meeting. My ladies and I sit on a bench near the door. My husband's wench is present, trying to keep out of my sight. For a moment, I wonder if Edwin likes the girl well enough to take her on to our next villa. I dismiss the thought. Edwin gets bored quickly. Paulinus bows to me and turns his attention back to the king.

"Your Majesty, may I present the letter Pope Boniface sends you?"

Paulinus kneels before the king and holds up a carved casket. Edwin examines it, opens the lid, and lifts out the document with its heavy embellished parchment. He weighs it in his hand and examines the calligraphy. I see he is impressed.

Hildeburg, Princess of Northumbria

The queen was sick this morning. While her nurse held her head and her ladies fanned the fire's smoke away from her, Hereswid and I fetched fresh clothing. I thought the queen would excuse herself from the meeting between the king and Paulinus, but she's strong-willed and wants everyone to see she's with child.

Last week the queen appointed Hereswid and me to her court of ladies. I thought it would be fun, but the ladies just sew and read aloud, which is almost as boring as weaving. And we have such low rank, we hardly speak. Today, the queen brings her ladies with her to the king's chamber. We're the last to arrive.

King Edwin is fascinated by the pope's letter. He keeps feeling the parchment and holding it up to the light. Paulinus is nervous. I can tell he wants to snatch back the document before my uncle spills something on it or drops it.

"May I read the letter from His Holiness to you, Your Majesty?" Paulinus beseeches, and my uncle motions for a servant to bring more ale.

"What could he write that has any interest to me? He's too far away to be an effective ally."

"Forgive me, but that's not entirely true. Kings who follow the true faith are natural allies. With the pope's blessing, you'll gain more allies in the south. Not just Kent, but East Anglia as well. Please allow me to share the pope's thoughts with you."

"Do you agree, wife? Shall I listen to the man's letter?"

The queen stands and bows her head. "My lord, His Holiness rules in God's name over all Christians. He rules over Italy and Frankland, as well as

Kent. If you become friends with the pope, you'll be friends with other kings. You can control all of England, my lord."

My uncle turns his attention to Paulinus and hands back the letter. "Read me the letter, priest."

"Yes, Your Majesty." Paulinus clears his throat. "To the illustrious Edwin, King of the English, from Boniface, Bishop, servant of the servants of God: We have undertaken to extend our priestly responsibility to disclose to you the fullness of the Christian Faith, in order that we may impart to your sense also the Gospel of Christ, which our Savior commanded be preached to all nations, and may offer you the medicine of salvation."

"What is this medicine, Paulinus?" the king breaks in. "What illness can it cure?"

"It cures sin, Your Majesty."

Edwin frowns and swirls the ale in his beaker. "Do you say *I* have this sin?"

"Most assuredly, Your Majesty." Paulinus hesitates. "It afflicts all humanity. Shall I continue?"

"What sin do you have, priest?" my uncle asks.

Paulinus drops his jaw. "Um, well, Your Majesty." He swallows. "There are so many ways to sin, it's impossible for a man to know all his sins. This is why we need salvation."

"Even you?"

"Yes, Your Majesty. Shall I continue reading the pope's letter?"

My uncle nods, and I think maybe he just wanted to put Paulinus on the spot.

Paulinus looks down at the letter. "Your Majesty, His Holiness writes that God created the heavens and the earth—that He formed man in His image from the earth's dust and placed him above all creatures. Most importantly, His Holiness writes that kingship is conferred by God, not by man."

"He's wrong," my uncle, the king, says. "I am king by battle and by Woden's luck. Do you doubt it?"

Paulinus inhales and opens his hands. "Your Majesty is indeed king by force of arms, but true kingship has a spiritual element you haven't experienced yet."

My uncle is clearly irritated. He glares at Paulinus, who bows his head. The king's eyes look around the room and stop when his gaze falls upon the queen. "Wife, come forward."

The queen rises, walks with a firm step to the king, and sinks into a deep curtsy.

"Bring a seat for the queen."

My uncle leaves the queen below him—and even below Paulinus, who moves out of the king's direct vision—looking instead at his sons and closest warriors. He sends his mistress and the servants away.

"Wife, Kent made you soft. You, your priest, and the pope don't know anything. You don't understand how a warrior becomes a king, and you don't know Woden's luck. Shall I tell you something? Your God sent me a messenger."

"My lord," the queen says, "how can this be?"

"When my brother, Aethelfrid, killed our father, the king, I fled. First I went to Mercia, where I married the king's daughter. But Aethelfrid tried to reach me there. So I fled again and threw myself on the mercy of King Redwald of East Anglia. Once again, Aethelfrid found me. He told Redwald that if he surrendered me, there would be a reward, but how could he reward so rich a king? After that, Aethelfrid threatened war if Redwald protected me, but how could such a strong king be afraid?

"You see me now, powerful and mighty, because luck was with me. Look at me, wife. Shall I tell you what happened?"

The queen looks pale. Perhaps she's still sick. "Yes, please, Your Grace," she says, the words barely a breath. "Tell us how God blessed you."

"While King Redwald considered Aethelfrid's threat, a stranger came to me in the night. He asked me why I sat alone while everyone else was asleep. I was angry and told him it wasn't his concern. The man said he knew my troubles and asked what reward I would give someone who persuaded King Redwald to protect me. I said I would give any reward in my power, though I had no power.

"Then the man asked what I would give if I became king. I said I would be grateful, as only a mighty king can be.

"Finally, the man asked me if I would listen to someone who could predict such good fortune. I told him I would accept guidance from anyone who could solve my problems and place me on my throne.

"The man laid his hand on my head, urged me to remember my promises—and disappeared into *mist*. What do you think, wife? Did it happen as I just said?"

The queen swallows. "It must have, for here you are, a mighty king."

"Yes, here I am. I'm not so ignorant of spirits as you think. I have Woden's luck."

"My lord husband, forgive me. You said a stranger spoke to you. You said God sent you a messenger. Surely it was an angel directing you to the righteous path?"

"What say you, priest? Do you call this stranger an angel from your God?"

"Who else could it be, Your Majesty?" Paulinus's intent gaze captures the king's eyes. "The angel's promises came true. Now you must do your part. His Holiness calls you to account."

The king breaks eye contact and picks up his beaker. He holds it so tightly, I think it will shatter.

"Your Majesty." Paulinus's intense tone demands attention. "His Holiness urges you to renounce idol worship and believe in God, his Son, and the Holy Ghost. Then you will be free of sin and have eternal life . . .

"Your Majesty, Pope Boniface urges you to accept the Christian way so you may abide with God. Already he has great respect for you. He wishes only for you to join with other Christian kings." Paulinus shakes with the urgency of his plea.

My uncle sneers, shaking his head. "Enough, priest," he says, dismissing Paulinus with a wave of his hand. "You and the queen have permission to leave."

Paulinus sways slightly as he escorts the queen outside, with the rest of us in her train. We hear the scop strike his harp and begin a song.

We leave Yeavering soon after and journey south, stopping at Goodmanham for Yule. I think the King's Hall here is the most grand. An enormous Yule log burns at the center, and on the Winter's Day festival, King Edwin and his warriors toast Woden for the victories he brings us and the happiness of the king. His eyes find their way to the queen's belly, and they both smile.

The queen leads her ladies, including Hereswid and me, as we refill the warriors' cups. The men are glassy-eyed. The next toast is for Goddess Freya, for a good season and peace. I find this an odd wish, since the men want only to fight. But perhaps it means peace for the people.

Chapter 3

Anno Domini 625 – The Year Eumer of Wessex Fails to Assassinate King Edwin

Hildeburg, Princess of Northumbria

When the worst of winter is behind us, we celebrate Somonath at all the king's villas. At Goodmanham, the queen allows me to join in gathering the first four sods of soil during the night. The maids and I soak them in oil and honey before adding meal and baking fist-sized cakes. The next night we place the cakes under the first furrows in the field while we chant: *Field full of food for mankind, bright-blooming, you are blessed in the name of the gods who made the ground, grant us the gift of growing, that for us each grain might come to use.* The farmers begin planting our new crops, and by April, when we go to the king's villa on the River Derwent, shoots are coming up.

King Edwin brings us here every year to celebrate Goddess Eostre. Queen Ethelberga says her child will come soon, and we shouldn't jostle it, but much as my uncle anticipates the birth of his new son, he orders our journey here.

When she isn't wanted in the King's Hall, the queen stays in seclusion, keeping to her chamber. She's very ungainly. I remember my mother's story about my birth, and how she could hardly move. I think the queen is like that. It's hard to stay inside with her. I want to go to the riverbank and pick the small flowers that come up in spring. I want to listen to the river go by. But the queen says I'm too old to waste time.

Sometimes she lets me read to her ladies. She's interested in my progress and selects stories she thinks will teach our women about Jesus. For some reason the queen likes the one about Jesus and the adulteress. The woman was guilty, and the punishment was stoning to death. I ask the queen why a woman would do such a thing.

"Perhaps she didn't."

"But your book says she did."

"Hildeburg, reading isn't about just the words, but the meaning behind them. Bring the Gospel Book of St. John, and we'll read it together."

I rise from my seat below hers and sit beside her.

"Take my pin, and point at the words as you read them."

"*Adduct autem scribae et Pharisaei mulierem in adulterio deprehensam et statuerunt eam in medio et dixerunt ei magister haec mulier modo deprehensa est in adulterio,*" I recite dutifully. My pin pauses on the final word as I confess, "But I don't understand—it says the scribes and Pharisees brought a woman caught in adultery. So, she *must* have done it. How can you say maybe she didn't?"

"Hildeburg, you are correct. The verses clearly state the woman was caught in adultery, but who caught her? The accusers say someone caught the woman. They don't say any of them witnessed the incident."

I ponder the queen's words. "So, you don't think she did it?"

"I don't know. But they didn't know, either. Perhaps someone else brought the woman to them and said she was guilty. Maybe they investigated. Maybe they didn't. What is the king's punishment for a guilty wife?"

"It's nothing to do with the king," I say. "Her husband turns her out and flogs her through the village."

"And then what happens?"

"I don't know." I shrug. "But she isn't killed."

"Not deliberately—though she is ruined. Tell me the next part of the story."

"The Pharisees say she should be stoned, and they ask Jesus what he wants to do."

"Which punishment is harsher, do you think? Being flogged through the village, or being stoned to death?"

"Either one would hurt a lot," I suggest. The queen's lessons always make my head hurt.

"And what did Jesus say?"

"He said only someone who didn't sin should throw the first stone at the woman. She must have been afraid, my lady."

"I'm sure she was. Why do you think she was spared?"

Everyone stares at me as I try to think of something to say, but I don't know the answer. I look back in the book. "The book just says they went away. It doesn't say why. And then Jesus said everything would be fine. But how could it be? They'll just come back later, when Jesus isn't around."

"Do you listen when the bishop speaks to us in chapel?"

"I try, my lady."

"Every morning Bishop Paulinus explains that when a person is baptized, all her sins are forgiven and no longer exist. Jesus forgave the woman, and she had a new life."

"Yes, my lady. But the king decides what we should do, not this Jesus."

The queen's lips become a flat line.

"Hildeburg," she says, sighing. "You disappoint me."

Though Hereswid and I continue our lessons, the queen ignores us. She seems unwell and won't eat any meat, though the wise women tell her she must if she wants a strong child. The ladies who came with her don't eat meat either, so Hereswid and I have nothing to eat but bread, cheese, and sheep's milk. What's the point of being a princess, if we eat like peasants? Everyone else celebrates Goddess Eostre and spring, while we spend our mornings in the bishop's chapel. The queen insists we listen to Bishop Paulinus talk about Jesus's persecution. I still don't understand it. He's not anything like Woden. Why does the queen bother with him?

In the afternoon, while the queen rests, Hereswid tends to her sewing, and I go to the riverbank. New leaves burst from the dead branches as Goddess Eostre clothes the earth. The water is cold, but so clear I can see fish. Sometimes I try to balance on the rocks and walk across the river. I often slip, but it's worth it. Some days, the wind blows fluffy clouds across a clear blue sky. Everything is waking up, and I feel pure joy.

On the day of Goddess Eostre's feast, I wake up early to watch the dawn. Fingers of light chase away the darkness until the sun's rays appear in all their fullness. Reluctantly, I go to the queen's chamber. It's my turn to assist her preparations before chapel. But when I arrive, the queen is already departing. She stops when she sees me.

"Where were you?" she asks in a reasonable tone of voice.

"Your Majesty, forgive me." I bow my head. "You don't usually awake so early."

She looks at me with disapproval. "Your sister told me you slipped out to watch the dawn appear, when you should have been in my chamber."

For the first time, I see Hereswid among the queen's ladies.

"Why did you watch the dawn?" the queen asks.

I keep my head down. "No reason, Your Majesty. I just—" I look up. "I'm sorry, I just wanted to see the dawn today."

To my surprise, the queen smiles. "I know you were worshipping the spring goddess." She lifts my chin. "I pray that someday you will understand the true meaning of this day. It is Easter, the day our Lord rose from the dead. And, in His honor, I forgive your lapse. Come. Assist me into chapel."

Queen Ethelberga has difficulty walking now. I help her cross the courtyard. Paulinus greets the queen and her Kentish ladies with a kiss. As we file inside, I can't believe my eyes. There are flowers everywhere. The altar linens are fresh and white. Paulinus beams with joy, and lights what he calls an Easter candle. He tells us God raised Jesus from the dead, so we'll never die. Hereswid and I nod and smile. I don't know what my sister thinks, but I'm pretty sure everyone dies, no matter what they do. The queen and her Kentish ladies take their special meal with Paulinus. Then they recite a hymn: *"O mystery great and glorious, that mortal flesh should conquer death, and all our human pains and wounds the Lord should heal by bearing them."*

Suddenly, Hereswid shoves her elbow into my belly. "You're making a noise," she hisses. "Don't let the queen hear you."

"She's too busy singing," I whisper. I've never heard the queen sing before. She has a pleasant voice, but the tune is monotonous.

At last Paulinus dismisses us. I help the queen cross over to her hall to break our fast. The Queen's Hall is full of flowers and has fresh straw on the floor. Her scop sits near the fire tuning his harp. I guide the queen to her chair at the head of the table next to Paulinus. Servants bustle in with trays of food and beakers of sheep's milk. One lad runs into me in his haste. He almost drops his tray, but rights himself. "Begging your pardon, my lady." He tugs his forelock. I wave him forward.

Taking my place next to Hereswid and my mother, I smell a fragrance that's been missing for months. The cauldron bubbles with boiled meat. I want to grab some of the meat on the platter before Paulinus prays. Mother grabs my wrist. "Hildeburg," she hisses. I hang my head. I know the queen and her Kentish ladies will be served first, but I'm so hungry.

When we finally receive our share, I let the meat sit on my tongue so I can suck in its juices. Mother lets me have two portions, but instead of filling me with delight, the food sits heavily on my belly. Mother gives me a knowing look.

"It is best," she says, "to enjoy nature's bounty in moderation."

The scop strikes a final chord.

"My ladies," the queen says, "Easter is the most blessed day of the year. I pray that one day all of you will know the joys of God's blessings."

Outside, cooks prepare for Goddess Eostre's feast. Hereswid comes with me to gather flowers to wear in our hair in the King's Hall. Even though it's a celebration for Goddess Eostre, the queen will attend, and we'll be among the cupbearers.

Men gather near the hall before sunset, when the door opens to admit them. I like to watch the warriors, who usually keep their weapons close at hand, surrender them to the seneschal for safekeeping. Shields are hung on the wall in order of importance, as the men find seats on the benches running the length of the table. The youngest warriors lounge near the door. Visitors are the last to be admitted. Even if uninvited, everyone may enjoy King Edwin's generosity.

I make my way to the side door to join the queen's ladies. I think this will be Queen Ethelberga's last appearance before the child comes. The ladies maneuver her through the door to her seat, and we take our places around her.

The king's court enters, and finally, King Edwin strides to the giefstol, resplendent in the pope's golden tunic and a cloak of rich firs. He holds up his hand, and everyone strikes the table and cheers.

Queen Ethelberga stands to greet the king and the hall. She sends my mother to present the drinking horn to King Edwin.

"Take this cup, my noble lord," Queen Ethelberga declares. "It is for you, the one who shares treasure. May you be in good times, and cheerful to your men, ever mindful of the gifts you have received."

King Edwin nods to the queen, raises the horn, and drinks. "Let us be well and celebrate Goddess Eostre," he declares.

Acting on the queen's behalf, my mother makes her way through the hall, stopping before each warrior. The queen says words of welcome to each man and reminds the hall of his good deeds. The thane tells of an exploit that makes him look brave or strong. Since the last raids were at Carlisle, there isn't much to boast about. My uncle's *pyle* sometimes challenges the boast. *How brave do you have to be in a territory already conquered? What warrior did you slay?*

Eventually, my mother reaches the young warriors who boast much but have done little. They smile appreciatively as she pours mead into their drinking horns, and they compliment her dimples. Mother laughs and passes on until she reaches the end of the bench, and then she hesitates. I strain to see the reason why.

There's a stranger in our midst. King Edwin welcomes travelers to his hall, especially when we celebrate, because he is a generous king, and they tell tales from their homelands. This man, in his travel-stained garments, doesn't jest with the young warriors, nor they with him. It's as if there's an invisible barrier around him. The thanes notice we aren't filling their cups, and the hall becomes quiet.

"Stranger," my uncle's voice booms out. "What brings you to my hall?"

The man pulls off his gloves, stands, and bows. "My name is Eumer. I come with a message from Cwichelm, King of Wessex."

My uncle rises. "Welcome, Eumer. Come forward and join my court. I will hear your message after the meal, for I see my men are ready to tear the venison off the haunch."

"As you wish, Your Majesty." Eumer strides to the front, finding a seat at the bottom of my uncle's court. He has a grim expression as he fills his trencher and doesn't converse with anyone. Eumer eats methodically, as if chewing is a chore he must complete. I notice he drinks very little.

The king tosses his last bone to the dogs, rubs his belly, and belches. "Eumer," he shouts, "tell me King Cwichelm's message."

The stranger knocks back his beaker of mead before standing at the center of the dais, directly in front of King Edwin. "Your Majesty," he says and bows deeply. He begins to rise. Suddenly he leaps forward holding a two-edged dagger. Firelight glints off the metal.

Lilla, the thane seated closest to the king, sees Eumer's intent and leaps across the space to protect my uncle. Eumer, unable to stop his own momentum, collides with both men. His dagger plunges through Lilla before finding its mark and wounding my uncle.

Blood pulses over the dais and drips onto the floor. Thanes growl and roar as they converge on the enemy. Eumer grabs a sword, swinging it against the thanes who surround him. He kills Forthere and wounds several other men, before the thanes tear him apart.

While the battle rages, Coifi and the other priests pull Lilla off the king. Coifi raises his staff. "The king lives!" he shouts. As word spreads, a mighty shout goes up through the hall. The warriors leave Eumer's body and rush forward to view King Edwin. Coifi selects a few thanes to carry the king to his chamber and sends the others away.

I watch the scene unfold, shaking with terror. My knees give way, and I slip down the wall, pulling a tapestry with me. With horror, I realize I'm sitting in blood. Warriors lift the king onto a bench and carry him out of the hall.

The queen! What happened to her? Is she hurt? Did she get away?

I make my way to the entry door with tears streaming down my face. The night is black. I see torches around the door to the queen's chamber. I make my way there just as my mother comes out. Her face is grim, and her tunic bloody. She grabs me and pulls me to her.

"You're alive." She wipes my face.

"And Hereswid?" I ask.

"She's safe. She's inside with the queen." My mother drops her head, and I can tell she's upset about something else, that perhaps she isn't telling me everything.

"What's happened?" I pry, still trembling. "Is the queen hurt?"

"The child is coming—but it's too soon. It—" Mother pauses, and I feel my throat tighten with worry. "It may not live."

"Is it a prince?" I ask.

"I said the child is *coming*—I didn't say it was here. But there's so much blood. The midwives are with her. I have to go back inside."

"Shall I come with you?"

"No. Go to our chamber and rest."

"But…"

"You're too young to see this. Go."

The night is full of sounds I've never heard before: men shouting, women wailing.

My mother and Hereswid return at dawn.

Queen Ethelberga gave birth to a daughter. Both are still alive.

Paulinus, Bishop of Northumbria

Praying for mercy, I follow the thanes carrying King Edwin to his chamber. Coifi and his henchmen stand around a cauldron over the fire. The sickly sweetness of cooked honey fills the space.

The thanes lay the king on a bed of furs. Coifi cuts through the golden tunic and removes it from the wound. I pray the pope's gift can be mended.

The priests hold torches around the bed as Coifi uses tweezers to pluck threads from the wound. He encourages more blood to flow, stanches it, and smears the wound with a concoction of honey and salt. Then he sews the edges of the wound together.

I can't see how far the dagger penetrated, but I know if the thane hadn't taken the blow, the king would be dead.

Coifi begins wrapping the wound in fresh cloth. Then he gives the king a drink. When I ask, I'm told it combines carline thistle, meadow sweet, and agrimony boiled in ale and fermented with yeast. King Edwin makes a face, sees me, and shouts, "Praise to Goddess Eostre for her protection!"

"To Goddess Eostre," the men repeat enthusiastically.

"Your Majesty." A woman's voice competes with masculine noise. We turn toward the sound. Breguswid enters the king's chambers and falls to her knees. "The queen delivered a daughter."

"She lives?" the king asks in a raspy voice.

"Both mother and child are well."

"Praise to Goddess Eostre!" the king shouts again.

I must stop this pagan adulation now, while the image of death is fresh in the king's mind. "Your Majesty, I must speak," I say, and the king's eyes fall on me. "Your Majesty, you should thank God for his mercy, not a nonexistent goddess." I swallow. "You live because you wore the tunic carrying the blessing and protection of St. Peter. This is how your life is saved. And the queen and your daughter live because today is Easter, a day of God's grace. I will thank God with prayers on your behalf, but you must thank God by your deeds."

The king grunts and looks at me with loathing, as though I'm the traitor. He tries to rise from his bed.

Coifi presses him back onto the furs. "Leave now," the priest says. "Your false god has no place here. Go to the queen. The king doesn't need your prayers."

Ethelberga, Queen of Northumbria

I'm surrounded by pain, as if my entire body has been torn in two. But that's nothing, if the king doesn't live.

"Is anyone there?" I whisper.

"You must rest, Your Majesty," a hoarse voice replies. A woman waves a bundle of burning herbs above my head.

"No." I try to sit. "I must go. Does the king live? I must go to him." But I can't lift my head.

"Rest, my lady." I hear Breguswid's voice. "The king lives and is well." She thrusts a bundle at me. "You have a daughter, my lady."

Daughter…

No. That's not possible. I carried a son. The fairies must have taken him and left a girl in his place.

I turn my head. "Take it away. I don't want it."

Where did I fail? Why did God take away my hopes and expectations? The last queen produced two strapping sons. They practice their weapons every day under their father's proud eye. Without a son, I'm nothing in the king's eyes. Tears crawl down my cheeks. *I had such hopes.* My hands make loose fists. Breguswid pushes the swaddled infant at me again.

"Won't you look at her?" Breguswid coaxes.

"No! Let the fairies take her."

Every woman in my chamber gasps. "The fairies don't want her," they chant in unison. "She's too ugly."

"Let me see her," I command.

Breguswid brings the infant back to me and shows me her face. She purses her lips and has a sweet look about her.

"The king has no use for girls," I say and wave the child away. "But if she survives the night, he may acknowledge her as a princess."

I hope so.

⚜

Hildeburg, Princess of Northumbria

Three days after the attack, we wear our best clothing in honor of Lilla and Forthere, and walk to the cemetery. The king rides at the front of our cavalcade. He sits tall on his horse, as if he never suffered an injury from the Wessex demon. But he keeps his men close around him. I wonder if it's for protection, or in case he has a moment of weakness, but it can't be either, for a king has luck and needs no protection.

Behind the mounted thanes, lesser warriors walk with their finest swords and shields.

The queen's ladies follow. We dress for a feast in the King's Hall, because today we bid farewell to two great warriors: Lilla, who threw himself in front of my uncle without thought for his own life, and Forthere, killed in the struggle against the fiend from Wessex.

Woodsmen felled the trees and craftsmen built the double funeral pyre in three days. To take longer would be disrespectful. Coifi and the priests oversaw the washing and dressing of the dead men.

When we arrive at the cemetery shortly after dawn, the king gives the signal, and we watch as the corpses are lifted onto the pyre. I see their leggings and the fine embroidery of their tunics.

After the bodies are placed, men arrange four rams with their throats cut at the dead warriors' feet. Drinking horns lie by their hands, and gaming boards are ready for play. Lilla and Forthere have all they need in Valhalla.

We gather at the base of the pyre. The king nods, and men touch torches to the kindling wood. As the fire catches, the flames reach higher and higher. Sparks fly through the air. We join in our assent as our comrades travel to the home of all great warriors.

A crackling noise comes from inside the pyre as we take shelter. The scops sing songs of Lilla's bravery and Forthere's courage. The king ordered cattle slaughtered for the funeral feast in honor of his warriors. The fragrance of roasting meat floats through the air.

At dusk, we ladies begin the walk home. The flames have died down into a red glow at the base of the pyre. I think the men will stay until only ash and smoke remain. Later, the ashes will be gathered into a joint urn and buried in a barrow. I hope Lilla and Forthere are well-placed in Valhalla and not disappointed that they will miss the coming battle.

Ethelberga, Queen of Northumbria

As soon as I'm fit to travel, my husband the king moves to his villa at Sancton. I'm glad to be away from Derwent and its evil events. I wish never to go there again, but I doubt I can avoid it.

To my delight, my daughter thrives. She's a lusty eater, sharing the wet nurse's breast as well as mine. Paulinus tells me she must be baptized in order to bring the king closer to his own baptism. I stroke her small head with its downy hair and tell her she's ugly so the spirits won't take her away. I hand the child to her nurse, dress carefully, and summon my ladies for the walk to my hall.

When my husband arrives, I order a chair for him beside and slightly above my own. My ladies draw away so we can speak privately.

"How do you fare, wife?" he asks. "And the child—is she bonny?"

"She is strong, my lord, as am I."

"That is well." He draws on his ale. "When I return from battle, we'll make a prince. Would you like that?"

"What queen does not desire a prince, my lord?"

The king drinks more ale and finally tells me why he's here. "Your priest says my survival and yours are due to his god—not Woden. Do you agree?"

"Woden has no interest in women, so God may have saved my life. But as to yours, am I the person to ask? Coifi or Bishop Paulinus know more about gods than I."

The king grunts and drinks again. "What do *you* think, wife? If I choose to be baptized, will I be stronger? Will I have more allies?"

"My lord, I hardly know how you could be stronger than you already are," I reply diplomatically, "but you will have Christian kings in England and Frankland to send you whatever support you need. And you'll have more scribes to keep an account of your wealth, as Paulinus already does. Do you not find his records helpful?"

"I am a king, not a steward," he sneers.

"Of course, my lord." I drop my eyes.

"I must settle this matter," the king says abruptly. "Your priest says your god is stronger than Woden. I suggest a test. Send for your priest."

Paulinus arrives so quickly, I wonder if he was listening at the door. The king motions for him to come forward.

"Paulinus, I have a proposition for you."

"Yes, Your Grace?" Paulinus gives a low bow.

The king stands and looks down on my bishop. "Do you still declare your god is stronger than Woden?"

Paulinus takes a step forward. "If he wasn't, Your Majesty, you wouldn't have survived the assassin's dagger."

The king narrows his eyes. For a moment he looks as if he has two options in his mind. He makes his decision and turns toward me. "After we open the campaign season, my warriors and I go to Wessex. I shall kill the treacherous King Cwichelm and take his land. If I'm successful, as I know I will be, I shall grant the pope's request and renounce Woden. Would that please you, my queen?"

I hide my surprise. "My lord, I can think of nothing to please me more. We shall stand together before God, who will make you a mightier king than you already are. Is this not wonderful, Bishop Paulinus?"

There's a strange tableau in my hall. I sit rigidly, trying to assess my husband's motives. Though I keep my face neutral, his unexpected vow catches me by surprise. Above me, the king looks satisfied with himself, as if he's won a trick at the gaming board. Below me, Paulinus wears a dubious expression. He doesn't believe the king is entirely honest, and he's probably right. I wait silently to see what the king has in mind.

Paulinus breaks the frozen tableau. "Your Grace, your generosity of spirit does you credit, and I have no doubt God will grant you the victory," he says smoothly. "You will be the greatest ruler this island has ever seen. But, regrettably, kings often forget their promises. Not you, of course, Your Grace." Paulinus opens his hands in a placating gesture. "But there will be so much to distract you after your victory that you may overlook your promise to God. I suggest a pledge in advance."

My husband's jaw sets a little tighter; there's a flicker in his eyes. He's always been so unreadable, even to those close to him. I dare not look at Paulinus as the king waves a hand, summoning a thane forward.

"With Bassus as witness, I pledge that after your god grants me victory, I shall renounce Woden." He looks to Paulinus, a dare in his eyes. "Is that sufficient, priest?"

I think Paulinus will agree, but he doesn't.

"Forgive me, Your Grace, but something more concrete is called for."

The thane's face blanches. I expect to see Paulinus dragged out of my hall for his boldness, but my husband suddenly laughs.

"There you are—completely dependent on my pleasure, and without a weapon—and yet you *question me*. Your god makes you bold. So, tell me, what do you think is an adequate pledge?"

"Your daughter, Your Grace," Paulinus says confidently, as if he's the king's closest advisor. "Allow me to baptize the infant and her household on Pentecost so she may serve as a living reminder of your promise."

My husband stands, walks to Paulinus, and claps him on the back.

"Done!" he shouts, and leaves my hall.

Hildeburg, Princess of Northumbria

News spreads quickly. The new princess will be baptized in the chapel. When the day comes, we crowd into the small space. The queen enters in her finest tunic, followed by the nursemaids and other members of the princess's household. The altar glitters with gold vessels and a golden cross. Light pours through the doorway.

Bishop Paulinus waits at the altar in special robes and a tall hat. He talks a long time about why baptism is important, and tells us we must hope the king will allow us to be baptized. He takes the princess from the queen's arms and walks to a special stand with a large golden bowl.

"Does this child have a name?" he asks.

"She is Enfleda," the queen replies.

Paulinus dips his fingers into the water and lays them on her head. "Enfleda, Edwin's daughter, I baptize you in the name of the Father"—he dips his fingers again and touches her head—"and of the Son"—he dips a third time—"and of the Holy Ghost. Welcome to God's kingdom."

Paulinus and the queen smile. He passes the child to the queen, who gives Enfleda to her nurse.

After that, Paulinus has each person in Enfleda's household kneel, and he goes through the same ritual. Each time, he and the queen smile, and she gives the new Christian a token.

When it's over, we go to a banquet in the Queen's Hall. I'm starving, but I'm also out of sorts. The queen's ladies from Kent, and the people who got baptized today, all sit near the queen, even if they're only servants. The rest of us are banished to the lower end of the table. I feel like we're being punished.

While we celebrate Princess Enfleda's baptism, King Edwin prepares for his attack on Wessex. Supplies arrive from throughout Northumbria. Three hundred chiefs arrive with their men, each war band bringing its own livestock until there is no place for the animals to graze. Warriors hone their skills in the morning and gamble through the afternoons. Farmers arrive with their pikes.

When all is complete, King Edwin and Coifi offer prayers to Woden for a successful campaign. The men pledge their loyalty in oaths of brotherhood sealed by mead. Finally, by foot and on horseback, the king, his sons, his thanes, and his allies depart for Wessex.

After all the noise and excitement, Sancton is deathly quiet. Doubt creeps into my mind. What if Woden removes his luck from our king? What if King Edwin is killed? The queen could return to Kent, but she might not take my family. I shake my head, remembering it doesn't matter if Woden turns his back on Edwin. The queen's god has to help him in exchange for the princess. I only hope her god is strong enough to protect the king.

Weeks pass before word arrives. King Edwin is victorious, but many are dead.

When King Edwin returns, the King's Hall is busy with celebrations. The scop's songs tell us about the battle near the rivers Noe and Derwent. My heart beating with excitement, I feel as if I'm there, privy to my uncle's knowledge that King Cynegils and King Cwichelm are bringing their men north to join forces with Penda of Mercia. Our warriors arrive at the rivers first and take the high ground atop the hill we later call Win Hill. King Edwin orders his men to build a barricade and drag boulders behind it. The scop doesn't mention it, but I know our farmers did the work while the warriors supervised, because thanes never dirty their hands with menial tasks. Our farmers are strong, but even for them it must have been hard work to bring the boulders into place. The scop sings about our warriors looking down on the combined army of Wessex and Mercia across the River Noe.

We were badly outnumbered, which makes our victory song all the sweeter. The thanes bang the table and boast of their exploits. I rush to keep their cups full as they praise the king.

Before the battle, both armies pounded on their shields, ready to fight each other to the death. Warriors never survive the death of their king, yet each is sure he will be the one to slay the enemy's leader. I think how the foot soldiers trembled, unable to flee, and imagine the thanes filled with the lust of killing.

Everyone waited, while envoys from each army met on an elevated site where everyone could see, and some could hear the reason for battle.

First, King Cwichelm stretched out his arm and declared my uncle a robber who stole his father's inheritance. "This day you will feel his son's vengeance! Come forth with your chiefs. Let this valley witness the might and strength of justice!"

Lies! My uncle takes only what is his by right.

The enemy army banged its shields. But my uncle's envoy never faltered. "Perfidious wretch! Do you have another assassin for your cowardly purpose?

You boast in vain. Before nightfall, this river will leave its bed to flow over the mangled remains of your dishonored dead."

Hearing the scop's song, our thanes pound the tables in the King's Hall, and I rush to pour more mead.

A second scop takes up the song. He waves a hand dramatically whilst delivering his tale of each army giving a mighty shout that was so loud, it frightened eagles high into the air. Grouse flew away, and red deer fled. My heart pounds at the mental picture, and I imagine the roar of violence.

Men rushed forward to fight hand-to-hand until the ground ran slippery with their blood. Warriors maneuvered around the dead and dying.

We fought hard, but enemy warriors managed to stream into the valley like an endless river, the scop sings, and the audience gasps. The scop sits forward, eyes wide as he details the way we fell back, fighting every inch of the way, to our hill with its barricades. Our enemy's cries of victory filled the air as their warriors crossed the river and began climbing the hill.

When our enemies had climbed too far to turn around, we descended to meet them. Arrows rained through the air. The battle recommenced with greater fury than before, until King Edwin sprang his trap by retreating back up the hill to our barricades. The enemy thought we were running away. When it was too late for them to escape, our men unleashed boulders and massive stones to roll down the mountain, crushing everyone in their path and pushing the enemy to the bottom.

Tears run down my cheeks as the scops sing their songs. The thanes, now glassy-eyed, clasp each other in brotherhood.

When our thanes reached the bottom of the hill, the dead were too many to count. The River Noe was red with blood and flowed over its banks. Woden's ravens flew over the field of battle, noting those who died bravely—enemies no longer. I imagine their spirits at the gates of Valhalla.

The enemy army was destroyed, but their leaders, King Cynegils and King Cwichelm of Wessex, as well as Penda of Mercia, escaped. King Edwin returned to us in triumph, now Bretwalda of England, with none to defy him. And yet, I'm uneasy, for now our enemies want revenge, and the cycle of war will continue.

The victory feast lasts until the next morning, the thanes falling asleep among the floor rushes, where they collapse off the benches.

Hereswid and I return to our mother's hut. We fall upon the bed, too tired to remove even our shoes. My sister falls asleep quickly, lightly snoring. I remain lost in the scops' songs of victory. So many brave men dead and given up to Woden, almost half our warriors.

Ethelberga, Queen of Northumbria

I lie awake, listening to a roaring sound at my ear and smelling fetid breath in my nose. It is, of course, my husband, the king, who came to me last night and fulfilled his promise to give me a prince. He attacked my body like a final enemy, concluding his advance with a mighty shout of victory. I am full to bursting and pray the child will soon make himself known, so my husband may find pleasure elsewhere.

I slide across the bed, reach my feet onto the floor, and walk with a shuffling gate to the door where my ladies wait to greet me with food and fresh clothing. Dressed for the day, I wait until sunlight enters through the doorway. When it touches my husband's face, my ladies and I leave him to sleep and walk to chapel.

After chapel, Paulinus follows me to my hall and kneels before me, his face divided between hope and despair. I invite him to join me as I break my fast. Before I swallow my first bite, the bishop speaks to me without being asked.

"When will the king keep his vow?" he asks. "When will the baptism take place? Easter is most appropriate for postulants to enter the church, but I can bring the ceremony forward. Perhaps at Christmas? I couldn't catechize the king before then."

"The king has forgotten his vow," I say flatly.

"That cannot be. He pledged his daughter."

"I don't know how you can be here so long and still misjudge the king. He's Bretwalda of England by the strength of his arm and Woden's luck. The scops sing of ravens circling the battlefield. Warriors await their rewards. He will not turn away from the source of his victory."

"But, Your Grace," the bishop sputters, "the king made a vow."

Before I answer, I spit a pebble from my bread onto my plate and chew thoughtfully. I drink a beaker of sheep's milk.

"Who was present?" I eventually ask. "Did his warriors hear him? Did he stand on the dais and proclaim his intention?"

"He made a pledge. I baptized the princess. You attended the christening."

"Yes. I attended with my household of ladies. Did you see the king?"

Paulinus drops his eyes. "No, Your Grace. But he allowed the ceremony."

"The king allowed it—but he didn't proclaim it."

My bishop's face fills with misery. "Then I have failed."

I rise from the table and beckon Paulinus to my alcove. "You must pray as you have never prayed before, but prayers aren't enough. You must also work without ceasing. Mention to the king that even as Bretwalda, he needs support against Wessex and Mercia. Praise him for pledging his daughter. Proclaim that God will give the king to his enemies if he fails to keep his vow. Do these things with cunning. And pray that I carry a prince, for that will soften my husband most of all."

Chapter 4

Anno Domini 626 – The Year Coifi Destroys Woden's Temple at Goodmanham

Ethelberga, Queen of Northumbria

To my surprise, Paulinus takes my advice. He is ever at the king's elbow, telling my husband how many cattle he has and where. The bishop praises my husband's power and asks how long he will keep it if he doesn't honor his vow. He tells the king God granted him victory and made Edwin Bretwalda of England. But the king, he says, hasn't kept his word.

When we are about to depart for Goodmanham, the king comes to me in my chamber. Before he reaches for my body, I give him another reason to convert. I tell him I carry a prince.

"You told me that before, and gave me a girl," he says gruffly.

I bow my head. "Yes, my lord, but God turned that tragedy to good. You allowed Enfleda to be baptized, and she grows strong. Your son will be stronger than she. But…" I let the word hang in the air.

"But what, wife? Say what you have to say."

"My lord, our child lives, but can yet be taken away. And the prince in my womb may fail. And even you, my lord"—I stop again, allowing suspense to funnel in—"God may yet turn his back on you, if you refuse your vow."

I think of what my life will be like if the king dies, and allow unhindered tears to flow down my cheeks.

I kneel before my husband the king. "I beg you, my lord. Fulfill your vow, so all may be well with us."

I don't see my husband on the journey to Goodmanham, nor does anyone else. He keeps to himself, and I know he is pondering what he should do. If he turns his back on Woden, will his luck change? Will the thanes stay with him? Will Coifi curse him? I find myself as nervous as the king.

Paulinus, Bishop of Northumbria

The wind is brisk this morning. Mayhap it will blow the clouds away and allow sunlight to filter onto the villa. The king's men look forward to the solstice celebrations at Goodmanham. They hang their shields on the wall in the King's Hall and waste their time gambling and drinking. The farmers and servants struggle to complete their tasks. Today, woodsmen are here too, wrestling with the oxen to pull an oak Yule log into the King's Hall. The oxen strain under the heavy load, their hooves slipping in the mud.

It takes most of the day to position the log down the center of the hall, its branches stripped off to serve as kindling and fodder for other fires. The cooks order their boys to bring smaller logs that give off a high heat. I hear pigs grunting as swineherds drive them to slaughter. It's a ghastly, heathen orgy of sound and blood, but one voice is notably missing.

The king isn't present. He's not jostling with the thanes. He's not directing the woodsmen where to place the Yule log. He's nowhere near his hall. I know he isn't with the queen. In fact, since she told him of her child, he avoids her. The king's absence is like a palpable, living thing—an abandoned heart ripped from its body.

I sense this is the time. He is ready to turn to God.

I make my way around men and animals to the king's chamber. The entry stands open. I peer in to see King Edwin staring into the central fire. He sits on a bench, his elbows on his knees and his head in his hands. He looks small and unsettled.

I walk toward him and bow deeply. "Your Grace."

King Edwin looks up and motions for me to sit beside him.

"Your Grace, you seem troubled," I dare to say, taking a seat. "May I put your mind at ease? Shall I pray with you?"

"You serve me well, Paulinus. I have a great decision to make. One I know can destroy me. If I turn away from Woden, my luck will change."

"It will, Your Grace. God will bless you and your kingdom more than He already has. He will forgive your sins and grant you eternal life in paradise. The decision seems large, but it is a trifle. Trust God, and allow me—as God's servant and yours—to lead you and your kingdom into new life."

Hope flickers in the king's eyes. "Can this be true?"

I place my right hand on the king's head, the same way the angel blessed him in the vision at Redwald's court. King Edwin leans forward, almost falling into my arms. I catch his weight and settle him back on the bench.

"Your Grace," I say almost inaudibly, making it clear we're speaking in confidence, "you've taken the first step already. God rescued you from your enemies and granted you a kingdom. Accept and trust in Him. Keep your vow. If you obey His will, which He reveals to you through me, He will save you from everlasting doom. Accept baptism, Your Grace. Join God's kingdom. It is a simple act of eternal importance."

Color returns to King Edwin's face. "I've watched you long enough to know you're sincere," he says. "And I think you place my welfare above your own. Otherwise, you would have desisted in your arguments. I was wrong to ignore my vow."

King Edwin stands and stretches to his full height. "Bishop Paulinus, I and my people will accept your God."

I can hardly believe the words. He could yet change his mind, but there's a note of conviction in his voice. I think he's tired of the struggle. It's easier to surrender to God than to fight Him.

As if he knows my thoughts, the king adds, "But we must wait a little longer."

"How long, Your Grace? Disaster might strike tomorrow. Will you face it without God's support and protection?"

"You're right, but it is a fearsome thing to lead my thanes away from Woden. It must be discussed in the Witan, so we may all be baptized together. I'll summon the chiefs at the Solstice, and we'll discuss the matter. Everyone will have a chance to speak, and we will be baptized together.

"I am a happy king, Paulinus." King Edwin clasps my elbow, as warriors do. "I know what I must do and what will happen. You have only to plan it and wait until the Witan rules."

I rush to the chapel and fall to my knees, thanking God for blessing my work.

The New Age is here.

Solstice is the longest night of the year—a time when men fear Darkness will swallow Light for all time. Warriors, ready to fight at the slightest insult, nervously glance into the twilight. The night is bitter cold, and the thanes readily enter the King's Hall. King Edwin has invited his chiefs to the Witan. Each comes with his closest advisors, the men pressing and squeezing into the Hall's warmth. Coifi arrives with a retinue of priests. They know what's coming. They know I will speak of the one true God, and they have nothing to say against me. Woden will fail them, as surely as Baal failed his priests in the contest with Elijah.

I stand by the king, wearing my finest robes and a mitre on my head. Coifi also stands by the king. His large golden neck torc reflects the torchlight, giving his face an iridescent glow. Edwin wears the golden tunic Pope Boniface sent him and a fur cloak.

Raising his hands for silence, he greets his chiefs and sub-kings. "I summoned you to rule on a matter of grave importance. Many of you know Bishop Paulinus, but if you don't, let me introduce him as my friend and close advisor. I, and my fathers before me, have served Woden. No one is more assiduous in the rituals and ceremonies presided over by our High Priest. And Woden has responded with luck, victory, and treasure."

The thanes shout and bang the tables. Cupbearers pour mead. King Edwin smiles and holds up his hands for silence.

"Woden has been generous to us, but times change. As your king, it is my duty to raise the question of whether Woden is strong enough to provide for the Bretwalda. Woden did not grant us victory against Wessex and Mercia." The king pauses and, momentarily, I fear he'll back out—refuse to go through with what we discussed. But then his jaw tenses, his posture goes rigid, and I know he's steeling himself to speak the truth. "It was the God of Bishop Paulinus who showed us favor."

The chiefs and thanes gasp in surprise at what they see as sacrilege, but Coifi shows no discomfort. *Does he expect Woden to strike down the king? Or does he already know the king's mind?*

Edwin raises his hands again to quiet the hall. "You know of the battle we fought," he says, the cacophony of outraged voices fading. "We were outnumbered. Rivers of blood covered the battlefield. Woden's ravens flew over us, watching for valor. But this wasn't a battle between followers of Woden, each seeking extra support from him. No. Wessex and Mercia fought for Woden. But I, and therefore you, fought for the new God, and he brought us the greatest victory we've ever had. This is the God who brought me back from exile and made me king and Bretwalda. This God will bring us more victories and riches than we've ever had before."

The men, pleased by the promise of riches, cheer and slap the tables with such force that I think the walls must fall. King Edwin stands before them, arms akimbo, absorbing their praise and adulation. Servers rush to refill drinking horns.

After the men drink, King Edwin turns to me. "Bishop Paulinus, have you anything to say?"

It's the moment I've prayed for since my arrival. The opportunity to speak to the Witan and fulfill my life's purpose. I arrange and rearrange my thoughts. If I fail, the king may change his mind. He won't ask men to change their allegiance unless he is sure they will follow him. I pray for courage and begin with the sign of the cross.

"In the name of the Father, the Son, and the Holy Ghost, I greet you with God's peace." I speak clearly and with authority, imagining myself as an Old Testament prophet.

"King Edwin," I continue, "is wise in spiritual as well as fighting matters. He followed the ways of Woden with great respect. But, as he just told you, Woden didn't make him king. When all seemed lost, God came to King Edwin in a vision. God said Edwin would be king, and here he stands before you as Bretwalda."

The warriors erupt again, stamping their feet and shouting. I wait for the sound to subside.

"God protects King Edwin, even now. He survived the treacherous assassin because the pope blessed the tunic he wears today with the blessing of God's Apostle Peter. He led you to victory, because he fought with God's favor.

"Now he asks you to consider which deity you will follow. You must decide who will give you victory. God alone can give you luck, as He did in the fight against Wessex. The old ways are overcome. Woden is defeated. Will you follow the new path?"

I bow my head to the king and step back. It is in God's hands.

As Coifi steps forward, I brace myself, but God has cleared the way.

"Your Majesty," he says, bowing to the king. "We must consider this new god. I have for some time thought our service to Woden has no value."

The hall erupts in seething astonishment at Coifi's admission. Even the king looks surprised. Coifi has done my work for me, by demonstrating that the issue is about more than supernatural support on the battlefield.

"Coifi," the king says, "you've never given any indication our ways are false. You preside over every ceremony. You make every sacrifice. Just today, your priests harvested the mistletoe that hangs in this hall."

"That is so, Your Majesty. I said nothing because I had no inkling of the truth. But my own experience told me our ceremonies have no purpose. Consider—I am devoted to serving Woden, Freya, and all our gods, yet when you dispense honors, you don't give them to me. You show greater favor to men who do little. If Woden had power, I would have greater favor. Yet you raise Bishop Paulinus to your court, and I receive little reward. Why did Woden allow that to happen? It could only be because he hadn't the strength to prevent a usurper from gaining your ear. So, I conclude that if this new god is stronger—if he grants those who worship him better benefits—then we should accept the new ways Bishop Paulinus brings to us."

Coifi bows to the king and returns to his place. I'm speechless. If the chief priest considers Woden a false god, then surely the people must turn to the True God. The hall is filled with voices, but no one stands to speak until the warrior Bassus—who fights at the king's right side—rises, bows to the king, and holds out his arms for attention.

"Comrades!" His voice booms, as if he stands on the battlefield. "Coifi speaks the truth. I too have given these matters some thought. Like many others, I've been close to death, and frankly, I don't think about it much. Warriors fight and die. It is our life. It is the life Woden gave us, but as Your Majesty says, the world changes, and there may be something more." Bassus takes a swallow of mead.

"I think life may be like the sparrow that flew through this hall as Coifi spoke. It comes from outside to the warmth of the hall, where it's safe from the winter storms. But then, the foolish bird flies out the other side. I've seen this many times, while listening to the scops sing. And I wonder if life is like this hall. We are here now, but we don't know what came before or what will come after. Will we go to Valhalla, if it exists? I don't know.

"I will never stop fighting for our king, but battle is harder for me now. My wounds are deeper, the healing slower, and I wonder what it's like outside the warmth of our life. I think it would be good to know these things, and it may be that the teachings of Bishop Paulinus can give us new knowledge. Our king is right. Our high priest is right. We should move into this new world Paulinus offers." The men watch Bassus raise his drinking horn in my direction.

"When he arrived, I thought Paulinus was a lapdog for our new queen. But he's proven himself a loyal follower of the king and a man devoted to his god. The god who brought us victory. We should listen to Paulinus. That's all I have to say."

The men stamp their approval. Coifi stands again.

"Your Majesty, I would like Paulinus to explain more about his god, what he requires from us and what he will give us."

The king bids me speak. I stand once again, facing these men with renewed vigor as I explain that God—through His son, Jesus, and the Holy Ghost—offers blessings in this world and eternal life in the next; that through Him, no man will be alone with his fears. I tell them that no matter what bad deeds they have done, baptism will cleanse them of their sins and make them God's sons. I'm deeply gratified when the men put down their drinking horns and listen to me. I tell them I and my priests will teach them the way to eternal life, and God will welcome them to heaven, not because of what they have done, but because they are part of His family.

And, because it is Solstice, a mere four days from Christmas, I tell them about Jesus's birth, and the signs and wonders that occurred. To my surprise, they don't dismiss the idea of kings paying homage to an infant. The miracle I witness humbles me.

Coifi comes to stand beside me, his priests arrayed behind him.

"There is no truth in our worship," he says. "I see now there never was. But the truth Bishop Paulinus brings will give us life and eternal happiness. Your Majesty," Coifi adds, turning to face the king. "I request that the temples and altars dedicated to false gods be destroyed."

The hall falls completely silent. We look to King Edwin.

"The matter is decided," declares Edwin, using a tone of voice that must ring over the battlefield. "I hereby renounce the worship of false gods. I accept this new god Bishop Paulinus brings us, and I command Paulinus to teach us so we may be baptized together."

The men roar their approval so loudly, I'm sure the building will burst.

"Who," King Edwin asks Coifi, "will destroy the false altars and temples? Who will obliterate their grounds?"

"I will do it myself," Coifi replies. "I built them. I worshiped at them. Who better than I to destroy the false god who never once acknowledged my service? Your Majesty, give me the weapons I was forbidden to carry and the white stallion I was forbidden to ride."

"Granted," the king says. "I give you this spear and sword with my own hands. My stallion stands outside ready. Let us waste no more time. Go, Coifi. Bring us into the new age."

Staggering slightly from the weight of his new weapons, Coifi walks through the hall and we behind him. A thane helps him mount the stallion. Coifi leaves for the sacred grounds near Goodmanham, riding like a madman. His white hair flows behind him like a halo.

Ethelberga, Queen of Northumbria

The villa is strangely quiet as my ladies and I walk to chapel. All through the night, the King's Hall heaved with spirits, as if some celestial battle was taking place. My husband's voice rang out, which didn't surprise me. But I could also hear Paulinus exhorting the thanes, his voice strong enough to ring through the night air to my chamber. My ladies and I spent the night in prayer, for I knew this was the moment. At last my purpose is fulfilled. It is a great relief that neither the pope nor Paulinus can chastise me for failing to convert the king. From now on, they will call me blessed for my faith.

Behind the chapel altar, Paulinus glows with exultation. As I take my place, I hear rumbling outside the door and the sound of weapons being stacked. The king enters, his thanes behind him. Paulinus gives each man a kiss of welcome and begins the service.

Coifi returns on Christmas Day. I tremble to hear reports of his actions. Coifi hurled his spear into the temple's center, profaning it for all time. He destroyed every image and set the entire temple complex on fire. I consider whether Woden ever existed or if, as Paulinus teaches, he was merely an imaginary figure. I can't help but think Woden must be furious, and I wonder if he will leave us be or use his followers to destroy us.

Inside the King's Hall we celebrate Christmas, as we do all feasts, with drinking and bluster. Paulinus announces he and his priests will begin preparations for the king's baptism after the Twelfth Day. The king gives his approval and toasts God.

Chapter 5

Anno Domini 627 – The Year King Edwin Is Baptized at York

Ethelberga, Queen of Northumbria

My husband paces, circling my chamber like a caged animal. Since Coifi destroyed Woden's altars, Edwin is in constant motion, as if Woden continues to struggle for my husband's soul. I hear the god's voice every time my husband growls in frustration.

"Come, my lord." I gesture to the stool near mine. "Sit down beside me. There are things to discuss."

Edwin stops to look at me and my rounding belly. "About what?"

"It hurts my neck to look up at you. Please sit." I hold up a cup of ale.

Edwin begins to take another step, stops, and sits down next to me. "What do you have to say, wife?"

To divert my husband's attention, I take his hand and place it on my belly.

"Will it be a prince this time?" he asks in a calm voice. "God should reward my decision to worship Him."

"Indeed, He will." Edwin withdraws his hand and looks away. "Husband," I say softly, so that he leans over to hear me. "You have so much on your mind."

He grunts. "So I have, wife. It is a fearsome thing to change a people's allegiance. Perhaps I betrayed the kingdom."

"No, my lord husband," I say with conviction. "You lead our people into eternal life. For the rest of time, people will bless your decision."

Edwin finishes his ale. I refill his cup, hoping this quiet moment will last a bit longer. We share the silence. I take my husband's hand and capture his eye. "It is time to decide," I say hesitantly.

"I have decided," he says in a husky voice. "You and I will worship the same God."

I hate destroying this rare tranquility between us. "My lord, you must choose where your baptism will take place."

Instantly, our peace is shattered. Edwin throws his cup across my chamber and stands. "Haven't I given my word to your priest?" he growls. "Haven't I rejected the god of my fathers and lost my luck? What more does your god want from me?"

"Husband, pray, sit down," I beg. "*Your* baptism will be a grand occasion with *every* Christian king, *every* chief, and *every* warrior in attendance. Your church will glitter with gold."

My husband narrows his eyes, imagining the occasion.

"It will be the greatest spectacle anyone has seen," he says. "*I'm* Bretwalda of England."

"Through the blessing of God," Paulinus's voice rings out from the doorway.

"So you say." My husband grunts and sits down, motioning for more ale.

Paulinus strides in, shattering the brief intimacy between my husband and me.

Paulinus, Bishop of Northumbria

I bow before their majesties and take a seat below the queen. King Edwin and his thanes attend chapel every morning, after which they come to the King's Hall for catechism lessons. The thanes watch the king, accepting direction only after he agrees. But the king seems to be of two minds, accepting instruction but still unsure of his choice. Lent began yesterday. Only forty days before the king's baptism, and there is still so much to be arranged.

"Your Majesty, this baptismal ceremony will prove to everyone your power and faith in God, who made you the strongest Bretwalda this island has seen."

"You flatter me," Edwin says harshly. "What do you want?"

"Your Majesty, we need to select your sponsor. May I suggest…?"

"You're the bishop. You do it."

"Your Majesty…" But the king is off on his own topic.

"I've been thinking about what you said. First, I thought to build the church at Goodmanham, but I like your idea better. As Bretwalda, I am as mighty as… who was the Roman emperor crowned at York?"

"Constantine, Your Majesty. The first emperor to recognize Jesus as his Savior. A man—" I pause. "A man much like yourself."

"That is true. God appeared to him, as he did to me. He turned away from false gods, just as I did. I am as great a ruler as he. Yes, I will be baptized where he became emperor. I will announce it tonight. You there!" The king shouts, pointing to one of the queen's ladies. "Bring in Aelfgar. I shall order him to start building my hall there at once. One large enough for all the men of England." The king nods to me. "And a church, of course. You can arrange that. I want it filled with gold and silver dishes on my altar."

"*God's* altar," I correct.

"Of course, Bishop, God's altar."

Aelfgar enters with two other thanes, bringing with them a scent of horses and cattle that overcomes the gentle fragrance of lavender and sage favored by the queen. Her Majesty inclines her head toward her husband and leads her ladies outside. The king is so filled with his plans, he doesn't notice her absence.

King Edwin stands and stretches. I rise.

"Why are you still here?" he asks. "Don't you have a church to organize?" Edwin strides toward the door.

I stand, gaping. Servants come in to light the wall sconces. The short winter day is over.

"Your Majesty," I call out as forcefully as I can. The servants watch from the corners of their eyes. Edwin turns from the entry door.

"If you have something to say, speak. I cannot dally here all night."

"Y-your Majesty, we still need to discuss your sponsors."

"I'll order King Eorpwald to be baptized with me," Edwin says dismissively. "I'll sponsor him."

"The king of East Anglia?"

"Yes. Write the letter. I'm sure he'll agree." King Edwin flashes a cunning smile. "I'll send out messengers. Everyone can contribute to the feasting. After all, I'm providing the hall. Come, it's time to join the warriors in my hall."

The king claps his hand on my shoulder. *It would be so easy to let him have his way.*

"Your Majesty..."

"Next time you write the pope, tell him I've named you Archbishop of York. A Bretwalda requires a priest of equal standing."

"Your Grace, my lord King, I really must insist..."

The king gives me a dark look. "Is the rank not to your liking?"

"I-it is, Your Majesty," I stutter. "It's far more than I deserve."

Edwin grunts and turns to leave, but I refuse to let him avoid the issue. "Your Majesty, I insist we decide on a sponsor for your baptism. There is a way to turn the office to your advantage."

Edwin has no more patience for me. I can see that his thoughts have left the room. "Speak quickly," he says in an irritated tone.

"The Kingdom of Rheged, Your Majesty. If you invite King Rhun to sponsor you, it gives you another ally, and I'm sure he'll see the value of supporting your cause."

King Edwin's expression turns from irritation to disgust. "Rheged." He spits the word. "*Celts.*"

"Yes, Your Majesty." I wet my lips. "They have no real standing—but would it not be better to bring them to your side before Penda and our enemies entice them to fight against us?"

King Edwin stares at me while his mind engages with my idea. I watch him consider my strategy, twisting it until it becomes his own idea.

"I will think on it."

Ethelberga, Queen of Northumbria

My husband the king moves us to York in the middle of Lent, though the halls are barely habitable. The weather is bitter cold and wet, the pathways swamped in mud. We keep the fire as well as we can in the Queen's Hall, but the workers put up the building too rapidly, and damp seeps through even the thickest tapestries.

I keep my ladies busy embroidering altar cloths and hangings for the church being built of timbered planks. The cloth is shot through with gold threads and has gemstones embedded in the stitchery. The flowers have rubies at their centers. We must finish and turn our attention to our gowns for the ceremony. I can hardly think for the stench.

Shepherds and swineherds drive animals to pens at the edge of the enclosure. Each chief brings cattle for the Easter feast. Everywhere smells of manure—and I have no fragrant herbs to mask the smells of animals and men.

King Eorpwald arrived yesterday. He and Edwin met Paulinus in the King's Hall immediately after chapel this morning, so my bishop ... no, now he's the king's archbishop. I'm overcome by events, and by the child kicking in my womb.

Easter Morning
Hildeburg, Princess of Northumbria

So much has happened since last Easter: Princess Enfleda was born and baptized; King Edwin almost died, but God saved him; the old gods fled from Northumbria; and today, King Edwin and his household will be baptized in the new church—and everyone will see I'm part of the king's household. The church will be beautiful with the hangings we've embroidered. I shift from foot to foot, waiting for Hereswid to fasten my torc.

"Hold still," Hereswid says. "You're jumping like a hare."

The torc is thick, twisted gold. And I have golden armbands. They look well with my new tunic. I'm also wearing a headdress for the first time. It's heavier than I expected and gives me a headache. Hereswid and I look like twins, except she's slightly taller.

We walk to the King's Hall, where the seneschal arranges us for the procession into the church. The archbishop and priests will go in first, followed by my uncle, King Eorpwald, King Rhun, and eventually the king's sons, Osfrid and Eadfrid. We are last.

Behind us, the highest-ranking chiefs and thanes stand shoulder-to-shoulder as witnesses. We're as crowded as pigs in their pen. I can't see what's going on.

My uncle's voice rings out as if he's on the battlefield. "I renounce him!"

"What does the king renounce?" I ask my sister.

"The devil," she whispers back. "We all have to do it."

"Is the devil Woden?"

"Probably. Look. The priest is coming. I think it's our turn now."

The priest walking toward us is clean-shaven and wearing a white cloak. He's the one who gave us the catechism lesson yesterday. He smiles, turning to lead the queen's household to the front of the room. As we pass kings and princes, Queen Ethelberga stops so we can bow. Those of us being baptized pass in front of the queen and the ladies she brought from Kent. We have to stand in front of them so they can sponsor us. I count my steps until I reach my place. Finally, I look up.

The altar is filled with gold and silver. A cloth of gold covers the table, with a gem-encrusted gold cross at the center. There are several vessels of gold and silver. I never realized how wealthy King Edwin is. All these dishes and utensils came from my uncle's hoard, and he gives them to God. I wonder how much more treasure he has.

Archbishop Paulinus stands before us, flanked by priests wearing white cloaks. Paulinus wears white robes trimmed in gold and an enormous triangular hat. He makes the sign of the cross and speaks in Latin. I don't understand all the words, but I know Paulinus chants them to chase the demon he calls the devil away from us, and all the false gods will leave with him. I suppose Goddess Eostre is gone now. We never praised her this season. I wonder if she feels lonely without us, and if she will still take care of our crops.

The priests separate. Each takes three of us, so Mother, Hereswid, and I are together. Our priest spits on his hands and touches our noses and ears.

"Be opened to the odor of sweetness. You, Devil, be put to flight, for God's judgment is here."

I shiver. *What if Woden doesn't run away? Will he punish us?*

The priest takes holy oil and anoints each of us on our breast and between our shoulder blades to strengthen us against the devil.

The archbishop asks the questions I memorized.

"Do you renounce Satan?" *He means Woden.*

"I renounce him," we each say, nervously glancing at one another.

"Do you renounce all his works?" *Does he mean Woden's luck? Woden didn't bother with women, so perhaps this doesn't affect us.*

"I renounce them," we reply, hesitantly.

"Do you renounce all his pomps?" *Do I have to throw away my charms? Will anyone know if I keep them?*

"I renounce them," we say, our words sounding like a sigh. *Who knows what this new life will bring?* My heart thumps in my chest, and I feel dizzy.

The priest puts his hands on each of our heads, and we individually recite our new allegiance: *"Credo in Deum, Patrem omnipotentem, Creatorem caeli et terrae. Et in Iesum Christum, Filius eius unicum, Dominum nostrum: quo conceptus est de Spirite Sancto…"*

The priest then takes each of us to a large bowl filled with water. When it is my turn I kneel in front of Archbishop Paulinus. He dips his hand into the water three times and touches my head each time.

"Hildeburg," he says to me, *"ego te baptizo in nomine Patris, et Filii, et Spiritus Sancti."*

When the ceremony ends, the queen gives each of us a kiss and leads us to the area set aside for us, in front of those who aren't baptized. The chiefs mumble and shuffle their feet. They don't like women being placed ahead of them. That alone could make them change from Woden to God. The archbishop and his priests begin another ceremony. Clouds of fragrant smoke surround the altar. Paulinus stands with his back to us, waving his arms as he does in the queen's chapel. He turns around, holding a silver plate, and nods to my uncle, the king.

King Edwin steps forward, followed by everyone who is baptized. The others watch as each of us receives a piece of bread. Mine has a pebble in it, but I don't dare spit it out. I hold it in my cheek and swallow the dry bread.

Paulinus pours red wine into a jewel-encrusted goblet. He offers a drink to the king, the queen, and the princes, while the rest of us watch.

Finally, Paulinus leads the priests out of the church, followed by the king and his family. I hope we'll feast in the King's Hall now, but when we get to the door, I see Paulinus and the king standing on a platform with the priests fanning out into a crowd of people from every class. The witnesses from the church stand in front of the crowd.

The archbishop asks who will step forward and join King Edwin. Who will reject idolatry and accept baptism? A great shout goes up.

Everyone will follow the king.

Ethelberga, Queen of Northumbria

Paulinus is the king's man now. He leads daily worship in the Great Church, while my ladies and I attend chapel led by a mere priest. Once Paulinus relied on me to intercede with King Edwin, but no longer. He's the archbishop, the man who will usher Edwin into heaven.

Paulinus told my husband an eternal God must have a church built of stone, so when people enter, they know the building will stand for eternity. Edwin agreed, and ordered foundations dug around the timber structure. I doubt Edwin cares what God wants, but he's impressed by the stone ruins of the Roman garrison. I know my husband. If the Romans built in stone, he will do the same.

I'm restless. I spent many hours preparing for the king's baptism, and now that it's over, I don't have a focus for my thoughts. Hildeburg reads aloud while my ladies ply their needles for new tapestries in my hall. Hildeburg's reading and understanding are much improved. She'll soon be fluent in Latin. Even Paulinus comments on her abilities.

I walk to the doorway and peer outside. I wonder when we'll leave York. It's two weeks since Easter. King Rhun was the first to leave. Gone back to Rheged, his kingdom in the wilderness. Edwin flattered him with honors and fine gifts of gold and horses. The next time I hear of him, he'll be Edwin's sub-king.

King Eorpwald accepted baptism. I expect the new alliance with East Anglia to be settled with a marriage. Hildeburg would be a good choice, but she's still too young. Hereswid is of a more suitable age, and it's time she married.

Hildeburg, Princess of Northumbria
June

The king decides to stay in York until it's time to leave for Yeavering. We arrive two days before the queen's birth pangs begin. This time I nurse her—cooling her brow and changing her linens. She's been crying and moaning for what seems like days. We get her up and walk her around. We put her in the birthing chair. But the child won't come out. The midwife and my mother confer, but they have no balm to sooth the queen.

The archbishop prays for the queen, when he's not too busy catechizing the villages.

Mother sends for an herbalist who makes the queen drink a vile-smelling concoction. We put the queen back in the birthing chair. When the pains start again, the midwife kneels down below the chair.

"Push!" my mother shouts as I hold up the queen's head. "Push!" Her eyes roll back. "Push again."

There's a shriek. The babe appears in a river of blood.

"Hildeburg—quick, take it." My mother passes me the blue-tinged newborn.

I grab the slippery burden, while the midwife stanches the blood.

"It's a prince!" I cry. I wipe the child's face and rub it. He makes a small mewling sound. "He lives!" I shout.

"Praise God," we all say.

"Send a messenger to the king," Mother orders. "He has a son!"

I wrap the child in swaddling and sit holding him near the fire. The women carry the queen back to her bed. She's pale as a newborn lamb. Mother wipes the queen's face and lifts her head for the birthing drink.

The prince looks up at me with tiny eyes, though I don't think he can see anything yet. I wonder if he's hungry. I place him in his mother's arms.

"Your Grace, will you feed him?" I ask several times before her eyes open. She gives a slight smile and puts the child to her breast.

"We need the wet nurse," Mother says. "The queen isn't strong enough to provide all he needs."

I hear shouts outside. King Edwin is in the King's Hall celebrating his new son.

⌘

After three days, the queen sits up in her bed. King Edwin sends word he's ready to meet his son. We scurry around the chamber, removing all signs of the birthing ordeal. We burn aromatic herbs and lay a warm fire. Most of all, we make the queen presentable, pinching her face to give it color. We brush her hair and arrange it around her face.

"Stop making such a fuss. He's here to acknowledge the prince, not to see me."

I wipe the queen's sweaty forehead.

"This chamber is too crowded," the queen complains. "All of you, wait in my hall. No. Hildeburg, you stay," she says, holding my hand, "and nurse, you hold the prince. Everyone else, get out."

The king arrives soon after the others leave and crosses the chamber in four broad strides.

"Show me the prince," he says, clearly delighted.

The nurse unwraps the infant, who gives a faint cry. Edwin touches the tiny face with his calloused hand.

"Swaddle him. The ugly creature will catch a chill."

"Do you acknowledge him?" I ask.

The king nods. "The first of many princes the queen and I will make together. My archbishop will baptize him tomorrow. Send him with his nurse and three ladies of your choosing."

The queen looks crestfallen. "Can it not wait until I'm on my feet?"

"No," the king says, gently. "Woden lurks to do us mischief. We must secure my son's health and future."

"What will you call our son?"

"Ethelhun, noble bear."

When Paulinus anoints Ethelhun's head with baptismal oil, something flutters above his head. Perhaps it's smoke from the incense. Or perhaps it's Woden's revenge.

The prince dies a week later.

King Edwin and Archbishop Paulinus take Ethelhun to York. He's the first occupant of King Edwin's crypt in the new stone church.

Queen Ethelberga is inconsolable, shrieking and tearing her hair. We fear for her life. Since the king's return, she refuses to see him, and he finds solace elsewhere until the fall harvest begins. On the night of the full moon, Edwin arrives at the queen's chamber unannounced and without attendants. He waves us out of the room.

"What do you want?" I hear the queen say.

"I want a prince, and I will have one."

By the time we celebrate Christmas at Goodmanham, the queen has a child in her belly.

Anno Domini 628 – The Year Prince Osfrid of Northumbria Takes A Wife

July

Ethelberga, Queen of Northumbria

Enfleda toddles around my chamber, followed by her nurse. She's a good girl and doesn't go near the fire. I thought she might want to hold baby Ethelthryd, but she has no interest in her sister. I hold out my arms so Enfleda can crawl into my lap. I take off her cap and stroke her baby-fine red hair. She has Edwin's temper when she doesn't get her way.

"It all began with you," I whisper in her ear. "You were the first baptism in Northumbria."

Enfleda squirms, and I put her down. I'm not recovered from Ethelthryd's birth, though it was easier than her brother's. I'm cursed to have only daughters. You would think a king as strong as Edwin would sire sons. He did well enough with his other wife. But he followed Woden then. Has the false god cursed me for taking Edwin away from him?

Outside, men jostle and gamble. Yeavering is full of chiefs and kings here to enjoy Prince Osfrid's wedding. Edwin's men strip the countryside of cattle to keep them fed. The King's Hall is filled with boastful warriors. I attend, but Hildeburg stands in for me, leading my ladies and taking the cup to each warrior.

Anno Domini 629 – The Year Prince
Wuscfrea of Northumbria Is Born

March
Hildeburg, Princess of Northumbria

After Prince Osfrid marries, the queen loses whatever luck she once had. Young princess Ethelthryd fails to thrive and dies, just as Osfrid's bride announces her pregnancy. And when we enter Lent, Osfrid's wife gives birth to a prince named Yffi. The child keeps two wet nurses busy.

The queen carries another child, and I pray she gives birth to a living prince. I'm certain another disappointment will kill her. She spends hours praying for God to protect her and grant her a prince, and she has little time for her duties. Hereswid and I oversee the household in place of my mother, who suffers pains in her legs.

∽◈∾

October

Queen Ethelberga's birth pangs begin before we're settled in the villa at Sancton. The wall hangings aren't even up. Hereswid and I walk with her around the room, though she begs to lie down. Sweat rolls down her face. She refuses the birthing drink. The queen shrieks and then moans.

Mother looks at us, shakes her head, and confers with the midwife. The pains become stronger and closer together. I think the queen will die. She hasn't eaten or slept in three days. We put her on the birthing stool.

"Push!" We shout as if our lives depend upon it. The midwife reaches up to take the child.

Mother puts her head next to the queen's. "Ethelberga, when the pain starts again, you must push with all your might."

The queen takes a deep breath and pushes.

"A prince! We have a prince!" the midwife shouts.

She slaps the baby. Nothing happens. She slaps it again, and we hear him cry.

I touch the charm I hide in my pocket. "Thank you, Freya," I whisper. "Keep the queen safe."

We send a messenger to the king and hear shouting from his hall.

A few hours later, King Edwin enters.

"Will the queen live?"

"We pray that she will," Breguswid replies.

"Show me my son."

I unwrap the infant and hold him in my hands.

"He's very ugly," the king says, tickling his son's chin.

"I don't know how you can bear to look at him," my mother replies with a smile. "Do you accept him?"

"The archbishop will baptize him today," King Edwin declares.

I swaddle the prince.

"What will you call him?" I ask.

"Wuscfrea, so he may have the cunning of a wolf."

Wolves belong to Woden. Is my uncle asking Woden to protect his son?

The queen heals slowly, her attention entirely occupied by her son and my sister's wedding to Prince Aethelric of East Anglia. Ethelberga orders the finest cloth from Frankland for Hereswid's gowns and tunics. The king has goldsmiths preparing gifts for her husband, Aethelric.

My uncle waited a long time to make this alliance. He thought he had bound King Eorpwald to him, but after Eorpwald was baptized, his wife persuaded him to return to Woden. Then he was assassinated, and East Anglia fell apart as God's punishment. *Or was it Woden's?* After three years, King Sigeberht came back from exile in Frankland and returned East Anglia to God, so now the alliance can go forward as though the wickedness had never happened.

"Stop fidgeting," Queen Ethelberga commands. "How am I to adjust this headpiece if you keep moving?"

"It's too heavy," I complain.

"All the more reason to practice wearing it. Stand still."

Hereswid smiles at my discomfort, too nervous to laugh. Finally, Queen Ethelberga is satisfied, and we begin our procession to the King's Hall. We enter through the queen's entrance, making our way to the floor. With Hereswid and I on either side of her, and the other ladies fanned out behind us, Queen Ethelberga escorts us to the king's giefstol. We make deep curtsies and wait for the king's word.

"Rise."

A stool stands ready for the queen. I see Archbishop Paulinus standing just below the king and to his right. Hereswid and I stand together, below the queen.

"My lord husband, I present the Princess Hereswid, daughter of your brother, Prince Hereric. At your word, she is prepared to meet her husband, Aethelric of East Anglia, and join our two kingdoms together."

The hall is as silent as a room filled with warriors can be. The seneschal holds out his arm to escort my sister forward.

"I can't," she whispers.

"You must, for the sake of our father." I want to give her an encouraging smile, but I'm afraid of dislodging the headpiece, so I squeeze her hand.

The seneschal waits, his face expressionless and his arm outstretched. My sister accepts his gesture. She looks small beside him. When they reach the giefstol, the king stands and turns Hereswid to face the hall.

"Here stands our pledge to East Anglia. Do you find her worthy?"

The men bang the table and thunder their approval. Before they become too enthusiastic, Paulinus raises his hands to command silence. He begins a long prayer of thanksgiving and asks God to bless my sister with safety and fertility.

"Amen!" King Edwin shouts.

"Amen," the thanes respond.

Paulinus makes the sign of the cross and returns to his place.

King Edwin holds up his chalice. "Tonight, Lady Hereswid welcomes you to my hall. Tomorrow, she departs to meet her bridegroom, and we take to the field against Cadwallon of Gwynedd. Drink up."

A thunderous noise breaks out, more at the thought of victory than my sister's beauty. The thanes will quickly forget her in their lust for battle.

Hereswid descends the dais, and together we play the role of hostess, stopping before each thane to fill his drinking horn. Each man praises her beauty, boasts of his past exploits in battle, and swears to die for the king.

The scops sing a song for Hereswid before retelling the story of King Edwin's victory at the Battle of Win Hill and Lose Hill.

Anno Domini 633 – The Year King Edwin Is Slain at the Battle of Hatfield Chase

Ethelberga, Queen of Northumbria

Every year my husband leads his men in battle. We need cattle, tribute, and slaves so we can reward our warriors. My husband's enemies need the same thing. Raids and counter-raids are an endless cycle, justified because our enemies follow Woden. Penda of Mercia to the south enjoys Woden's special favor, not always winning, but never truly losing. Cadwallon of Gwynedd is another matter. He professes to be Christian, but behaves with a ruthlessness beyond Penda's reprisals.

Now Penda and Cadwallon fight together, their alliance upheld by Cadwallon's marriage to Helen of Mercia. I warned my husband. I told him he was pushing too hard and taking too much. I told him they would join forces, but he laughed. "What does a woman know of battle?" he asked.

As soon as the campaign season opened, Edwin assembled his army and set out to find his enemies and destroy them. He took everything we have. The cattle and pigs are gone. The King's Hall is empty. Only I am left with my ladies, the children, the serving women, and a few sheep and chickens. The only men we have are those unable to fight.

I'm uneasy. Edwin isn't leading his army on an annual raid. He wants to destroy his enemies and take their land. There will be no bribes or hostages, only death.

⤐⟡⤏

Hildeburg, Princess of Northumbria

A hare dashes out from the edge of the forest, quickly followed by two young wolves. The hare changes direction, which I think is a mistake. The wolves follow it into the open area outside the villa. I keep my eyes on the hare's fast movement. One of the wolves gains ground and nips at the hare's hindquarters, but doesn't bring it down. The hare accelerates, changes direction again, and heads back into the forest—just as a few thanes stagger out.

I rush to the Queen's Hall. "Thanes are coming this way," I announce, and the queen's eyes widen with fear.

She stands, her hand at her throat. "How many?"

"Three, I think."

The hall explodes with activity. Servants rush to bring food and drink. In the courtyard, the men remaining with us assemble, in case these thanes are enemies come to destroy us. Archbishop Paulinus emerges from the church, adjusting his robes. Three men stand before us at the gate—or should I say *ghosts* of men, for they sway as if they are halfway to Valhalla. In the center is Bassus, my uncle's most trusted warrior. A bloody cloth covers his forehead, and there are tracks of blood through the mud on his face. I don't know how he can see. Perhaps he can't. Another thane drags his leg as he holds on to Bassus's shoulder. The third thane—I think his name is Giles—walks with a thick staff.

Their presence speaks of disaster, and there is only one reason Bassus would leave the king. Breath leaves my body, then returns with a gasp. Two servants and I rush forward to help the beleaguered warriors to the villa. When we reach the men, I grab Bassus. "Come, there's food and ale inside. The wise woman will bind your wounds. You're safe here." I don't know if Bassus hears me. His eyes are glazed. I link my arm in his. "Lean on me."

"Take me to the queen," Bassus gasps.

"I will, after we bind your wounds."

"There's no time. I must see her now."

I take Bassus's weight on my shoulder, and we cross the field. For once, I don't care where I step. It starts to drizzle. By the time we reach the villa's courtyard, the drizzle surrounds us in a heavy mist. Queen Ethelberga stands bareheaded in the courtyard, with her ladies around her.

"Bassus," she gasps in recognition. "Tell me there's another reason you're here. Tell me—"

Bassus falls to his knees in the mud. He kisses the queen's hand. "Your Majesty, you know the truth already. The king is dead."

Queen Ethelberga emits a low moaning sound that quickly turns into a shriek. She lifts her face up into the mist and begins to tear her hair. The queen's ladies lift her up and carry her to her chamber. I turn my attention to Bassus. Paulinus and I lay him on a bed of furs inside the Queen's Hall. The wise woman lifts his head and gives him numbing drink. We take off Bassus's bandage and wash the wound. I hold the edges of Bassus's skin together while the wise woman closes the gash with broad stitches. She smears the skin with a honey poultice and pulls me away.

"He and his comrades will live," she says. "But you must leave this place. No one here has their wits, so you must think for them."

"I? I don't know what to do," I wail.

The wise woman touches my head and my heart. "Think, and you will understand what happened and know what needs to be done."

I put on a cloak and walk outside, away from the queen's cries of anguish. The mist swirls around me. I remember the wolves chasing the hare I saw earlier today. *Wolves are Woden's companions.* I realize Woden wanted me to know of his victory.

In the Queen's Hall, the thanes and I sup on bread and cheese, waiting for the queen.

Bassus draws on his ale. "Where is the queen?" he asks. "We must depart before dawn tomorrow."

"You and the others aren't fit to travel," I counter. "Rest here for a day at least."

Bassus shakes his head. "There's no time, my lady."

I nod. "We will be ready."

When the queen opens the door, a cold wind blows through the hall. Bassus starts to rise. "Stay seated," she orders, "and tell me what happened to my husband."

Without a scop to sing a dirge for the king, we hang on every word Bassus utters. "We traveled south to meet Cadwallon of Gwynedd and Penda of Mercia in honorable battle. We underestimated their army, Your Majesty. And we thought God was with us."

Paulinus's faces flushes. He gazes at the rushes on the floor, unable to meet anyone's eyes.

Bassus swallows more ale. "We met the enemy on a moorland near the River Don, where we hurled insults at each other. I remember ravens circling the battlefield. I suppose they were attracted by the noise." Bassus falls silent.

"We were ready for battle." Bassus says suddenly. He looks at us as if we doubt him and wraps his hand around the beaker as if to crush it. "We held our lines, but Cadwallon's men pressed us away from the high ground. Prince Osfrid—" Bassus's eyes dart, as if witnessing the battle. "Osfrid fought without stopping, taking all comers, until—I don't know what happened. He fell." Tears leak from Bassus's eyes. "Then, King Edwin caught us by surprise. He rushed forward into the enemy like a madman. We couldn't reach him."

Bassus sobs. *Who could believe a thane would shed tears?* "The enemy," he continues, "they rained blow after blow on our king until he was defenseless, and then pierced his body with their swords. There was nothing we could do."

The queen's face is ashen. "You saw my husband defenseless and left him to die alone?" she asks incredulously.

Bassus hangs his head in sorrow.

Paulinus approaches Queen Ethelberga to comfort her. "The king is with God, Your Majesty. He and all our fallen have eternal life."

"No, bishop," the queen says without emotion. "He is dead. Is there more to say, Bassus?"

"I will never forget the sight, Your Majesty. When King Edwin fell, our army broke and ran away, slipping in the blood and mud on the battlefield. Woden's ravens swooped down to feast on the fallen, flying away with carrion in their beaks. Sprawled in the muck wondering if I was dead or alive, I watched Penda cut off the king's head and pound it into a stake as a sacrifice to Woden."

Paulinus moans and crosses himself.

"What will become of us?" I wonder. "How will we ever escape?"

Chapter 6

Anno Domini 633 – The Year King Edwin Is Slain at the Battle of Hatfield Chase

Hildeburg , Princess of Northumbria

We travel furtively, like robbers. After the battle, Penda withdrew to Mercia, but Cadwallon lays waste to Northumbria. He raids cattle, burns villages, and kills everyone he can find. We stay away from the roads as we make our way from Yeavering to the fortress at Bamburg, and from there to the sea. What will we do if the fishermen are gone? How will we get a boat?

Ethelberga, Dowager Queen of Northumbria

I am a displaced queen with two princes to protect: Yffi, my husband's grandson, and Prince Wuscfrea, my husband's heir. Both are too young to protect themselves in a world gone mad. My daughter, Enfleda, may become valuable again. But what will I do with my son? It's only a matter of time before someone seizes the throne and seeks to kill him, just as Aethelfrid tried to kill my husband. God made my husband king. Will he do the same for Wuscfrea?

Paulinus, Archbishop of Northumbria

"Out of the depths I cry to you, Lord. Hear my supplications. Save us, Lord. Please, I beg you on my knees. My hands are wet with my tears. Save us, Lord God. How can I serve you if I'm dead? Please bring us safely to Kent. Save us from the heathen monster."

I pray while tears stream from my eyes. I beat my chest and tear my clothing. I think we shall never reach the sea, and if we do, there will be no boat. Our clothing is tattered, and our bellies are empty. We live in terror of the devil's henchman. I am sure we will die.

Hildeburg, Princess of Northumbria

Caw, caw, caw.

I look up expecting to see ravens taunting us. Instead, seabirds with yellow bills swoop past us. We've done it. We're almost at the ocean. God hasn't abandoned us after all.

When we reach the sea, the fishermen are gone and the village deserted. We search each house for food and clothing, gladly consuming what we find. Bassus sends our few servants into the forest to trap game. Miraculously, they return with rabbits and squirrels. We roast them on spits over an open fire, tearing the meat off before it's fully cooked. Paulinus babbles about Jesus feeding five thousand people from one loaf of bread and two fish. But Jesus isn't here.

I approach Bassus and say, "This won't do. We can't stay here—we'll starve. The young princes fall ill already. King Edwin trusted you with our survival."

"I've gotten us this far."

"But we need to get to Kent. You yourself said Cadwallon is looking for us. It won't be long before he knows we're here. Please, Bassus, find a way. Get us on those boats."

Bassus rubs his hand over his head. He has lice like the rest of us.

"I can do that, my lady, but I've no one to sail them, and no one to fish."

"How hard can it be? The servants can row. If we keep the coast in sight, we won't get lost. And we can fish well enough to survive."

"Warriors don't fish."

"They do if it's the only way to eat. Give the order and transfer us to the boats."

"*Boat*," Bassus corrects me.

"We're too many for one boat. The queen's household, the archbishop's priests, servants, baggage…One boat can't carry us all. We need at least two. Three would be better."

"My lady, you're right. We must leave. But we sail in one boat. I won't risk becoming separated. We take one boat, or we stay here until we find the fishermen."

Bassus and I glare at each other.

"Then search for them. Find a pilot who can take us south."

Bassus spreads his hands. "They're gone."

"They're in the forest. Hunt them down the way you do poachers."

Bassus shakes his head and turns to walk away. *You won't get off so easily.*

"Or shall I tell the queen and the archbishop you're a coward? That after King Edwin died, you ran away?"

Bassus swings back around to face me, his weathered face glowing red. "That is a lie," he growls. He raises his hand, as if to strike me.

Inwardly quaking, I stand my ground. "Perhaps, but everyone will believe it. Your reputation and that of your family will suffer for generations."

Bassus drops his hand and looks inland to the forest. "You drive a hard bargain, my lady," he says before stomping off to confer with the other two thanes. They trot toward the forest. I watch until they disappear into the trees.

Please, God, let me be right. Let them find fishermen to handle the boats and someone who knows the way south.

⚮

I go to the queen's wagon and tell her we have too much baggage to fit in three boats.

The queen looks at me in astonishment.

"We have little enough, and I can't fit my household onto one boat. The children … my ladies … What about our tapestries and plate?"

"I'm sorry, Your Majesty." I turn to the ladies who came with Ethelberga from Kent. They found husbands, only to lose them on the battlefield at Hatfield Chase. "Everyone, wear your warmest clothing. Bring blankets, not tapestries. Bring whatever gems you have. Nothing extra. There isn't room."

"But presents!" Queen Ethelberga exclaims. "I must have the tapestries as presents for my brother. I can't arrive empty-handed."

I shake my head sadly. "Better to arrive empty-handed than not at all, Your Majesty."

The queen looks at me with hollow eyes before turning to her treasure box.

⚮

The priests set up an open-air altar with a wooden cross made from tree branches. They kneel before it, begging God to rescue us. I hope God sends the fishermen I requested. Archbishop Paulinus kneels in front, his black robes billowing behind him in the wind.

"Archbishop," I call.

He stops praying, crosses himself, and comes to me. The others open their eyes slightly but continue praying.

"Does the queen summon me?"

"No, she's busy paring down her baggage, and you must do the same. As soon as Bassus brings men to sail the boats, we leave. The boats are small. Bring only warm clothing and treasure. Nothing extra."

99

For a moment I expect Paulinus to argue, but he simply nods and returns to his prayers.

❧≈❧

Waves creep up the shore. If we aren't aboard the boats when the tide is high, we'll have to wait for the next cycle. The remaining servants we brought with us from Yeavering bring our baggage to the high tide line. The men slip away, a few more each day. Bassus doesn't go after them, and we can't feed them anyway.

I hear shouting and swearing. *Praise God!* The thanes prod a dozen men roped together. I wait outside the queen's wagon until Bassus comes to me.

"My lady, we have enough fishermen to sail the boats, and a pilot who knows the way south." Bassus prods a stooped, grizzled man forward. "Tell the lady your name."

"I be Hud."

"And you know the route to Kent?" I ask.

Hud shrugs. "I been past the Humber. I can get you there."

"And beyond?"

Hud shakes his head and laughs in a way that shows his yellow teeth. "None of us knows that."

Hud doesn't inspire me with much confidence, but he's the only pilot we have. "How did you persuade those men to help us?" I ask Bassus.

"I said if they didn't come with us, I'd kill them where they stood." Bassus glances at Hud. "I may kill them yet."

❧≈❧

Ethelberga, Dowager Queen of Northumbria

When the tide is low, we splash through shallow water to the boats. They sit tied to logs, listing a bit to one side. Paulinus, surrounded by his priests, clutches the golden altar vessels Edwin gave the church. Hildeburg makes a game with the children, pointing out seabirds. The princes join in, waving their arms, but Enfleda walks with me, pulling her feet up from the wet, sandy bottom.

What a shattered group we are. How could God let this happen? I persuaded Edwin to convert. I bore a living prince. And now I return to my brother as a beggar with nothing to my name. It is a great humiliation. I glance at Paulinus. He, I'm sure, will find another post. But there's no place for the widowed queen of a conquered kingdom.

Bassus cups his hands around his mouth. "Your Majesty." He shouts and gestures. Waterlogged nets float beside him. "Your Majesty, may I suggest we use these fishing nets to lift you and your ladies to the deck?"

I'm speechless. How could I fall so far?

Bassus responds to my hesitation. "The only other way is the rope ladder, and, well…"

I ignore him, calling Hildeburg forward. She arrives at my side, cheeks red and lips chapped by the wind rolling off the grey coastline. I shiver against it. "Bassus tells me the only way to board this ship is in a net or on a rope ladder."

The girl looks from me to the ship, and then to Bassus, who shrugs. "I suggest the children use the net," she says. "If the thanes support us, we can climb the ladder."

And so we do.

Paulinus and his priests choose the net. Watching Paulinus hold on to the sides of the net as he's hoisted aboard the next boat, I almost laugh out loud. The sea air will do him good.

Hildeburg, Princess of Northumbria

At twilight, we pull the boats ashore, because the fishermen won't sail at night. We disembark and search for whatever we can find: firewood, edible vegetation, the occasional small animal or bird we can catch with our hands.

During the day, we run fishing lines off the sides of the boat. We're wet, sick, and terribly afraid.

At first light, Paulinus quickly leads us in prayers, and we launch the boats as soon as the tide allows. I almost wish our puny vessels would sink and relieve us of this desperate journey. But they struggle on in their wobbly dance upon the sea. I stop bailing seawater from the bottom of the boat to look at the horizon.

A voice in my ear. "Have courage."

It's Hud. The man we forced to come with us. I move away from him.

"We cross the mouth of the Humber soon," he adds, as though that's any consolation.

I sigh, keeping my eyes fixed on the horizon: an endless stretch of grey water. Gulls dive into the sea, looking for their next meal.

Finally, I turn, looking back at Hud. "And then what?"

Hud shrugs. "Who knows what tomorrow will bring? I never thought I'd be here."

We cross the mouth of an enormous river and almost lose sight of our boats. We pull the boats ashore before sundown so Bassus and his thanes can find out where we are.

They return with men and several wagons.

"My lady, come quickly," Bassus shouts from above the tideline.

Queen Ethelberga and I scramble up to the wagons without assistance. A man wearing a king's badge kneels before us.

"Your Majesty, I am Saewine, reeve of King Eadbald's villa at Reculver. On behalf of the king, I welcome you to Kent."

Queen Ethelberga holds out her hand for him to kiss.

"Rise," she says. "Take us to my brother's villa."

Bassus leads King Eadbald's men to the shoreline to unload the boats and summon our men. Archbishop Paulinus and his priests are at their prayers.

The moment they realize our salvation is at hand, they raise their hands to heaven and prostrate themselves on the sand. Paulinus quickly springs up to join us, leaving his priests to follow.

Hud passes me on his way to the last wagon and nods his head. "Your courage gave God time to test you before answering your prayer. He has great things in store for you."

"Are you a priest as well as a pilot?"

"I am neither. I'm a man who reads signs and waits in stillness."

I shiver as he walks on, and climb into the queen's wagon.

Ethelberga, Dowager Queen of Northumbria

We're home at last in my brother's domain. Saewine assigned us Queen Emma's chambers. I wonder what she's like. Everything here is perfect, and it's not even the most important villa. The timbered wall planks are set exactly next to each other and decorated with bright colors. Smoke from the fire escapes easily through the roof without tainting the air.

Servants bring us warmed red wine in glass beakers. And food. Meat, not fish. Cheese and sweetmeats. Servants bathe my children, wrap them in furs, and settle them to rest.

A maid picks lice from my hair and washes out the saltwater. I scrub sea foam off my body. I sleep. When I wake, there is new clothing for me. Linen undergarments, a soft wool tunic, and shoes made of supple leather. I wonder if they come from Frankland. I braid my hair tightly and cover it with a new cap.

I ask Lady Hildeburg if I look good and twirl in front of her. My ladies come to me wearing new garments. Saewine invites us to the Queen's Hall. When we arrive, I offer my hand and allow him to escort me to the queen's chair. Archbishop Paulinus takes a seat next to me. He should be below me, but now isn't the time to quibble. Saewine sits on a bench slightly below us and motions for Bassus to join him. Hildeburg and my ladies sit at the head of the table. The priests, dressed in new linen, sit below them, followed by Saewine's thanes. Servants fill everyone's glass beakers. I've never seen so much glassware; the table sparkles with it.

Lord Saewine rises, lifting his beaker. "Your Majesty, the king bids you welcome. On his behalf, I offer a toast of thanksgiving for your safe arrival."

The thanes bang the table—not in the jolting way of Northumbrians, but rather authoritatively.

I incline my head and say, "Lord Saewine, I thank my brother for his generous hospitality at a moment when our fortunes are somewhat reversed. When I am restored to my proper place, you and he will be rewarded." This is not the time to admit I have no place.

The scop strikes his harp. Already he's composed a song about our bravery and courage on the sea. In his rendition, I triumphed over my enemies to rescue my household. In truth, I spent most of my time at sea puking over the rail. I prefer the scop's interpretation of our escape to the harsh reality of fear.

"Lord Saewine," I ask, "where is my brother, the king?"

"At Lyminge, Your Majesty. As soon as he learned of your escape, he told me to watch for your arrival." He pauses to lift his beaker in Bassus's direction. "Indeed, Your Majesty, I looked for your men as earnestly as they looked for mine. Our meeting is a blessing from God."

Bassus raises his beaker in response, and motions for more wine.

Lord Saewine smiles, his gaze still fixed on Bassus, though he's speaking to me. "You are the king's most honored guests. My fastest messengers are on their way to tell him the good news. You have nothing further to worry about."

I mean to thank him again, but Archbishop Paulinus approaches. He's cleanly shaven, dressed properly once again—and smiling broadly, as though we haven't all been through hell since my husband's brutal death.

"My lord," Paulinus says with a sweeping bow.

Lord Saewine's brows raise. "Yes, Archbishop?"

"I should like to offer a service of thanksgiving tomorrow."

"Of course. The chapel near the King's Hall is at your disposal. I also sent a messenger to Archbishop Honorius at Canterbury. He'll want to meet with you."

"And I with him."

"Lord Saewine," I interject, "when shall I hear from my brother the king?"

"It will take about a week, or perhaps two. The quickest way is by sea, but we must round the peninsula, which can have storms this time of year. Rest assured—you'll be with His Majesty by Yule. Pardon me, Lord Archbishop, *Christmas*."

Every day for three weeks I watch the horizon for my brother's envoy, until he finally arrives with an escort of twenty thanes and an invitation. I'm too nervous to open it, so I send a servant to find Hildeburg.

"Did you send for me, my lady?"

"Obviously, or you wouldn't be here." I'm waspish with anxiety. What if my brother doesn't offer us shelter? "I have a letter from the king. Read it and tell me what it says."

Hildeburg takes her time unfolding the vellum. She smiles. "My lady, he invites us to spend Christmas with the court at Lyminge." Hildeburg raises her shining eyes to my face. "Lord Saewine said Lyminge is the king's favorite villa. I'm sure the celebrations will be wonderful."

"Does he write anything else?"

Hildeburg scans the letter again. "The king says it fills his heart with gladness to have you home in Kent again."

"Give me the letter, so I can see the words with my own eyes." I wave my hand. "You may go." I want to see if the letter is in my brother's own hand. It isn't. Not even the signature. I ponder what this means. If my brother is truly pleased I'm here, surely he would sign the letter himself. Yet he extends every courtesy to me. I wonder what plans he's making.

Hildeburg, Princess of Northumbria
Christmas at Lyminge

Incense billows around the altar and anyone near it. Archbishop Paulinus—attired in new vestments and wearing a mitre—presides over Christmas mass. The altar glitters with gold and silver dishes and paraments made from cloth of gold, but it's the walls that fascinate me. They are painted with images of Jesus and saints with eyes that follow everyone in the room. Paulinus calls these "icons."

Queen Ethelberga's ladies have new silks and furs. As the highest-ranking lady, I stand next to my queen but behind King Eadbald, Queen Emma, and their children: the heir Eorcenberht, who is about eight seasons, the same age as Princess Enfleda, and Prince Eormenred. Princess Eanswid is at a nearby monastery called Folkstone Priory. They say she rejected marriage to a pagan prince. She's either very brave to oppose her father or afraid to follow Queen Ethelberga's example.

Archbishop Paulinus is in his element here. This church is far more elaborate than the stone church at York. Princess Enfleda and the two princes squirm next to me. It's hard for children to stand for so long, but Queen Ethelberga insists they be present. She says it's important for everyone to realize that the rightful heirs of Northumbria are in Kent and that Oswald, who now rules Northumbria, is a usurper with no standing.

It's midday before we stroll to the Queen's Hall to break our fast. The aroma of roasted meat and a warming fire fed by a yule log laid down the center of the hall greet us at the door. We take our places in order of rank. Queen Emma reverences the king and welcomes us to her hall.

Ethelberga, Dowager Queen of Northumbria

We spend the Twelve Days of Christmas at my brother's court. Every day we feast and enjoy entertainments. Now the season is over, and we Northumbrians are summoned to the king's chamber. I dress carefully, so my brother can see I am a queen equal to his wife, despite the fact that I arrived in rags. My undertunic is linen with embroidery at the neckline and hem, and I fasten the overgarment with my own brooches. I clasp my armbands and neck torc, the gifts Edwin gave me on our wedding day. Their golden hue glows in the firelight. I also brought buckles to attach on my shoes. My silk headdress wraps around my head and shoulders, reducing the effect of my jewelry. I'm not entirely pleased with my appearance, but the garments support my status as queen. I take a deep breath.

Lady Hildeburg, also dressed in new garments, arrives to escort me into my brother's presence. She, too, wears golden armbands and a neck torc. I was afraid she might have lost them. Hildeburg bows to me. When I bid her rise, she kisses my cheek.

"Do you think my brother will send us to a monastery in France?" I ask. "There are several there for high-born ladies. Perhaps we could go to Chelles."

Hildeburg shrugs. "I hope, for your sake, that he does as you wish."

My brother's seneschal is at the door. Hildeburg takes her place two paces behind me. It is time to meet my fate.

"Dear sister." King Eadbald kisses my cheek and takes my hand. "Come near the fire. May I offer you wine while we have our discussions?"

I accept a beaker, holding its warmth in my hand.

My brother selects a sweetmeat and chews thoughtfully, before wiping his fingers on a linen cloth. "We've been so busy in this holy season, we've hardly kept up with events in Northumbria."

"I know enough," I say, after sipping my wine. "I know my husband's enemies laid waste to our lands and butchered our people."

The king shakes his head. "Such heathens," he says. "Events will run their course; order will return."

Run their course? Penda and Cadwallon burned our villages, took our cattle, and left the people to starve in the cold. They put my husband's head on a pike. I squelch my emotions.

The seneschal escorts Archbishop Paulinus into the room. He bends his knee to my brother, sitting before being invited. He used to be so obsequious; now he ignores every propriety. I'm surprised my brother allows such behavior. Perhaps it's because he's sending Paulinus away from his court.

"My lord archbishop, how good of you to come. I know you must wonder where God calls you. I have a letter from Archbishop Honorius at Canterbury. It's unusual to have two archbishops within one kingdom, but the diocese at Rochester is vacant. Archbishop Honorius recommends it for your use. Will that do? It's the only place able to support your rank."

A relieved expression crosses Paulinus's face, quickly followed by disappointment and a slight flush of anger. *Did he think he might go to Canterbury? Surely not.*

"Your majesty is most kind to share this unexpectedly ... joyous"— Paulinus clears his throat—"news."

"Archbishop Honorius writes he will receive you at Easter, before you take up your responsibilities. Travel will be easier then. Do you concur?"

"Of course, Your Majesty," Paulinus responds, his face completely blank. "You do me great honor. As always, God's will is done."

"Good. That's settled. Until then, pray continue leading the churchmen here. It benefits them to be near a man of your learning and piety."

Paulinus glances in my direction. He knows my position will fall beneath his. A widowed queen is no queen at all. Within the folds of my garments, I clench my fists.

"And you, dear sister," my brother goes on. I school my expression into neutrality, trying to master myself. "How shall we settle your affairs?"

I clear my throat, staring at my beaker. "My first thought is for the princes. I should like to send Wuscfrea and Yffi to Frankland. I thought to put them under King Dagobert's protection."

"The poor lads are in a dangerous position. So young and no father…"

"Yes, Your Majesty," I interject. There's no need to reflect on our situation. I appeal to my brother. "The boys have only your good offices to secure their future."

My brother's brow furrows. "Yet you don't ask *me* to protect them. You want to send them to King Dagobert."

"I thought, perhaps, since your good queen is from Frankland…"

"And what of yourself, dear sister? Surely you wouldn't leave us after we've been so long apart?"

What does he mean?

"I'm their mother. I must go with them. I can join a convent, perhaps at Chelles, or…"

"No. I won't allow the entire Northumbrian royal family to go to Frankland. You might set up a court against me," he confesses, and I feel my blood run cold at the accusation, "or pit your boy against mine for the throne in Kent."

What! Why does he think that?

"Your Majesty, dear brother," I say, truly taken aback, "I never thought of such a thing. I thought only to protect King Edwin's princes."

"As a proper mother should." He pats my hand. "Do you like it here at Lyminge? It's my favorite villa. I come here as often as the land can support my court. The sea air makes it a healthful place. Don't you think so?"

"It's a wonderful place, Your Majesty."

"Wouldn't you like to stay?"

"With your court?" I ask hopefully.

"Alas, no. My court has only one queen," he says, a sparkle in his eye. This is clearly something he's planned. "But there is a way you could stay."

He smiles broadly and sends for more wine.

"Archbishop Paulinus tells me you have a pious nature. You and your ladies. He credits you with the late king's conversion, and I'm sure he is right. Our mother, Queen Bertha, told me herself that God has a special task for you. Was she right?"

He's laying a trap for me, pushing me away from the princes. I glance at Paulinus, who keeps his face expressionless.

"Your Majesty, dear brother, I'm merely God's handmaiden. It was Paulinus…"

"Yes. You are right. God's handmaiden. That's you. Your ladies aren't the only Kentish women without family. There are many women of high birth who lack the means to enter a convent in France. As God's handmaiden, you must help them."

"I? I have nothing."

"But I could give you the means and receive God's blessing for my generosity. Your archbishop and Archbishop Honorius agree. We need a women's monastery where such useless women may go to live their lives in service to God—and you are the very person to lead the endeavor."

"But…" *What is he doing? No! I don't want to lead a women's monastery.*

My brother keeps talking, and there's nothing I can do. "You can build on the Roman ruins on the other side of Lyminge," he says. "They aren't much now, but I'll send men. And you and your sisters can stay in one of the halls here until all is complete."

My future is gone. Instead of going to the aristocratic house in Chelles, I'm to lead my ladies in prayer, locked away forever.

"Your Majesty…"

"It's all settled. Before we leave, your archbishop can administer holy vows to you and your household. Princess Enfleda will join Queen Emma's household. When the weather improves, Bassus will take the princes to Frankland. I've thought of everything." My overfed brother rubs his hands together. "Are you pleased, Ethelberga—soon to be Abbess Ethelberga?

I bow my head. *I'm not pleased at all. I force myself to say,* "You're most gracious, Your Majesty. May I ask, what of the Princess Hildeburg? She's no kin to me. Her sister married into East Anglia. Perhaps..."

"Yes, of course. Perhaps they'll pay a bride price for her."

⤜∞⤛

The next morning, I explain everything to my ladies. They are as shocked as I was. I never envisioned being shut away.

A servant announces Archbishop Paulinus and brings in wine.

"My lady." He nods his head.

"Archbishop," I say flatly. "Come to gloat?"

The smile disappears, replaced by a sharp intake of breath.

"I came to offer my congratulations," Paulinus says with sincerity. "You are chosen to build the first women's monastery in Kent. You will set the model of service to God. What greater blessing could there be on earth? You are both abbess and dowager queen—a high rank in both realms."

He makes the sign of the cross over my head, while tears of frustration quietly run down my face.

"I don't want to be shut away from decent company," I confess.

"You think you will be lonely, but you have God and your ladies. Gentlewomen from all over Kent and other kingdoms will come to you for solace and guidance. When I leave for Rochester, you'll be the spiritual counselor closest to the king, if you choose to make the most of the opportunity God gives you."

"And you, Paulinus... Are you pleased to be placed at Rochester?"

"Well, I can hardly displace Archbishop Honorius of Canterbury. After using my strength in the service of God and King Edwin, I'm not sure I could adequately carry out the duties of his office. God blesses me."

"And what do I tell my children?"

"That God calls you in one direction and them in another. It is the truth, after all."

Hildeburg, Princess of Northumbria

On a dry, blustery morning, the royal households assemble in the timber church. I walk with Queen Emma's ladies, a prince holding my hand on either side and Enfleda walking next to her brother. Ethelberga and her ladies spent the night in the church, prostrate on the cold floor. By the time we arrive, servants have built up a fire. Priests surround us, waving censers back and forth. The women, dressed in somber clothing, kneel before the altar.

I thank God I'm not among them. I'm only twenty years old, too young to have my future taken from me.

Archbishop Paulinus stands before each woman, asking questions I can't hear. After they all answer, he prays. They stand and walk past us to exit the building. Ethelberga is the last to leave, with unshed tears in her eyes.

Part 2

ENFLEDA

Anno Domini 642 — Anno Domini 664

Chapter 7

Anno Domini 642 –
The Year Princess Enfleda Learns Her Fate

Hildeburg, Princess of Northumbria

I often ponder the way God's favor passes from one king to another, as capricious as fortune's wheel. Our family's misfortune brought back the princes my uncle drove out of Northumbria when he returned from King Redwald's court. King Edwin said he ruled by Woden's luck. Later, he gave credit to God. But he was only a small piece in a cosmic struggle. When gods dispute, kings die. Edwin's princes are dead; his queen in a monastery; his daughter, Enfleda, neither nun nor princess; and I am less than that.

The kings of East Anglia have no use for a dispossessed princess, so King Eadbald marries me to an old man who served him well in battle. I bind my husband's weeping wounds, keep his hall supplied, and warm his bed. In his battle-hardened way, he is kind, and I am grateful.

Ethelberga, Abbess of Lyminge

Lyminge Abbey extends farther than my eye can see—and it belongs to me. The community began with only myself and my ladies, but well-bred women join us almost every month. Most are widows. Some are young women who, for various reasons, will never find a husband. A few even *request* a life of spiritual seclusion. We leave the prayers to those who enjoy them. Most of us are content to embroider while a scop sings. To my pleasant surprise, I find it is better to be God's handmaiden for eternity than even the wealthiest widow dependent on the winds of fate.

Yet when my daughter asks to take her vows, I refuse. I don't want Enfleda in a monastery where monotonous litanies make every day the same. I want her presiding over her own court beside a powerful king, as I did. She can come here later. But not now, in her first blush of womanhood.

Enfleda comes to my chamber after morning prayer.

"Lady Mother," she says, kneeling for my blessing. I offer it gladly, pleased with the way she always complies with my wishes. Now I must give her guidance she will try to avoid.

"Come sit beside me," I say, gesturing to the weather-beaten wooden bench I've commandeered. When she does, I look at her, brushing her straw-colored hair out of her eyes. "Do you remember what I told you when you asked to take your vows?"

"You said I should marry a king instead." Enfleda smiles. "Have you found one?"

"As it happens, I have."

Enfleda's chin drops. Her breath makes a soft, whooshing sound of surprise.

"King Oswy's wife is dead, and he requests your hand in marriage. You will be queen of Northumbria, as I was."

"No," Enfleda replies coldly, her posture suddenly rigid. "I won't return to Northumbria. Nor do I wish to be a queen."

"Enfleda, you don't know what you're saying. I've no doubt Oswy will become the most powerful king in England, and you will be an excellent queen."

Enfleda covers her ears with her hands and shakes her head, as though she can escape reality by retreating into her mind.

I edge closer to her and grasp her shoulders. "Enfleda, stop it," I say gently. I pull her hands off her ears. "The arrangements have already been made. You're to marry King Oswy next summer."

"I don't want to marry a king!"

"I didn't want to be an abbess, but here I am. It's a good life, one you will have after you serve as Queen of Northumbria."

"What makes you think I'll outlive the king?"

"I'm sure he'll be killed in some battle, like your father was. Now stop this nonsense and accept your fate." I kiss my daughter's forehead. "It is done."

Anno Domini 643 – The Year King Oswy of Northumbria Marries Princess Enfleda of Northumbria

Enfleda, Princess of Northumbria

My mother sends me to Queen Seaxburg's court the same day she announces my marriage. A refugee for the second time, I struggle to please the queen.

"Everyone will hold me responsible," she says. "Your mother taught you nothing but prayers, Latin, and embroidery."

The queen sends to Frankland for silk and cloth of gold. My traveling chests fill with linen undergarments, ermine cloaks, glassware and beads, buckles for my shoes, and brooches as clasps for my tunics. I wear gold torcs and armbands.

"It is too much," I protest.

"You are a queen now," she says. "You cannot shame us with coarse garments from your mother's monastery."

At Christmas, the queen places me in charge of entertainments. I and my ladies—young girls who should still be at their lessons—fill the warriors' drinking horns and ask them about their deeds of valor. My kinswoman, Lady Hildeburg, and her husband come to court for the season, but not my mother. King Eorcenberht doesn't favor the villa at Lyminge and prefers to be near Canterbury.

An escort of priests and thanes led by Utta arrives before the campaign season opens. I attend them at a welcome banquet in the King's Hall, trailing behind Queen Seaxburg as she welcomes our guests. "Welcome to King Eorcenberht's hall," she says. "Drink, and tell us of your king."

Hildeburg, Princess of Northumbria

Princess Enfleda circulates among the priests, who don't drink, and the thanes, who do. She reminds me of her mother at the same age.

King Eorcenberht gestures toward his cousin. "Is she not a perfect bride?"

The thanes shout, bang the tables, and raise their drinking horns.

"Utta, come forward. Tell us your wondrous tale of how you calmed the ocean waters. My scops will set it to music."

Utta, conspicuous in his rough robe and sandals, rises from his place and strides forward.

"Your Majesty." He bows. "The tale belongs to God and Abbot Aidan, who gave us God's holy oil. When storms blew up to lead us astray, we poured the oil upon the sea, and the winds died so we could make our way in peace."

"Could you not make it a better story?" King Eorcenberht complains. "Tell us how high the waves rose. How did you place the oil in a churning sea?"

"We are simple priests, Your Majesty. I can't describe what happened, only the blessings of God."

"Did you save any of this oil for your return?"

"Enough so Princess Enfleda can sail without fear."

Princess Enfleda invites me to her chamber for a private farewell. Her boxes sit strapped and ready for the journey. We share beakers of wine, its ruby color glinting through the glass.

"Have you remembered to take wine with you?" I ask to break the silence.

"Of course, though I think wine flows further north now than it did when my mother went to Northumbria."

"No doubt it does. King Edwin was but a short time on the throne when he sent for Ethelberga. King Oswy's family have been in place for a decade, restoring order and trade routes."

Enfleda nods and picks at the embroidery on her tunic.

"Your future is safe in God's hands. Don't be nervous. I'm told King Oswy is handsome and clever."

"It's not that."

"Are you worried about the wars with Mercia?"

"A bit. The Mercians..."

"Fight for power. Enfleda, that is a fact you will never escape. Even in Kent, we are vulnerable to warfare. I know you're afraid of what might happen in battle, but there's nothing to be done except trust God." I grasp her hand. "Do you have something else on your mind? The marriage bed? Surely the queen or her ladies instructed you..."

"Yes, of course." Enfleda takes a gulp of wine.

"What, then?" I tire of this virginal inability to speak plainly. "King Oswy's other women? What of them? King Eorcenberht keeps concubines. They take nothing away from the queen."

"I don't care about that side of things. My lady mother told me she was happiest when my father visited other women. What I want to know is whether there will be a war between King Oswy and Oswin of Deira. Will I have to flee again?"

"It depends on who wins the struggle to unite Northumbria. Oswin is your nearest living kinsman. By Edwin's blood, he has rights to all Northumbria. But King Oswy's brother, Oswald, ruled Northumbria before his death. Naturally, Oswy wants what he believes to be his. With you as his wife, he too has ties to King Edwin. And your children will have Edwin's blood. But there's nothing you can do to protect yourself from wars between kings. You have to trust God. He brought us safely to Kent. I'm sure he'll keep you safe in Northumbria."

"I don't understand how something that has nothing to do with me controls my life." Enfleda gives me an intense look, as if I can change her fate. "I can't help who my father was," she declares.

I cup Enfleda's cheek in my hand and speak with authority. "Enfleda, a woman's purpose is to further her husband's ambition and give him sons, as I'm sure your mother told you." The girl drops her eyes. "Look at me." When I have her attention, I explain, "Your father wanted an alliance with Kent and, eventually, with the Roman church. Your husband wants to unite Northumbria by both arms and blood. That is the way things are. You must accept it."

We sit together long enough for me to finish my wine and hope it brings some of its color to my cheeks.

"And my uncle gave my mother Lyminge ... ?" she says hesitantly.

"As a reward for her service to Kent and the church. Queens aren't like kings. A king holds his place by success in battle. If he loses, he dies. But women, by the grace of God, have other spaces. If King Oswy loses his quest, you will find another home." I squeeze her hand. "With me, if I'm living."

Enfleda finishes her wine, smiles, and walks outside with me. The crisp air and birdsong promise that a lovely summer will appear in a few weeks. I squeeze Enfleda's hand again.

"Thank you for your wise counsel," she says, her face as serene as it once was troubled. "I'm ready to face my future now."

At the church, Archbishop Paulinus presides over a service of thanksgiving and blesses Enfleda's marriage, as he once blessed Ethelberga's.

"May you be fruitful," he says. "May you serve God."

"Do you wish you were going with her?" my husband asks.

I consider the question. There's no place for me in Northumbria. I take my husband's arm. "No," I reply. "My life is with you."

My husband smiles and taps my hand. "I'm glad to hear it."

Enfleda, Queen of Northumbria

My husband reminds me of my father. Edwin had a barrel-sized chest, a red beard, and a rheumy nose from drinking too much mead. He was Bretwalda of England, his only concern victory and power. He cared little for my mother, nor she for him.

Oswy is younger, taller, stronger—his hair a golden halo that streams behind him when he trains for battle. He's determined to be Bretwalda of England, like my father. Like his brother. He married Princess Rieinmelt on his brother's orders, so Oswald could attach Rheged to Northumbria. Oswy put away a woman he cared for to make the match. Court gossip says she was an Irish princess. No matter. Gossipers also say Oswy rejoiced when Rieinmelt died, that she blocked his ambition. I try not to listen.

I'm drawn to Oswy like a moth to a candle flame. When I arrive at Bamburg, my little ladies dress me in my finest tunic and costliest gems. On the shore, my husband stands like one of the old gods. He holds out his hand. I take it and set my face to the north.

The king comes to me every night until I can no longer hide my pregnancy. Oswy smiles, then scolds me for keeping the child a secret. The next morning, he sends me a ruby pendant for protection.

Months later, I rub my belly and feel my son kick. And then, something else: a pain so sharp, I'm bent over. The little ladies rush to my aid as the pain washes over me. They walk me around the room and wipe my brow. When the old woman arrives, she pokes and prods. She gives me a vile concoction to drink. My ladies keep me walking until I beg to sit down. Then they prop me in the birthing chair. I'm exhausted with it all.

My ladies hold my head up.

"Push," the midwife commands. "Push again."

What does she think I'm doing?

"Keep bearing down. I can see his head."

I grit my teeth, give the most powerful push I can imagine, and expel my infant. The child cries.

"You have a prince, Your Majesty."

I've never heard sweeter words.

The ladies clean me, put me in bed, and put my swaddled son to my breast. *He's beautiful.*

"He is shriveled and ugly," my husband says to keep the fairies from taking him. "Too weak to be a warrior. I will call him Egfrid, the sword's edge."

When I'm strong enough to sit in a chair, Abbot Aidan walks from Lindisfarne to Bamburg. In a timbered church, Oswy presents my son for baptism. Five-year-old Alhfrith stands by his father, accepting congratulations from the warriors. His sister, Alchfled, barely out of small clothes, stands with my little ladies.

Abbot Aidan stands before me with a smile and twinkling eyes. "Unwrap the child, please."

"He'll catch a chill," I protest.

"Not from me."

I unwrap my son's swaddling. The abbot lifts the naked baby from my arms, carries him to the font, and dips him into the water.

"Egfrid, I baptize you for the Father," he says.

He's giving Egfrid to the water. The nymphs will take him. I struggle to stand.

He dips my son again. And then a third time.

"Return my son," I beg.

The abbot covers my crying son with a linen cloth.

"Why were you afraid?" Aidan asks. "Egfrid is safe with God."

Anno Domini 646 – The Year Abbess Ethelberga of Lyminge and Princess Hildeburg of Northumbria Meet for the Last Time

Hildeburg, Princess of Northumbria

The summer sun warms my face as I wander through Abbess Ethelberga's herb garden. Each section has its own fragrance. I pick a sprig of mint and crush it between my fingers before tasting it.

Sister Wassa touches my shoulder and asks, "Do you have indigestion, Lady Hildeburg? Shall I mix a tisane for you?"

"I'm fine. I just like the taste."

"Take some with you." Sister Wassa ties together a small bundle. "Take rosemary, also. For the fragrance."

I smile and stroll back to the raised terrace, where my kinswoman sits reading her Psalter.

"Where were you?" she asks.

"Just in the garden. See? Sister Wassa gave me these."

Abbess Ethelberga sniffs my sprig of mint.

"Sit by me," she says. "I think this is my last summer, before God calls me to heaven. I mention it because if you join my monastery, you will naturally become the next abbess."

My heart jolts with a premonition of loss. "Why do you say that?"

"That it's my last summer, or that you could be abbess?"

"The abbey isn't complete yet. You must oversee the work."

"The abbey isn't complete, but my tomb is."

"What do you mean?"

"My chapel is on the north side of the church. All that's left is to put me in it." Ethelberga chuckles. "So, will you take vows? Your husband's been dead a year. Surely you've thought about it."

"I have a sister. Do you remember?"

Ethelberga looks past me to the horizon. "No. Remind me."

"Hereswid. She married Aethelric of East Anglia. She sent me a letter. She's made arrangements to go to the convent at Chelles and invites me to go with her."

"A princess should be an abbess. You won't be an abbess in Chelles."

"No, but I'll be with Hereswid." I reach for Ethelberga's hand. "Your hospitality is gracious, and Lyminge is more beautiful than heaven can ever be. But I want to be with my own family when I cross over."

"I understand. You're the only family I have left who cares for me. Will you stay until summer ends? I'll ask King Eorcenberht to grant you safe passage to the King of East Anglia's court."

I don't want to stay, but I agree. Ethelberga could have married me away from the court. She could have left me behind. But she brought me to Kent, and I've been happy here.

Ethelberga, Abbess of Lyminge

My nephew sends twenty thanes to escort Hildeburg and her ladies to East Anglia. After we embrace one last time, I watch the wagons pass through the gate, and I remember the girl I taught to read.

She mustn't go to Frankland and be lost to us. I go inside to write a letter to Abbot Aidan. Surely someone at his abbey can translate Latin.

⌒⌒⌒

Hildeburg, Princess of Northumbria

Like Kent, East Anglia is a fertile and wealthy kingdom. I'm so excited about seeing Hereswid, I scarcely notice. *Will I recognize her? Will she remember me?* But when I arrive at King Anna's court, I discover Hereswid didn't wait for me. I wrote to her and said I'd be here in time to sail for Frankland with her. Why didn't she wait for me?

The queen gives me accommodation for as long as I need it. How long will I have to wait before sailing?

I sit, brooding, trying to come to a decision. Shall I try to travel to Chelles now? Would it be better to wait until spring? I can't decide. I send for my nephew. Perhaps he can advise me.

After chapel the next morning, a slender youth enters my chamber and kneels before me with his head bowed. "Lady Aunt? I am Ealdwulf."

I feel a ripple of surprise and pleasure. "Rise, please. It is I who should bow before you."

He's a tall young man with hair the color of corn tassels and deep blue eyes. I search his face for a wisp of my sister, but find none.

"Please sit," I say. "Tell me about your mother."

"I'm sorry she's not here. If she had known ... She didn't want to wait until next spring. Anglia has no house for royal women. And she wasn't sure you would come."

He looks helpless in his explanation.

"You look like my mother," he says.

"Did she think I would stay at Lyminge?"

"I don't know. She waited for you all summer." Ealdwulf gives me a reproachful look. "You can stay at court and cross over in the spring. My uncle will arrange it."

Anno Domini 647 – The Year Princess Hildeburg Returns to Northumbria

I pass the winter months in prayer, directing my mind to give up worldly pleasure in favor of contemplation. My ladies and I embroider vestments to take with us to Chelles, and take turns reading scripture aloud.

At last, all is ready. The winter storms die down. We pack our chests for the journey. Ealdwulf comes to wish us Godspeed and gives me a letter for his mother.

I'm finishing my farewell letter for Enfleda when a visitor arrives. His feet are bare, his hair unkempt, and his tunic torn. He holds a staff and wears the largest cross I've ever seen.

"We haven't met," he says. "I am Abbot Aidan from the Holy Island of Lindisfarne."

"Lindisfarne?" I repeat dumbly. "In Bernicia?"

"Your family home. Do you remember it?"

I don't know what to say. I send one of my ladies for wine and refreshments.

"Forgive my manners. You must sit, Your Grace."

"I'm a mere monk. Call me Aidan."

"You've had a long journey. Why are you here?"

"You, Princess Hildeburg. I am here for *you*." Abbot Aidan's eyes twinkle, as if we share a wonderful joke.

"I don't understand. Who sent you?"

"God—and in a roundabout way, Abbess Ethelberga, God rest her soul, and King Oswy of Bernicia."

"Enfleda's husband?"

"The very same." Abbot Aidan eats an oatcake with great enjoyment. "Abbess Ethelberga wrote of your plans to join the convent at Chelles. She thought you should establish a house in Bernicia, and I agree. It seems I arrived just in time."

"Your journey is wasted. I'm going to Chelles."

"God doesn't want you there."

What! Who is this man to tell me what God wants or doesn't want? "How do you know?"

"I talk to him. You should too. God will tell you that your duty, as a Christian woman and a princess, is to serve His people in the north."

All these months my mind has been at the monastery at Chelles. I prepared tapestries and altar hangings. I practiced the litanies. I turned away from society in favor of contemplation. And now this scruffy monk comes from Northumbria and says God talks to him. *No! I refuse to accept his word for it.* Aidan looks at me and smiles. I shake my head. "We don't even believe the same things," I argue.

Aidan spreads his hands to reason with me. "You and I profess the same faith in the Father, Son, and Holy Ghost. We believe Christ died for our sins. We have the sacrament of baptism and celebrate Easter. We're the same in our hearts. Don't let the difference between the Columban rite King Oswald brought to Northumbria and the Roman rite of your baptism confuse you. Pray upon it, and you'll know God calls you north."

"I'm going to Chelles," I say with defiance, even as my resolve weakens. "I want to be with my sister." My voice drops off.

Abbot Aidan shakes his head and smiles. "Daughter," he says simply, "there is nothing for you to do at Chelles. In Bernicia, you can serve God. You can uplift his church. Feed the hungry. House the poor. You can sing the offices, if that's what you want to do."

"I have to think."

"No. You have to pray, perhaps for the first time. Here is my suggestion: come north with me, bring your household, and establish a monastery. I will personally instruct you in the Columban Way. If after a year you still want to go to Chelles, King Oswy will arrange it."

Abbot Aidan looks at me expectantly, as if he already knows my answer. He is right. I grew up in King Edwin's court. I belong in Northumbria, serving his kingdom to repay his kindness to me.

My monastery by the River Wear is a poor affair: a timbered church, living quarters, one hide of land to support us and the people who work the land. Aidan says my first lesson is humility. My second is to establish a way of life.

When we arrive, Abbess Hieu, a wizened woman of few words, raises her eyebrows.

"You don't need all that," she says and sends our wagons to her monastery at Heretu.

She directs us to our cells. Small rooms with no fire or wall coverings to keep out the chill—only a sleeping area on the floor and a candle.

"Abbess Hieu, I protest our accommodation. My ladies and I can't live under such conditions."

She looks at me with rheumy eyes. "I was a hermit before I was a nun. Completely on my own until Abbot Aidan consecrated me. You're never away from your women. You can't hear God over your chatter."

"We keep silence."

"You chatter in your heads. You sign with your hands. Your prayers are hollow. When you learn how to pray, Aidan will teach you how to rule a community. I hope you learn soon, so your sisters can follow your example."

Hieu sets us on a schedule. So many hours reading scripture. Worship throughout the day. Labor to establish a garden. We learn to bake bread and boil porridge. And we pray in strict silence until I, at least, can converse with God. And if my "sisters" don't believe me, they accept my word for it.

When the summer days begin to shorten, Aidan returns.

"Sister Hildeburg," he says. "Hieu tells me you and your sisters are ready to take your vows, and that you're ready to lead them as their abbess."

If I become an abbess, I'll lose this life of contemplation I've come to love. I'll have to protect my sisters from the world's predators: from kings and bishops and the devil's temptations. I turn my face away. "I don't know what you mean," I say. "The position is too much for me. My faith is too weak."

Aidan smiles. "Hieu says you're ready, as I knew you would be. The only question is whether you accept God's call and King Oswy's request. If you remain in Bernicia, your connection with Edwin supports the king's claim to the throne."

I shake my head. "Queen Enfleda does that," I protest. "The king has no need for my services."

"Oswy is a careful man. The closer he seems to Edwin, the stronger his claim to power. But that's nothing to do with God's claim on you. There's no point in resisting," Aidan says.

We sit in silence until I realize Aidan is right. My desire to be with my sister in Chelles is an illusion. I don't even know if she lives. And I've come to crave the silence of prayer. It was Penda and Cadwallon who cast me out of Northumbria, not Oswy. Besides, his queen is my kinswoman.

Aidan and Hieu hear my vows and those of my sisters. We reject the world's vanities and vow to serve the poor. We continue our life together, self-sufficient in our own world, until I receive news that I'm appointed Abbess of Heretu.

❦

Anno Domini 650 – The Year King Penda of Mercia Attacks the Fortress at Bamburg

August

Enfleda, Queen of Northumbria

Penda's forces ravage Bernicia. He raids our cattle and sets our fields on fire. And King Oswy, that bellowing warrior, can't stop him. Now Penda's army camps outside Bamburg, our strongest fortress, unable to enter and refusing to leave.

I peer down from the wall overlooking our lands. Every day wagons stacked with thatch and fencing materials pull up outside the walls. Men unload wood, wattle, thatch—all dry in the August sun. The stack of kindling grows higher each day. They will burn us out, if my husband doesn't force them away.

A small hand tugs at my sleeve. "Lady Mother, come below."

"Egfrid, it's not safe here."

My son clutches a small wooden sword. He reaches out his left hand.

"No," he agrees. "Come below."

We go to my chamber. I wonder which is worse: being burned alive or being slain by a sword. Alchfled, my husband's daughter, hands me a beaker of ale.

"It's a hot day," she says, as if our lives don't hang by a thread.

Sometime in the night, the wind shifts. Penda's men light their fires. The only escape is the seaward entrance where our enemies wait for us. The thanes watch for my signal to open the gate. I hesitate. Surely it's safer to remain inside.

"Your Grace." A young thane kneels before me until I signal him to stand. "We cannot remain inside." He directs my attention behind me where the flames burn hot enough to melt stone. The wind blows embers onto my skirt. I look at my son's soot-stained face. "You must open the gate, Your Grace. I swear on my life, I will see you to safety."

I nod and say a small prayer that we will not drown. Just as I raise my arm, the wind changes again, bringing cool air from the sea. The fire begins to retreat as men beat it back with anything they can find. The wind continues blowing against the fire until there is nothing left to burn. I fall to my knees with my son by my side to thank God for his mercy.

The scops sing of our divine rescue. Aidan saw the flames and said, "Lord, see what evil Penda does." The wind shifted, and those who would burn us found themselves in the fire.

Now that it doesn't matter, Oswy is back.

"Why didn't you come?" I ask my husband. "Why did you leave us here, helpless?"

"It was a ruse," he says. "Oswin of Deira, your cowardly kinsman, lured our army away. Our forces were massed and ready near Catterick. He saw our army, knew he couldn't win, and sent his men home. Coward! We rooted them out of their hovels. They won't take up arms against us again."

"And Penda?"

"Gone south to prey on East Anglia." Oswy laughs. "Woden's luck won't help him in Bernicia. I named Oswald's son Ethelwald sub-king in Deira. He's loyal and fights well."

"What happened to Oswin?" I ask. "Did you kill him?"

"No, not I—Hunwald, his own man, betrayed him. He sent word Oswin was hiding at his house, so I sent my thane Ethelwin there to kill him."

I'm aghast. "But that's murder!" I exclaim, "How could you give such an order? God will punish you. We must make amends."

"Oswin ran away from battle. He plotted with Penda to take Bernicia. He deserved to be killed."

"In the heat of battle—not in cold blood. Will you confess to Aidan?"

"I'm sure he knows already."

A week later, Aidan dies. I think he was too good a man to see my husband's treachery. My husband has no such qualms, but to atone for his perfidy, he joins me in founding a monastery where our kinsman Abbot Trumhere leads prayers for Oswin and my husband.

We have a few years of peace while Penda competes his conquest of East Anglia and appoints his son, Peada, as sub-king. Immediately, Peada requests Oswy's daughter, Alchfled, as his wife. At first, I think he must be mad to suggest such a match. Alchfled is a child, not yet ready for the marriage bed. But then I see the advantage. Oswy's daughter will be a promise to guarantee peace.

"I won't do it," Alchfled stamps her foot. "Two years ago, his father tried to kill us."

"Penda and I have an understanding," Oswy says. "He rules the south and I the north. It's natural for equals to declare their connections with a marriage. At least until we're strong enough to fight again." My husband smiles, showing his teeth.

"Husband," I interrupt tentatively. "Your heir married Penda's daughter, Cyneburg. Surely that secures the peace?" Oswy narrows his eyes but doesn't stop me, so I continue. "There's also the matter of religion. Peada follows Woden. You cannot marry your daughter to a pagan."

Oswy laughs uproariously, as if I'd just told him a joke. "Such religious scruples, Enfleda," he says, still chuckling. "Everything is arranged. Peada will be baptized, and I'll stand as his godfather."

"What about Penda?" I ask. "Will he allow it?"

"He will if it keeps the peace."

Abbot Finan baptizes Peada and his warriors at Wattbottle. Peada is so sincere, he returns to Mercia with four priests. Alchfled is a lovely, if reluctant, bride.

❧❧❧

Anno Domini 652 – The Year Queen Enfleda of Northumbria Sponsors Wilfrid's First Pilgrimage to Rome

Enfleda, Queen of Northumbria

A young man in monastic garb, but without a tonsure, kneels before me. I met him five years ago. He was a cocky lad then, sure he could find a place at the king's court. "He's too young," my husband had said. "Too thin. Perhaps you can find a place for him. His manners are too good for a thane. Mayhap the scops can teach him to sing." My husband had tousled the boy's hair then, and laughed.

But Wilfrid didn't want to sing. He wanted to study with Aidan's monks at Lindisfarne, so I sent him to Cudda, one of Oswy's thanes who had retired there. I hadn't expected to see him again.

I decide to let him off his knees.

"Rise," I say. "What brings you here? Did you decide not to become a monk after all? Were the studies too difficult?"

"Quite the opposite, Your Majesty. They were too simple. There's nothing more I can learn at the abbey. I memorized the psalms and the gospels. I adhere to all the observances, but I find them hollow. Your Majesty, will you help me?" he says earnestly. "I must go to Rome. I must study with the great scholars and learn the ancient traditions."

There's a fire in his eyes.

"Rome? Do you realize how far away Rome is? It's on the other side of the sea and the mountains. You'll never survive the journey."

"I must try. Please, Your Majesty. Will you help me?" He looks so sincere with his scraggly beard and reddish hair.

"I can't send you to Rome, but I'll write a letter of introduction to my cousin, King Eorcenberht of Kent, asking him to help you find your way."

"May God bless Your Majesty. You are forever in my prayers."

⤜✣⤛

Anno Domini 654 – The Year King Oswy of Northumbria Trades Princess Elfleda For Victory Against King Penda Of Mercia

Queen Enfleda of Northumbria

The marital peace between Mercia and Northumbria doesn't last long. In less than two years, Penda launches another sequence of cattle raids. He needs treasure to reward his thanes. Oswy gives him my son, Egfrid, as hostage for our good behavior, but Penda continues his border raids.

I don't think Penda will be satisfied until he is Bretwalda of all England and our family disappears forever. Oswy empties the treasury and rides out one last time to offer a bribe in exchange for peace. Penda laughs in his face. There will be no truce.

While Oswy is away, my daughter, Elfleda, comes into the world. She feeds well and waves her arms and legs when we remove the swaddling. I love her with a ferocity that frightens me, and I vow to keep her close by.

When Oswy returns, he acknowledges Elfleda as his and summons every thane in Northumbria to a Witan. With Abbot Finan by his side, Oswy makes a deal with God.

Oswy vows to meet Penda in open battle, and calls on God for victory against Woden. In exchange, Oswy pledges my precious babe to the church as a consecrated virgin to serve God forever. *Please take her,* I beg God. *Keep Elfleda safe.*

Oswy bargains with God as he would with a king.

"Not only will I give you my daughter," he says, "but twelve of my estates, where I will build monasteries to serve you in perpetuity."

Anno Domini 655 – The Year King Oswy of Northumbria Kills King Penda of Mercia at the Battle of Winwaed

Hildeburg, Princess of Northumbria

The scops will sing of King Oswy's victory until the end of time. How Oswy, with his heir beside him, led his army south to the River Winwaed near the border with Mercia. Did God march beside Oswy? He must have, because Penda was ready to fight. His army—gathered from Mercia, East Anglia, and Wales—dwarfed ours by thousands. Woden's ravens circled the battlefield, ready to swoop down on our wounded.

King Oswy never faltered, pushing tirelessly against the enemy. Penda's Welsh allies pulled away, as did the traitor Ethelwald—Oswy's nephew. God sent rain to swell the river and flood the battlefield. When Penda's men tried to run away, they drowned.

Our forces ended Woden's luck once and for all. He is a spent god. Penda died fighting with his sub-kings and war chiefs. The ravens feasted and flew away with full bellies, never to return.

Chapter 9

Anno Domini 656 – The Year It Is Said Queen Alchfled of Mercia Murdered Her Husband, King Peada

---

Hildeburg, Abbess of Heretu

The wind never stops at Heretu, whether it blows white clouds across the sky or whips rain and fog into my face. Today, however, is a happy day filled with sun and celebration. God granted King Oswy his request and mine. Never again will Penda attack innocent people and steal their cattle. Oswy keeps his vow to God and sends his infant daughter to me.

I think of God granting Sarah the child Isaac in her old age. Now he grants me Elfleda.

"Abbess Hildeburg." Queen Enfleda stands at my chamber door.

I greet her with a welcoming kiss. "Come in. Rest. You've had a long journey."

Enfleda glances around my chamber. It's spacious, with tapestries on the wall to keep out the chill. I have a cradle in readiness for the child.

"Come, Egfrid, greet Abbess Hildeburg," she says, and a thin boy comes forward and bows to me. "The Mercians kept him hostage so long, I thought I'd never see him again. I thought they'd kill him in revenge."

"Surely not. Peada is King Oswy's son-in-law. Besides, if any harm befell Egfrid, Oswy's retribution would be terrible."

"Even so," the queen mumbles.

"Egfrid," I suggest, "why don't you go to the apothecary's workshop to see how medicines are made? Your mother and I have much to talk about. Enfleda, introduce me to your daughter."

Enfleda takes the child from her nurse and hands her over to me. I hold Elfleda's chubby little body, thrilled to feel such life in my arms.

"You are God's chosen one," I coo. "You'll stay with me forever." I settle the child on my lap.

"I'm glad you have Elfleda." Enfleda smiles. "She'll be safe with you. She won't be married off for a false peace agreement, or held hostage in another kingdom."

I shake a rattle and hand it to Elfleda so she can examine it.

"I can't promise the king won't change his mind," I say. "Do you think he'll keep his word?"

"Oswy is superstitious. He won't risk breaking his vow."

"Rest assured, Elfleda will want for nothing. I'll supervise her education and train her to be abbess after me. Between us, we'll care for the king's spiritual well-being." I hand the child back to her nurse. "She's wet."

"Heretu isn't anything like my mother's abbey at Lyminge. It's so isolated. Why did you choose this place?"

"I didn't. Abbot Aidan and Abbess Hieu founded Heretu. I merely pick up where Hieu left off. We're not as isolated as we seem," I reassure Enfleda. "It's true we're on the headland, but we're at the mouth of the River Tees and on the sea lanes. We're prosperous, as well as spiritual. We copy books, weave textiles, educate children, care for the sick … It's so busy, there's hardly time to pray. That's why Hieu left to return to her life as a hermit."

"Do you wish you'd stayed by the River Wear?"

"Sometimes. But Abbot Aidan placed me here for a purpose. Heretu is here for the people, no matter how high or low."

"Is there a place here for me?" Enfleda asks. "You once said I have a home with you. I need to be with my daughter."

I force down my sense of disappointment. Perhaps it's for the best. Elfleda will need all the support she can get, if she is to survive in this world.

Enfleda stays several weeks before departing for Bamburg. When she returns the following spring, the queen is distraught—her clothing thrown together, her hair out of its cap. She doesn't look like a queen at all.

"Is Elfleda safe?" she cries. "Have they taken her?"

I send for the apothecary, as well as the child. "Elfleda is with her nurse," I explain. I put my arm around Enfleda's shaking shoulders. "Elfleda is coming. Tell me what's happened."

Sister Ethryd arrives first, before Enfleda can say anything. She cups her hands around Enfleda's face and says, "You are safe here, my lady. I have *maythen* for you. Drink it."

Enfleda makes a face. "You haven't heard, have you, Hildeburg? Peada of Mercia is dead, and that's not the worst of it." The tears start again. "They say his wife—Oswy's daughter, Alchfled—betrayed him. The fighting will start again. I can't bear it."

"You forget your husband is King of Mercia. Peada was his sub-king," I rationalize. "Oswy won't make war on himself."

The nurse appears with Elfleda. The queen takes her daughter and rocks back and forth with her.

Eventually, she looks up to me, eyes still wary. "Are you sure there's no danger?"

"We're always surrounded by danger," I tell her. "No doubt the Mercians want to revolt. Oswy will soon settle the matter. Trust God and your husband."

Enfleda moves onto the floor and begins rolling a ball back and forth to her daughter. The little girl has a magical laugh like crystal chimes.

⁓❧⁓

Anno Domini 657 – The Year Abbess Hildeburg Establishes the Abbey at Streoneshalh

The next summer, I take my last walk around Heretu. I've been here ten years, refining what Hieu built. Heretu is an orderly monastery of monks and nuns, each in their separate areas. All follow the daily office with a balance of work and worship. I hope God is pleased. I know Abbot Finan is. Today, my forty-third birthday, I leave Heretu to take up residence at Streoneshalh on the River Esk—a monastery of men and women built to my specifications. I pray it becomes a beacon of education and spiritual growth.

King Oswy granted me the lands to suit his own purpose, and I, as his kinswoman, agreed. He may lose lands he controls directly, but the land he gives the church will always serve him. Oswy looks to eternity. When our stone church is complete, whatever is left of my Uncle Edwin's bones will be placed there. Since Oswy doesn't have to prove his bloodline anymore, I pray his desire to create a family mausoleum to include Edwin is from respect rather than boasting.

My first year of residence is a revelation. Oswy's favor and Abbot Finan's authority make Streoneshalh a beacon for women and men seeking the contemplative life while they commit the Gospels to memory and study teachings from the church based in Rome, but we continue practicing the Columban Way. For most, studying Roman teachings is a search for further knowledge, but for one, it is more.

Queen Enfleda's protégé, Wilfrid, returns from Rome and seeks a place with me. I do not trust him. He is too quick to tell me about the holy relics he brought back—as if a saint's fingernail can do anything to help the poor. Wilfrid is arrogant in his conviction that the Roman way of calculating Easter is more accurate than the Columban computation.

I suggest that the exact date is irrelevant to the Easter event. There were no churches when Christ rose from the dead to save us all. Wilfrid smiles and says God will teach me he is right.

Enfleda visits whenever she can escape the court and spends most of her latest pregnancy here. Osthryth arrives gently, without causing her mother too much distress. At four years old, Elfleda is fascinated by her tiny sister and cries when the queen takes the infant back to court.

Anno Domini 660 – The Year Prince Egfrid of Northumbria Marries Princess Etheldreda of East Anglia

Enfleda, Queen of Northumbria

Egfrid waits until I finish feeding Osthryth before launching into his screed of frustration and anger. "Lady Mother, speak to the king," he begs. "Don't make me go through with this marriage to an old woman."

"Hardly that old." I hand the baby back to her nurse. "She can still bear children."

"Can she? Then why didn't she have any children with her first husband?"

I chuckle. When my mother sent me to Northumbria, I thought it the cruelest of fates. Listening to my adolescent son complain reminds me that women aren't the only people pushed into fulfilling the will of others.

"Your father didn't choose his first wife, nor did your brother choose Penda's daughter, Cyneburg. Why should you be any different?"

"Father chose you," my son retorts with bitterness.

I shrug. "Not really. I united King Edwin's line with your father's. Egfrid, you are a prince and must behave as one. Etheldreda is the price for East Anglia." I smile. "You won't have to see her much to produce an heir. Gossip tells me you've already discovered how such events occur."

Egfrid has the grace to blush. "I didn't think you knew."

"Everyone knows, even Abbess Hildeburg."

"You won't send Ermen away?" Suddenly my son looks like a boy about to lose his favorite plaything.

"I'll make you a bargain: send Ermenburg to Streoneshalh for the birth. If you wish, she can leave the child there and return to court. In exchange, consent to the marriage. You cannot refuse it, but your agreement will make life easier for everyone, including the bride. Come give me a kiss of peace."

I stroke my son's fair hair and let him go.

Ermenburg, Prince Egfrid's Companion

The prince gave me glass beads from Frankland as a token. I twirl, and the motion swings the beads in front of and around me, so I can see them. I turn until I'm dizzy. When I stop, they fall on my chest. I collapse into the meadow, twisting flowers into a chain for my hair.

I daydream that when Egfrid arrives, he'll sweep me up, take me to the queen, and announce our marriage.

Two boots stand in front of me. Already, I know who it is.

"Ermen," my prince says with a lopsided smile. I jump up and cover Egfrid's face with kisses. We fall back into the grass together, and he cups his hand around my face. I reach for him, and his expression changes.

"Ermen, stop," he whispers, grabbing my hands. Something is wrong.

"What is it?" I ask, though I'm not sure if I want to hear the answer.

"Ermen, it's no good." The prince's eyes fall. "The marriage will go through."

"No." A flare of anger explodes from my heart. We're to be separated forever. I'll be forgotten and my child declared a bastard. I beat my hands on his chest. "You promised! You said—"

"Shhh," he coos. "I know what I said, but it cannot be. I pledge we'll be together, but I must marry Anglia."

"Who?"

"The Princess Etheldreda. It cannot be otherwise."

"No. No, no, no!" Again, I beat his chest, spilling my anger over him like a high wind. "You promised, Egfrid! I'm with child. You *have* to marry me."

"I cannot. The king will never allow it."

He keeps talking, but I'm too furious to hear him.

"The king is old," I say. "He'll die soon, and then you can send her away—"

"Never say that!" he interjects sternly, gripping my shoulders. I go still. "You'll get us both killed. Listen to me. Before the bride arrives, I'll send you to my kinswoman at Streoneshalh. You can have the babe there, and then come back."

I burst into tears. "You're sending me away," I sob.

"Only until you give birth. Then you can return." He lifts my chin. "When things settle down, you can send for our child and bring him up with the court. I'll never leave you, Ermen. You must believe me. We're one heart in two bodies."

"I—I thought we'd marry," I say with a sniffle.

Egfrid begins kissing me. "Someday, we will. I promise."

Etheldreda, Princess of East Anglia

It's a grand affair, this marriage. The King's Hall heaves with chiefs and their ladies. We sit at a table above them, so everyone can see the Bretwalda. King Oswy is in the center with his heir, Alhfrith, to his right. Alhfrith's wife, Cyneburg, sits next to him, filling his cup. Queen Enfleda sits to her husband's left, then my husband, Egfrid, next to her—and I next to my new husband.

I look at Egfrid through the corner of my eye. He's a comely lad. I hear he sent away his common wife. I pour wine into his cup and lower my eyes as scops begin their songs of the king's past deeds. The chiefs pay homage to the royal family with their toasts. Egfrid enthusiastically drinks up.

Eventually, after we consume honey cakes, Queen Enfleda rises and leads the ladies out of the hall. In my chamber, she personally removes my jewelry, laying each torc and armband on a carved table. She and Cyneburg lift my scarlet tunic over my head. Enfleda rubs my undergarment between her fingers.

"This isn't linen," she says with disapproval.

"No, Your Majesty. I keep coarse wool next to my skin to prevent vanity."

She purses her lips. "Yet your tunic is silk."

"My penance is before God, not men."

"My kinswoman, Abbess Hildeburg, doesn't go to such extremes. Are you more in favor with God than she?"

"I cannot judge, Your Majesty."

Enfleda removes my undergarment and replaces it with one of fine linen. "My son married a princess, not a beggar. Do not meet him in coarse garments."

My husband and his men bang on the door. Egfrid enters and clasps my hand as the abbot prays over the marriage bed, wishes us a good night, and leads everyone out of the chamber.

"They left us some wine," Egfrid says and hands me a beaker. "Drink up. We have work to do tonight."

I lay my hand on Egfrid's arm. "I have something to tell you first. I made a vow before God to remain chaste. I will never voluntarily consummate this marriage."

Egfrid's face flushes, though I'm not sure if it's the wine or anger. I hope it's the wine.

"You're a widow. How can you have a vow of celibacy? When did you make it?"

"Before I married Tondberht. I assure you, I'm untouched by any man."

"Did you trick him as you have me?"

"I committed no falsehood. My father knew of my vow when he arranged the marriage to Tondberht and then to you."

"And Tondberht respected your vow?"

"More than that. He joined me in it." I drop to my knees and hold my hands up. "I beg you, husband, to do the same. Sanctify your body to God for eternal glory. Let us kneel together and pledge ourselves to God."

Egfrid throws his glass into the fire. "I am a warrior, not a monk!"

I didn't expect this response. When I explained my vow to Tondberht, he dedicated himself to God and good works.

"Please, send me to a monastery. I swear I will pray for you daily."

Egfrid turns to look at me, his face a mask.

"That will never happen. I will never give you what you want, while you deny me the heir I need. I forbid you to speak of your vow to anyone. You will perform the duties of your station and welcome my visits."

I stare back at him, unblinking. "You would force me?"

"I won't spend the energy. It will be your choice. But you won't gain any recognition for your ... sacrifice. You'll have only pity for your barren state."

"What of you?" I parry.

"I already fathered a child. If it lives, I shall raise it at court as a constant reminder of your ... inability to bear children."

Anno Domini 661 – The Year Abbess Hildeburg Nurtures Cadmon's Divine Gift

Hildeburg, Abbess of Streoneshalh

My clerk taps the door before entering my chamber. "Abbess Hildeburg, forgive the interruption, but Wemba, one of your reeves, begs to see you. A most unusual event has occurred."

I put aside my letter from Abbot Colman. "Send him to me."

The reeve is a man of middling height with weathered skin. He carries his cap in his hand and kneels before me. I bless him and tell him to rise.

"Pray tell me why you made the journey from the fields to the abbey," I say, studying the old man with his grey beard and serviceable footwear. "It's a long way to walk."

"My lady abbess, I can't explain it—but it seems that God has spoken to one of my cowherds. He came to me. He's a sober man, my lady. A solid worker."

I send for ale, sensing this will be quite the story. "Sit with me," I say, "and tell me what happened."

"The cowherd rushed into my cottage this morning and told me God spoke to him."

"There's more to it than that. Begin at the beginning."

"Well, you see, the cowherds are a rough lot. They don't know much beyond seeing to your cattle and driving them from pasture to pasture."

He stops and strokes his chin, as if unsure what to say next.

"Go on." I nod encouragingly.

"Well, my lady, there's not much to do in the pastures. Sometimes, when things are quiet, the cowherds have a sort of party after they sup. They pass around a harp and sing songs. This lad isn't much for singing. He isn't much for anything except work. He never has a joke or much of a smile. But he's a good worker and has a light touch, if a cow is poorly. He's a bit of a loner. Keeps to himself. So when the harp gets closer to him, he sneaks away from the party and sleeps with the cattle. Bit odd, that, if you ask me."

"We all have the strengths God gives us."

"That's just it, my lady. This fellow was never good at anything except cows."

"Does he have a name?"

"Beggin' your pardon, my lady. The man's name is Cadmon. I should have said so from the start. So this Cadmon comes to me this morning all excited, saying God spoke to him in a dream."

My brow furrows. "No doubt."

"I don't think it was like that, my lady. He doesn't take a lot of drink. After he left the party, he went to the cowshed and fell asleep. He told me someone spoke to him and told him to sing a song about God creating the world."

"Did he sing it for you?"

"After a fashion. When I heard it, I thought I should bring him to you. In case it's important, like. You being a holy woman and all. He's just outside. Shall I get him?"

The reeve brings in a boy so overwhelmed by his fate, I think the story must be true. He pulls his forelock and bows his head.

"You can look at me." I smile. "I won't bite. Would you like some oatcakes? I have some here."

Shyly, Cadmon reaches out his hand.

"Wemba tells me God spoke to you. How did that happen?"

"It was a dream. A man came to me. 'Cadmon, sing me something,' he said. I told him I canna sing. That's why I left the feast."

The lad shifts from foot to foot.

"And what did he say?" I ask gently.

"He said I had to sing for him. That I had to sing about God creating the world. So, I can't believe it, but I did. And the next morning, I remembered the dream. I didn't know what to do, so I asked the reeve."

"If I give you a harp, will you sing the song for me?"

"I can't play, my lady."

"I'll make the chord. You sing, so we may all share in God's word."

I take my harp down from the wall and tune the four strings. "I haven't played in a long while." I smile at Cadmon and play a short tune, as the lad bobs his head along with the music. I end the tune on a single note, and listen as the lad sings in a clear voice.

"Now we must praise the heaven-kingdom's guardian,
The Measurer's might and his mind-plans
The work of the Glory-Father, when he of wonders of every one
Eternal Lord, the beginning established.

He first created for men's sons
Heaven as a roof, holy Creator;
Then middle-earth, mankind's Guardian
Eternal Lord, afterwards made —
For men earth, Master Almighty."

The last note dies away. From the mouth of a simple cowherd I hear God's word, not as Aidan spoke it, but as common people do.

"Cadmon...," I say, truly taken aback. "You must leave the cowshed and live in the monastery."

A look of panic crosses his face. "Oh, no, my lady—I didn't mean to offend. Forgive me."

"You misunderstand. I want you to live here so you can teach us your songs. I want you to learn more stories, so you can share them with people like yourself. God chose you above all others to tell His story. He wants you to take holy vows."

Anno Domini 663 – The Year Prince Alhfrith, Sub-King Of Deira, Gives Ripon Abbey to Wilfrid

Enfleda, Queen of Northumbria

The wagons climb to the abbey entrance above the cliff face. I lift my head to face the gentle wind blowing inland. Osthryth sits beside me pointing at every cow we pass, and I laugh from sheer joy, because while I'm at Streoneshalh, I live freely.

When we enter the nuns' area, Hildeburg waves.

"Where is the new prince?" she calls.

The nursemaid places him into her waiting arms.

"Elfleda, come meet Elfwin, your new brother," Hildeburg says.

My daughter peers at the swaddled bundle, then turns to her sister. "Come on," she says, "we have new lambs."

The girls scamper off, one of the novices keeping pace with them. I follow Hildeburg into her meeting area.

"I had a letter from Abbot Eata," Hildeburg says. "He writes that Oswy's heir took the abbey at Ripon from him and gave it to Wilfrid. Why would he do that? Aidan trained Eata personally. Enfleda, tell me what's going on in Deira."

"I wish I knew." I shrug. "Before I left the villa, my husband the king said he's increasingly vexed over Easter. Oswy thinks he and I should celebrate Easter at the same time. I told him we can't, because he follows Aidan's teaching and I'm attached to the Roman rite. Why should he care after all these years?"

"You could easily change, if you wish. After twenty years, no one would fault you if you changed to the Columban church. I did, after all. The Columban Way is far less confining."

I pick up a beaker of ale and swirl the liquid before drinking. "Dear Hildeburg," I say. "I don't think that's how the wind blows. Oswy takes no interest in religious festivals. I'm sure our mutual protégé, Wilfrid, has his fingers in the pie. He's all but declared himself for Rome, and he's close to Alhfrith. From what I hear, they're thick as two thieves. Alhfrith gave Wilfrid the monastery at Ripon to prove something to his father."

Hildeburg's eyes widen. "You don't think…"

"I do. I suspect Alhfrith wants to build ties with the southern kingdoms. He doesn't want to wait until Oswy dies. He wants to be king now, and he's seized on the church as a way to further his interests. It's clear to me that Wilfrid whispers in his ear and boasts of his connections to Rome."

Anno Domini 664 – The Year of The Great Synod at Streoneshalh

Hildeburg, Abbess of Streoneshalh

"My lady abbess, I have a message from the king."

I send the messenger to the kitchen for a meal and break the seal on the heavy parchment. My eye runs to the bottom and King Oswy's mark before I read the document.

King Oswy can no longer tolerate two churches in Northumbria. We must, his scribe writes, all follow the same calendar so that he and Queen Enfleda can observe the penance of Lent and the joy of Easter at the same time.

When I was a child, King Edwin said he followed God because God brought him victory. I smile. Woden didn't depart without a struggle. All King Oswy worries about is a calendar, but he emulates Edwin's example. He will convene a synod at Streoneshalh this fall. There will be chiefs, princes, and prelates from throughout Northumbria, and I am to play hostess.

I send for my steward. We have a lot to prepare before September.

Chapter 9

Anno Domini 664 – The Year of The Great Synod at Streoneshalh

---

Hildeburg, Abbess of Streoneshalh

The conflict between our Columban church and the Roman church shatters the very heavens. In May, as summer begins, the moon covers the sun. Then disease stalks the land and frightens people so badly that instead of praying, they throw themselves into the sea for a quicker death. Others fear the old gods are back and begin reciting charms against diseases caused by elf-shot—the arrows shot by capricious elves to cause mischief.

After King Erconbert of Kent succumbs to sickness, his widow, Queen Seaxburg, retires to Lyminge Abbey. God takes Archbishop Deusdedit of Canterbury, leaving us without a high-ranking churchman. Many monasteries in Northumbria are affected. We isolate the sick in the infirmary and pray for relief.

Through it all, we continue to build huts and lay up stores at Streoneshalh. I worry we will fall short of food or shelter at this great meeting.

The winds pick up when the season shifts from summer to fall. I order more wood to be chopped for the guest houses. The visitors will be here soon.

Two days before King Oswy's synod is supposed to start, Abbot Colman and the monks from Lindisfarne arrive. Bishop Cedd travels north from East Saxony to meet them. I suggest we three discuss the issues to be raised at King Oswy's synod. I suspect the king favors Rome for political reasons, and if we remind him of how the Columban Way came to Northumbria—and what it means to his family, as well as the people—we can recall him to his roots.

"King Oswy's brother, King Oswald, brought the Columban Way from Iona to serve all the people," I observe. "Not just the nobles, but *every* person in *every* village."

"Oswald didn't spread God's word," Colman objects. "It was Aidan who taught the people."

"They worked together," I insist. "Oswald translated for Aidan until he could speak Anglo-Saxon—and it was Oswald who sent for Aidan after Cadwallon destroyed the land and drove my family away. Aidan healed the people. He trained all of us to continue his work." My voice wobbles. "This synod is a travesty."

"Abbess Hildeburg, why are you so concerned?" Bishop Cedd asks. "Both paths to God are valid. Both bring people to God."

"How can you be so unaware?" I say. "This isn't about the church. It's as political as King Edwin's conversion."

Abbot Colman looks at me with tenderness. "It's God's church. He will sort it out. I believe as I always have, and as Aidan taught us. We serve from monasteries among the people. Bishops' trappings make no difference to us."

At first, I agree with Abbot Colman and admonish myself for my lack of faith. Then Prince Alhfrith arrives bringing Bishop Agilbert. The bishop came to Ripon to ordain Wilfrid and remained in Northumbria to attend the king's synod.

Coincidence? I think not. Without Agilbert, the Roman party has no one of any standing to argue their case. Now they have a bishop to counter our abbot.

Wilfrid is also in the party. I don't trust him. As a lad, he appealed to Queen Enfleda because he wanted to go to Lindisfarne. No sooner was he praised for his humility and studious demeanor then he asked the queen to sponsor his trip to Rome. He went for vanity, and returned convinced of the Roman way. I think he found it more compatible with his love of status and pageantry. He quickly ingratiated himself with Alhfrith, and together, these two young men gathered enough support to push King Oswy into declaring this sham of a synod.

Wilfrid isn't the only young priest longing for status, and Alhfrith is a beacon for young men seeking their fortune through battle.

I worry and fret. I even pray—something I don't do often enough. When King Oswy summons me for a private audience, I think my prayers may be answered. Perhaps the king is having second thoughts.

I arrive at the guest house after the midafternoon service. Oswy sits alone with only his seneschal present to serve the wine. We sit quietly until Oswy breaks the silence.

"You are well, cousin?" he asks.

"I am honored that you chose Streoneshalh for a meeting of such importance. Scribes will write of it and scops compose songs in salute of your wisdom."

"You flatter me."

What else can I do in the presence of the king?

I bow my head.

"You will be the famous one," he says. "Whenever anyone remembers this synod, they will remember it was here, and you were the abbess. You're a great friend to our family. Trees that bend don't break. Do you understand me? Streoneshalh holds a special place in my heart. My bones will rest here. My daughter will preside here. Streoneshalh will always be known for its learning and for the abbess who made it so."

I search the king's eyes for a hint of why he called this meeting of princes and prelates, but he reveals nothing. "Your Majesty is generous in your praise," I reply humbly.

"Streoneshalh is important to me. Whatever decision is made, I urge you to accept it as God's will."

"What else could it be?" I give the expected reply, knowing King Oswy thinks God's will is the same as his own.

When the synod convenes, my refectory becomes King Oswy's Great Hall. After the visiting prelates and chiefs find positions at the rear of the hall, the competing parties process two by two and take their places facing each other. The Roman party enters on the left-hand side, which will be to the king's right. The priest known as James the Deacon, whom I haven't seen since I left Northumbria as a child, leads them in. Queen Enfleda tells me he often attends her court, especially for the celebration of Easter. Her own chaplain, Romanus, follows James.

Wilfrid holds the center position between inconsequential priests and the bishop's party. Prince Alhfrith probably thinks Wilfrid should head the delegation.

Bishop Agilbert shuffles his way down the aisle, while his priest takes the place between him and Wilfrid.

Five learned men are here to present the case for Rome, visually overwhelming our three advocates. I nervously clench my fists in the folds of my tunic. Abbot Colman takes his seat across from Bishop Agilbert. Colman is a spiritual man, perhaps too spiritual for the debate about to take place, considering he finds it as difficult to defend the Columban Way as he would the need to breathe. Next to him is Bishop Cedd, Abbot Aidan's pupil. He understands the issues far better than Colman does, but the abbot won't give way to him. I'm the last person seated. But though I am kinswoman of the king and abbess of Streoneshalh, my thoughts aren't required at a public discussion.

We remain standing until King Oswy enters—his heir, Alhfrith, on his right, and Egfrid on his left. Oswy strides forward purposefully, looking straight ahead so he doesn't seem to prefer either side. He wears a gold diadem and a white silk tunic with golden borders. Beside him, his sons, though taller, seem smaller somehow. Egfrid, still a slender youth, treads lightly. His brother, attired in a scarlet tunic, turns his head slightly toward Wilfrid as the procession passes. The royal party reaches the dais and turns to face us.

"Bishop Agilbert," King Oswy says, "you're a guest at our court. Pray for the wisdom of this group of learned churchmen to determine how God wants us to worship Him."

Abbot Colman looks crestfallen, as if he knows the king has already made his decision.

Bishop Cedd rises. "Your Majesty, since Bishop Agilbert doesn't speak our language, may I interpret his prayer so that all may understand it?"

The king nods his head in agreement. Bishop Cedd stands near Bishop Agilbert, translating his Latin words—which most but not all of us understand—into Anglo-Saxon. The bishop's prayer begins with God's creation of the world and concludes with the promise of eternal life. It is a relief when he gets to the Pater Noster.

King Oswy says, "I've been troubled for some time that in our united kingdom of Northumbria, we have two rules of Christian life. I should not be in Lent when the queen celebrates Easter. All who serve God should have one rule of life, because all hope for the same kingdom of heaven. I called this synod to discover the way of life that is the truer tradition. Whether we should be governed by ecclesiastic structure given to us by the Roman church, as my son suggests, or continue with the rule brought to us by Abbot Aidan, as I have always done.

"In deference to my own way of life, I call upon Abbot Colman to explain the Columban tradition and whether it is truly the observance closest to the first church."

While King Oswy speaks, Bishop Agilbert's priest and Wilfrid change positions. Wilfrid puts his head close to Bishop Agilbert, making himself interpreter. I purse my lips, hands clasped in my lap. *I don't like seeing those two heads together.*

Abbot Colman stands slowly.

"Your Majesty," he says, "I find myself bewildered by your confusion. Your brother, King Oswald, brought Abbot Aidan to Northumbria to teach us God's ways. Indeed, he schooled Abbess Hildeburg before she took her position here. Aidan taught us a way of simplicity, dedication to scripture, service, and contemplation of God's mighty works. He taught us to consider the fruits of behavior—not the method."

Abbot Colman clears his throat, glancing at me. I nod encouragingly. *Remember what we discussed.*

"It seems Your Majesty is most concerned over the observance of Easter. I understand it is difficult to celebrate the same festival on different dates—a man wants his wife by his side to share in the joy of the resurrection. But in the spirit of generosity, you accepted the queen's different ritual, and she, likewise, never tried to train your children in a system foreign to your own practices. Your Majesty, may I trouble you for something to drink?"

Oswy nods. Colman takes a long time swallowing his ale.

"Abbot Colman," Oswy goes on, "will you continue? Or shall Bishop Cedd tell us about the observance of Easter?"

Aroma from the cooking fires seeps into the hall. I feel myself growing nervous. *Colman needs to speak quickly before the king becomes distracted.*

"I'm just coming to it, Your Majesty. Thank you for your indulgence. The Easter customs I observe were taught to me by Abbot Finan, and to him by Abbot Aidan, all the way back to St. Columba of blessed memory. They are the teachings your brother, King Oswald, brought to us from Iona—the very teachings you were baptized into as a small boy. All our forefathers, men beloved by God, observed these customs.

"They cannot be condemned or rejected, because the disciple St. John, loved by Jesus, established these customs we faithfully follow and will always follow. St. John witnessed Jesus's suffering. He knew Jesus's heart. I will never stop following the way he set out for us, nor will any person faithful to the teachings of Iona."

He pauses, and I hold my breath.

"Your Majesty," he goes on, clearly edging toward his conclusion, "it is not for me to persuade you. It is for your own heart to understand the truth."

Prince Egfrid looks toward me with a sorrowful expression. We both know Colman's quiet testimony won't sway the king. Oswy looks to political advantages that come with a change in faith; he doesn't care about Easter one way or the other. Oswy waits until Colman sits before turning his attention to the bishop.

"Bishop Agilbert, explain the origin of Roman customs and why we should find them to be more in keeping with God's intent."

Agilbert rises, beckoning Bishop Cedd to translate.

"Your Majesty, I find it difficult to speak through a translator. Please allow Wilfrid, my colleague and your countryman, to speak for me. We are of one mind on these issues, and he can explain my view more clearly than I."

Again, my heart sinks at this notion. *We're lost. Wilfrid will completely overshadow Colman with his youth, energy, and skill at debate. It's as if his entire life has been for this moment. His oratory will sweep all before him.*

Instead of speaking from his place, Wilfrid takes a position directly in front of the king and bows.

"Your Majesty, the points you raise are of utmost importance for our salvation and for the unity of the church in Northumbria. As you observe, the issue is not merely a date for Easter celebrations, but for unity in our spiritual lives."

The king nods.

"You are Bretwalda of England—yet the Easter customs observed here aren't followed anywhere else, except in Ireland. The customs observed by Bishop Agilbert and me are universally observed in Rome, where the blessed apostles Peter and Paul lived, taught, suffered, and were buried.

"Abbot Colman spoke of the Apostle John, but I testify that the Roman customs of Peter and Paul are observed throughout Italy and Gaul, where I traveled for study and prayer. And not only there—everyone in the world, except on the two small islands of Briton and Ireland, observes Easter according to Roman customs. Those who stupidly follow Iona contend against the entire world."

Abbot Colman is on his feet, his gray hair flying around his face. "You go too far, young man. You call us stupid when we uphold customs that rest on the authority of the apostle who was considered worthy to lean on our Lord's breast, and whose great wisdom is respected throughout the world. You insult Jesus Christ himself!"

Abbot Colman sways slightly. A young monk rushes forward to steady him. The Abbot waves him off.

King Oswy stands.

"Order," he commands. "We are here as a Christian body of brothers. We will not behave in a riotous fashion. Abbot Colman, if you wish to say something, you have only to ask. This is not a time for anger, but for the discernment of God's will."

God's will, indeed. Oswy is only ever concerned for his own will.

"Wilfrid, do you wish to add anything to your statement?" Oswy asks.

"I regret that Abbot Colman misunderstands my purpose. Far be it from us to charge John with stupidity, because he literally observed the Law of Moses at a time when the church followed many Jewish practices. The apostles could not immediately dismiss observances of the Law once given by God, lest they give offence to believers who were also Jews.

"This is why Paul circumcised Timothy, offered sacrifices in the temple, and even shaved his head at Corinth. People didn't understand it was a new age—but today is different. Today it's unlawful for Christians to be circumcised or for animals to be sacrificed in a temple."

The king leans forward to catch every word from Wilfrid's golden tongue.

"John, following the Law, began Easter on the evening of the fourteenth day of the first month. He didn't care what day of the week it was. But when Peter, who founded the church, preached in Rome, he remembered that Christ rose on the day after the Jewish Sabbath, and he understood when Easter should be celebrated."

Wilfrid embarks on an explanation so involved that the king begins a side conversation with Egfrid. Wilfrid turns to face Colman.

"It is quite apparent, Colman, that you follow neither the example of John, as you imagine, nor of Peter, whom you contradict. You follow neither the Law nor the Gospel in the celebration of our greatest festival."

Colman's chin drops. "Do you maintain that St. Anatolius of Laodicea taught contrary to Law and Gospel when he established the computation of Easter? Or that Father Columba and his successors thought or acted contrary to Scripture? They are both saints. I shall never cease to emulate their lives and customs."

"I agree Anatolius was a holy man, but you don't follow his directions either," Wilfrid counters. "And with regard to Father Columba and his followers, whose holiness you claim to imitate, I can only say that many will say to our Lord on the Day of Judgment, 'Have we not prophesied in your name, and cast out devils, and done wonderful works?' The Lord will reply, 'I never knew you.'"

With every word Wilfrid pronounces, Colman shrinks. *Put on the shield of faith,* I want to tell him. *Lean on Christ for support.* But he sits silently, as though in meditation. Perhaps he's stopped listening—but the king hasn't. Wilfrid has a flair for the dramatic that carries his message beyond mere explanation. He is a king's man. But which king? King Oswy, or his heir, Alhfrith?

"No doubt," Wilfrid continues, "these men loved God in primitive simplicity and devout sincerity. Their ways of keeping Easter caused no harm, when there was no one to show them the correct way. But if you reject the decrees of the universal church, you and your followers are guilty of sin. Although your fathers were holy men, do you imagine that they—a few men on a remote island—should be preferred before the universal Church of Christ throughout the world?

"Can Columba take precedence over the most blessed Prince of the Apostles, to whom our Lord said, 'Thou art Peter, and upon this rock I will build my church, and the gates of hell shall not prevail against it, and I will give unto thee the keys of the kingdom of heaven'?"

The hall falls into deep silence. *How can anyone discredit an argument so eloquently made? How can the oral tradition left to us by Columba stand against words written in the Gospel by those who were there? And how can anyone refute Wilfrid's eloquence?*

"Is it true, Abbot Colman?" the king asks quietly. "Did our Lord speak those words to Peter?"

Colman doesn't bother to stand. "It is true, Your Majesty."

"Can you show that a similar authority was given to Columba?"

"No."

A triumphant smile plays around the edges of Oswy's mouth. He strokes his chin before speaking. "So you both agree that these words were addressed to Peter in the first place, and that our Lord gave him the keys to the kingdom of heaven?"

"Yes," Abbot Colman says.

"Yes," Bishop Agilbert and Wilfrid say in unison.

Oswy's smile grows. "Then," the king announces, "I conclude that Peter guards the gates of heaven. I will obey his commandments in everything to the best of my knowledge and ability. If I don't, when I come to the gates of heaven there may be no one to open them, because he who holds the keys has turned away."

Oswy smiles, as if he has a private joke.

Abbot Colman leaves the meeting a disappointed man.

I will never forgive Wilfrid for twisting God's truth.

In the days to come God turns His face against Columba's followers. Bishop Cedd returns to his monastery at Lastingham, succumbs to plague, and dies within a month.

Prince Alhfrith, flush with victory, persuades his father to appoint Wilfrid Bishop of York, a diocese equal to Canterbury. Wilfrid believes he must be ordained by bishops sanctified in the Roman rite, so Alhfrith persuades his father to send Wilfrid to Frankland where Bishop Agilbert—who is now Bishop of Paris—will consecrate him.

Abbot Colman prayerfully considers what to do. Unable to accept the king's decision, he resigns as abbot of Lindisfarne and takes about thirty monks with him to Iona. Those remaining elect Tuda abbot, until he succumbs to plague. Eata, the abbot Wilfrid evicted from Ripon, is now my colleague at Lindisfarne. Like me, he abides by the new rules without discarding Columban ways.

Prince Alhfrith, impatient to be king, launches a revolt against his father. Oswy seems unsurprised and appoints Egfrid as sub-king of Deira. When the southern kingdoms learn the synod results, they give their support to the king—and Alhfrith vanishes, whether from disease or battle, no one knows.

We do have some changes at Streoneshalh. We are required to observe the Rule of St. Benedict, and to ensure that we do, I am forced to admit Benedictine monks. They have a prior to look after them, but their presence disrupts my soul. As often as possible, I escape to a small hermitage I built in nearby Hackness. There, I and my companions worship as I once did by the River Wear.

Part 3

ELFLEDA

Anno Domini 670 — Anno Domini 706

Chapter 10

Anno Domini 670 – The Year King Oswy Dies and Egfrid Becomes King of Northumbria

Hildeburg, Abbess of Streoneshalh

I lean on my staff, holding it firmly while the sea below roils with high waves and misty rain swirls around me. The damp penetrates my clothing and pulses through my bones. I focus my eyes on the shore below, determined to see Oswy's coffin loaded onto the wagon.

It's impossible to believe a man so blustery, conniving, and vibrant died in his bed. In January, King Oswy and Bishop Wilfrid busily planned a visit to Rome in the spring. As if God personally disapproved, the king fell ill and died without warning.

The oxen begin pulling Oswy's hearse up the hill.

A hand touches my shoulder.

"You must come to the courtyard now," Elfleda says. "Our guests will arrive soon."

We walk to the church with the wind pushing us and whistling around the workshops. The courtyard is full of monks, nuns, and villagers holding their caps in respect.

The carts stop at the church door. Egfrid helps his mother disembark and then turns to shoulder the front right corner of his father's coffin. He and seven warriors carry their burden to the sanctuary area below the altar, where it will lie in state until the funeral tomorrow.

Bishop Wilfrid, lately restored to his see at York, wears a black cassock as he circles the coffin in a clockwise direction, waving a censer to sanctify the area. Dowager Queen Enfleda stands next to me, quietly weeping.

"I cared for him," she says. "I thought we would be together longer. Is he in heaven, Hildeburg?"

I don't know. Can any king be virtuous enough for heaven?

"He must be," I say. "King Oswy faithfully followed church teaching. He was about to make a pilgrimage to Rome. I'm sure God accepts him into heaven."

"He died in his own bed. How many kings can say that?" Enfleda sniffs and gives a slight smile.

"Lady Mother, shall I take you to your chamber?" Elfleda asks. She puts her arm around Enfleda's shoulders. "The children are already there."

Wilfrid walks up, wiping a bit of ash from his sleeve. "Abbess Hildeburg, three priests along with three of King Egfrid's men will watch the king's coffin and keep the mortuary candles burning."

I nod.

"They will be relieved after the Matins," Wilfrid instructs.

"Of course." I bow my head.

Wilfrid leads his priests out the south door to meet the Benedictine monks who joined us after the synod six years ago

Enfleda, Dowager Queen of Northumbria

Elfleda shared my bed last night, as she does whenever I visit. I suppose that will change now. When we finish mourning the king, she'll take her vows. From today, I'm a dowager queen as my mother was. And like her, I shall withdraw to a monastery, but I don't have to build it myself. Hildeburg's monastery on the cliffs of Streoneshalh has been my true home these past years.

I break my fast and dress in a quickly dyed black tunic. I tuck my hair under a plain cap. As a last touch, I add the ruby pendant Oswy gave me for my first pregnancy and a gem-studded ring he presented me after Elfwin's birth nine years ago.

Elfleda enters in her plain grey nun's habit. I long to dress her as a proper princess, but she is safer at the abbey, away from kings and their ambitions.

"Lady Mother, we must hurry. Father's requiem will be held at Terce."

Outside, a weak sun tries to warm the air but is defeated by the ceaseless sea winds. We walk to the church. At the door, Hildeburg greets me with a kiss.

"Lady Mother," my son says, "Queen Etheldreda will walk with you when we enter the church."

"I'm going to walk with Abbess Hildeburg," I tell him.

"You'll have the rest of your life to walk with her. Today, you walk with the new queen."

"It is nothing, Your Majesty," Hildeburg says to me. "Those who watch need to see the king's family together."

The monks and nuns enter and stand on opposite sides at the back of the church. Abbess Hildeburg and Elfleda enter last.

Queen Etheldreda appears at my right hand.

"When will you move to the abbey?" she asks.

"I'm already here."

"I pray God that soon I may join you."

"I'm sure Abbess Hildeburg—" Before I finish, the choir boys Bishop Wilfrid brought from York begin singing.

"Eternal rest give unto them, O Lord, and let perpetual light shine upon them."

Queen Etheldreda and I enter, followed by my son, King Egfrid, an apparition in black wearing a gold crown. Onlookers fall to one knee as he passes and takes his place before a chair at the front. The choir passes us and stands in the aisle on the monks' side of the church.

The censor is next, waving his container of billowing incense. The smoke alone will cleanse us of our sins. Several priests follow. Last is Bishop Wilfrid, wearing a mitre and walking with a crozier.

How my husband would laugh if he could see this. He put no store in ceremonies.

Elfleda, Princess of Northumbria

The choir leads us in the Kyrie: *Lord have mercy—Christ have mercy—Lord have mercy.*

I sense the sound floating up to join the incense. Bishop Wilfrid removes his mitre and takes a seat near the altar, while another priest leads the prayers. I study him as closely as I can through the smoke. I haven't seen him since he convinced my father to abandon the Columban rite in favor of the Roman. Mother Abbess still hasn't forgiven him.

My father's coffin seems lost amid all this ceremony and chanting, as if his death is merely an excuse for a grand service.

We pray for my father's entry into paradise, and for my brother, the new king. The choir sings Psalm 39. *"Behold, thou hast made my days as a handbreadth; and mine age is as nothing before thee: verily every man at his best state is altogether vanity."*

The service continues, punctuated by incense, until finally Bishop Wilfrid pronounces the Benediction.

King Egfrid leads the bearers who pick up my father's coffin and place it in the crypt with the remains of my uncle, King Oswald, and King Edwin.

Hildeburg, Abbess of Streoneshalh

The candles flutter in the mausoleum's damp air. Wilfrid's priest censes the small space with pillows of fragrant smoke. I wonder if something similar happened when they buried King David, another warrior king who died in his bed.

Oswy is in the third niche. My uncle, King Edwin, rests in the first space; Oswy's brother, King Oswald, rests in the second. The space after Oswy is for Egfrid, though I don't expect I'll live long enough to see him in it.

I glance at a far corner where my own bones will lie. I would rather be on the cliff with my sisters, but I have a duty to lie near my uncle since his family cannot.

Elfleda squeezes my hand. Besides God, she alone knows my heart.

Wilfrid makes a final prayer. We leave the crypt in darkness and follow a monk holding a candle aloft. The monks leave to attend the office of Sext in their own church. The king and queen retire to the guest quarters.

Alone, free from ceremony and praying with my sisters, I'm at peace.

Anno Domini 671 – "In this year there was a great mortality of birds." –Anglo-Saxon Chronicle

Etheldreda, Queen of Northumbria

I kneel on the stone floor, facing Bishop Wilfrid, and confess my sins— particularly vanity.

"Forgive me, for I have sinned," I beg.

Bishop Wilfrid looks at me with a bland, expressionless face. "What is your sin, daughter?"

I touch the gold torc at my neck. "I cannot tear myself away from worldly adornment."

Bishop Wilfrid looks slightly bored. "Have you any other sins to confess?"

"No. I spend my days keeping the holy offices and embroidering vestments."

"I wasn't speaking of vestments, but of your duty to your husband."

"My duty to God is greater."

Bishop Wilfrid sighs, makes the sign of the cross over me, and says God forgives my vanity, so long as I strive to overcome it.

We retire to my chamber's warm fire. Wilfrid rubs his hands together before picking up a glass beaker of wine. I notice the glass has a greenish tint.

"Your Majesty, your husband, King Egfrid, is greatly troubled by your refusal to consummate your marriage. He tells me that never in ten years have you shared his bed. As your spiritual counselor, I must ask if you married the king in good faith. Were you honest when you said you had no impediment? Is there a true reason why you won't consummate your marriage?"

It's a bit late to ask me now. I remember my husband's expression on the night we wed. When I told him the truth, his entire face twisted in fury. But God protected me from my husband's wrath then as he does now. "There was no deception on my part," I say with a clear conscience. "Marriages are arranged for political reasons, with no concern for the bride or groom. Egfrid finds his comfort in Ermenburg's arms. I find mine in prayer." I shrug. "Why are you concerned, Bishop Wilfrid?"

"It is my duty to uphold the sacrament of marriage," Wilfrid says smoothly. "A wife, particularly a queen, is expected to provide her husband with sons. Your refusal to consummate your marriage flouts God's law and risks a political crisis. Surely you understand the issues at stake."

I narrow my eyes and bore them into what remains of Wilfrid's soul. "I understand many things, Bishop Wilfrid," I say. "When I gave you a portion of my dower land for your monastery at Hexham, you agreed that a vow to God is greater than any promise made to a man, particularly one made under duress."

Wilfrid squirms under my gaze and looks away. "At the time of your marriage, the king knew nothing about your vow to God. Had he known, he might have chosen a different bride. In essence, Egfrid believes you tricked him into marriage."

I gasp and clutch my throat. "As God is my witness, that is a lie. I pledged myself to God before I married the first time."

"And your previous husband never pressed you?" Wilfrid says incredulously.

"The Lord moved his heart to join me in worldly sacrifice. Egfrid has no heart to move."

"You are harsh, Your Majesty."

"I am truthful," I emphasize. "Why are you concerned? Did the king engage you to intercede for him? You can tell him my position is unchanged."

"The king needs a legitimate heir. Is it so much to ask? Give the king a son, and he'll release you."

I shake my head. I am truly sorry that the sin of greed has led Bishop Wilfrid to flout God's law. "What does the king give you to change your loyalty?" I ask softly.

Wilfrid has the grace to look embarrassed. He opens his hands. "King Egfrid shows me favor."

"My loyalty is to God alone," I say, emphasizing every word. "It will not change. The only way Egfrid will get a child from me is by force. Tell him I will fight to the death to defend my vow."

⌒⌯⌒

Unable to resolve the issue of my marriage, the king banishes me to Coldingham, a small double monastery of monks and nuns presided over by my husband's aunt, Abbess Ebbe. I pray God I never see my husband again.

After Prime, a novice escorts me to Abbess Ebbe's chamber. The girl strikes me as less than sincere in her vocation. I doubt she wears rough wool next to her skin, as I do. A gold brooch attaches her tunic. In fact, many of the sisters wear glass beads, gold bracelets, and other forms of jewelry.

The novice knocks and opens the door to Abbess Ebbe's chamber. She pours wine and adjusts chair cushions before leaving the room. Though it is spring, a fire burns. The abbess invites me to sit.

"Is there anything you need to be more comfortable?" she asks.

The question shocks me. "I didn't come here for comfort, but to practice self-discipline in God's service."

Abbess Ebbe wrinkles her forehead in confusion. "I'm not aware God commanded us to exchange comfort for austerity," she says. "Bishop Wilfrid himself travels with a king's retinue. Surely, as queen, you should have no less. My nephew didn't send you here to be a pauper."

"I don't know why he sent me here." *Why would he send me to a place where I can find happiness serving God?*

"Perhaps your husband hopes you won't like the life here. He probably thinks you'll return, as the former queen returned from her visits to Streoneshalh."

I shake my head. "No. I will never willingly return to the king's household."

Abbess Ebbe gives me an appraising look. "I suggest you stay with us through the summer and then return to your marriage."

"Do you doubt my resolve? I took an oath before God to remain untouched. Surely you understand what that means. You never married. How can you deny me the life you chose for yourself?"

"Who told you that?"

"King Oswy. When he discovered I refused to lie with his son, he said I was just like you. Headstrong and willful."

Ebbe laughs. "He was always a rascal. I'll tell you what happened: When I was sixteen or thereabouts, I caught the attention of Prince Aidan. With my brothers' support, I founded this monastery, but Aidan refused to accept defeat. When I heard he planned to kidnap me, I prayed day and night. God held the waves at high tide for three days, until Aidan relinquished his suit.

"It appears he's done the same for you. These past ten years, my nephew never forced himself on you, and now he sends you to me. Have no fear, I accept your resolve."

I say a quiet prayer of gratitude.

"Bishop Wilfrid suggests you join in our observances and learn how an abbey is governed. Stay through the summer, and see us at our best. Will that suit you?"

I kneel and kiss Abbess Ebbe's ring. "Thank you."

"Come, it's time for Sext, and then our midday meal in the refectory."

I embrace life under Abbess Ebbe's rule. She is pious, gentle, and fair—though I do think she's lax. She doesn't discipline those who fail to perform the offices, nor does she enforce the simplicity of a nun's habit. When I ask her why, she tells me that when a nun truly gives her heart to God, she changes her behaviors and adornments.

Abbess Ebbe assigns me to the apothecary, so I learn how to pick healing herbs and administer them to their best advantage. When I ask why she doesn't give me work in the scriptorium or making vestments, she says there's no point giving me work I already know how to do. After two years, Ebbe appoints me as the abbey's prioress.

I beg Bishop Wilfrid to persuade my husband to release me, but Egfrid is stubborn and vindictive. Though he has ignored me for two years, I'm afraid one day he'll send men to drag me back to Bamburg. Then, I have an idea. If I can get to my dower lands at Ely in East Anglia, I'll be safe. Egfrid won't drag an army that far south.

The days grow longer with the onset of summer. Soon Egfrid will begin his campaign season. If he decides to ride north to the Scottish border, he'll pass Coldingham. Every day I pray at dawn before walking around the abbey's borders. I look past the promontory's edge to the beach below. There's a path fishermen use to reach their boats. At the shoreline, I can hire a crew to take me below Bamburg and be on my way south. I confide my plan to Abbess Ebbe.

"God be praised!" The abbess grabs my hands. "Your plan could work. But you cannot travel alone. Any man on the road could attack you." She thinks a minute. "You can't wear your habit either. Word of an unaccompanied nun would draw the king's attention."

What am I to do? "What if I disguise myself as a beggar?" I ask. "I can exchange a fresh suit of clothing for beggars' garb. No one will recognize me in soiled rags with dirt on my face."

"A great blessing for the beggar," Ebbe observes with a smile. "Now then, who shall accompany you?"

We sit in silence until I identify my perfect travel companions. "With your approval, I will ask Sisters Sewara and Sewanna to join me."

"Yes," Ebbe nods. "They are both faithful and discreet. I will call them away from their duties and send them to you."

We clasp hands again. Abbess Ebbe makes the sign of the cross and gives me her blessing.

Several days later on a moonless night, the sisters and I bid farewell to Abbess Ebbe and depart in our smelly rags. The actual pathway to the sea bears little resemblance to the one I memorized while standing at the abbey's hilltop. We jump at every noise. As we get closer to the headland, I hear a clanking sound. "Hurry, Sisters," I whisper. "I think the king's men are near." We scramble down the pathway until we reach safety at the base of the headland ahead of the rising tide.

The next morning, we look across the bay, and I see I was right about the source of the noise. Egfrid's camp stretches out before us. When the tide ebbs, he'll be able to reach us. If he wasn't looking for me earlier, I'm sure he is now that I've slipped through his fingers. The sisters and I fall to our knees and pray for God's mercy. We steel ourselves to hear the tide recede, fully prepared to become martyrs for God

But the tide doesn't recede. Every day and night, high tide blocks Egfrid's access to us. On the seventh day, Egfrid's men break camp, and I know the king will not pursue me further. When the tide ebbs, the sisters and I find a fisherman willing to take us as far south as the mouth of the Humber River. Once there, we find a boat to take us to East Anglia and across the marshes to my dower lands on the island of Ely.

I send word to my kinsman, King Ealdwulf, who graciously confirms my lands at Ely and sends workmen to establish my new double monastery. We build the church of stone and the other buildings of timber. As we progress, I appreciate the training I received from Abbess Ebbe. When her son is old enough to rule Kent, my sister, Seaxburg, joins me. Women and men from Kent and East Anglia become part of my new community. After testing me for so long, God blesses me more every day.

Anno Domini 678 – The Year King Egfrid of Northumbria Imprisons Bishop Wilfrid

Ermenburg, Queen of Northumbria

Egfrid nuzzles my ear. I reach my arm across him to stroke his head.

"I've dreamed of this day for ten years," I whisper, and he raises his brows.

"What day is that?"

"The day I wake up and call you husband."

Egfrid kisses my neck. "And I embrace my true queen."

My servant brings in bread and ale, as she does every day. She places her tray near the fire, pokes the embers, and leaves. Egfrid stands, as golden as he ever was. I watch with my eyes half closed. He brings me a cup of ale.

"You've ever been my true wife."

"If she hadn't run away, would you have put her aside?"

"I had no cause."

"You had every cause. She never lay with you. She made no effort to give you an heir. While I—" I stop. So many pregnancies and not one living child. "Do you think she cursed me?"

"The punishment is mine, not yours."

"Husband…" *How I love saying that word.* "Why did you work so hard to reconcile? Why did you give Bishop Wilfrid so many rewards of land and treasure when he made no effort to help you? He was her confessor. He could have ordered her to be a good wife." I pause. "Wilfrid dealt falsely with you."

"No. I am the king. Wilfrid's status depends upon me."

I sit up in bed and let my robe fall open. I make my eyes big. "Then why does he travel with a king's retinue? Why does he come to court so finely dressed a stranger might mistake him for you?"

Egfrid narrows his eyes. "Is that what people think?"

"I'm cold. Will you not warm me?"

Egfrid puts our cups to the side. The seed is planted. I know when Egfrid leaves our chamber, he'll gather reports and do an inventory of Wilfrid's holdings. Then I shall ask for the dower lands the last queen gave to Wilfrid.

To my delight, after Egfrid makes an inventory, he puts Wilfrid in prison at Dunbar for a time and then banishes him from Northumbria.

Hildeburg, Abbess of Streoneshalh

Sister Honoria gives me a vile concoction to drink.

"You should rest," she says. "Pray the offices in your cell. Prioress Elfleda can lead the observances."

"Very well. I confess I'm tired."

Sister Honoria picks up her things. "I'll tell the kitchen to send you a beef porridge. It will strengthen you."

She bows her head so I may bless her.

To my delight, Elfleda brings my meal. She sits by the bed and starts to feed me.

"I can feed myself," I snap.

"Then let me put a cloth in your lap. I have news. Archbishop Theodore is taking advantage of Bishop Wilfrid's absence—"

"*Banishment*," I interject with a grunt.

"—to divide Northumbria into four dioceses," Elfleda goes on. "Our bishop will be so surprised when he hears."

I detect a bit of humor in her voice.

"And the new bishops have their training in the Columban rite, as we do. God blesses us."

"Indeed. Tell me who is being given what."

"Once," Elfleda begins, "there was only York, but now…" She begins to count on her fingers. "Archbishop Theodore appoints Bosa as Bishop of Deira with his seat at York, and Eata as Bishop of Bernicia, including Hexham and Lindisfarne. Two men who share our customs. God's ways are mysterious." Elfleda's eyes twinkle. "Then, there's the territory at Lindsey that my brother the king conquered four years ago. The archbishop appointed Eadhead as bishop. So," Elfleda concludes, "where once Bishop Wilfrid controlled all Northumbria, now he shares authority with three new Columban bishops."

I pass my bowl to Elfleda and sit up. "No doubt Wilfrid left for Rome immediately after the announcement. I pray he takes up a post there."

Elfleda laughs. "It's in God's hands. At least he'll be away from Northumbria for a bit."

"Thanks be to God. I think King Ethelred of Mercia will try to get Lindsey back. I doubt Egfrid has the will to hold it."

Elfleda starts to answer, then cocks her head. "I must lead the prayers at None. Shall I send my mother to sit with you after prayers?"

"Please don't—I need to rest."

Elfleda drops a kiss on my cheek and departs.

∽༄∾

Anno Domini 679 – The Year King Ethelred of Mercia Kills Sub-King Elfwin of Deira In Battle

Hildeburg, Abbess of Streoneshalh

The more my vision fades, the more my eyes face toward heaven. Elfleda and her mother, the dowager queen, oversee Streoneshalh. I see few visitors, and clerks help me with correspondence. A messenger arrived this morning with a letter from Ely Abbey. I don't want to share its news, so I send for Elfleda. She arrives with her veil slightly askew, her mind clearly elsewhere.

"Come, Elfleda, I need you to read this letter to me," I say, and she looks at me with an expression of strained patience.

"Shall I send for a clerk?" she asks.

"No. The letter is from Ely."

"Ely? Etheldreda's monastery?"

I nod. Elfleda opens the parchment carefully, her eyes rolling side to side, studying the text. With a pale face, she says, "There was plague. Etheldreda has died."

A tear trickles down my cheek. "Who sent the letter? Tell me what happened."

"Abbess Seaxburg writes that when the plague arrived, Etheldreda predicted she and several sisters would die. She had a painful tumor on her jaw and claimed it was because of her vanity in the past."

Elfleda gives me a questioning look.

"Etheldreda kept many austerities," I explain, "but couldn't refrain from wearing her gold torc. I see the connection, but I doubt her jewelry caused her death. What else?"

"She asked to be buried with the other sisters who would die, and so she was."

"I'm happy for Etheldreda. She waited a long time to meet her true bridegroom. There was a sincerity in her vow that transcends the unhappiness she caused your brother. Elfleda, I'm not as humble as Etheldreda. When I leave for heaven, put me near King Edwin's bones. It's my duty to lie with my family. Promise you will do that."

"I will, but I pray you stay with us for a long while yet. I can't take care of Streoneshalh alone."

"I've taught you everything you need to know. And your mother is with you. You must know I'm tired. My fever comes and goes; each episode is more severe. I can hardly see. I pray God calls me soon."

Elfleda, Prioress of Streoneshalh

Mother and I stand in the courtyard watching the wagons navigate the path. We have a clear day for a change. I look forward to a walk on the cliffs with my sister. The wagon stops before us, and Osthryth scrambles off, too impatient to wait for assistance.

"Elfleda!" she calls. "I'm here."

I hold out my hands and laugh. "You certainly are."

As always, my sister's enthusiasm is a breath of joy. This is Osthryth's last visit to Streoneshalh before she marries King Ethelred of Mercia. My mother swears the wedding will end all strife over Lindsey. Mother Hildeburg disagrees. I embrace my sister before my mother grabs Osthryth's arm and leads her toward the guest quarters.

Three months after the wedding, Ethelred attacks Egfrid's men in Lindsey—the province my brother took from Mercia. Egfrid summons his chiefs. My brother, Elfwin, brings men from Deira.

My two brothers ride into battle, as my mother despairs. She has two sons fighting on one side—and a daughter held in suspicion by the enemy—and stays on her knees from dawn to dusk, scarcely pausing to rest.

I don't trouble Mother Hildeburg with what little news we receive, and she doesn't inquire. Her fevers grow more intense.

We receive news that Egfrid and Ethelred clashed near the River Trent. Egfrid won the battle, but the Mercians killed my brother Elfwin. My mother is inconsolable. He was only eighteen, her youngest child.

I appeal to Archbishop Theodore to prevent a war of revenge, and by the grace of God, he succeeds. In view of our family connections, Ethelred expresses his sorrow at Elfwin's death and pays Egfrid substantial wergeld for our family's loss. In exchange, Egfrid returns Lindsey to Mercia. I pray this time the peace will last, but I don't have much hope.

Chapter 11

Anno Domini 680 – The Year Hildeburg, Abbess of Streoneshalh, Dies

Elfleda, Prioress of Streoneshalh

Taking care of Streoneshalh and its people consumes all my daylight hours. My mother, mired in grief, gives little help and less advice. Mother Hildeburg lies in the infirmary. We give her constant care. I appoint a prioress to assist me and place her in charge of the offices. I stay by Hildeburg's bedside, feeding her as much as she will take until the day she turns her face away. I send to the monks for our priest so she may receive last rites in the sacrament of extreme unction.

All our sisters kneel at the foot of Abbess Hildeburg's bed and pray for her soul. Father Garvin arrives with his flagon of holy oil. I haven't seen him since the last time he conducted the communion service in our chapel.

The crowded chamber becomes close. Sweat rolls down my face, mingling with my tears. Mother and I clasp each other's hands. *What will we do without Mother Hildeburg? Without her good humor and sound advice?*

Father Garvin touches Hildeburg's closed eyes with oil and begins the ritual. "Through this holy unction and His own most tender mercy, may the Lord pardon thee whatever sins or faults thou hast committed by sight," he prays. He anoints Hildeburg's ears, nostrils, lips, hands, and feet, each time repeating the words meant to bring Hildeburg into God's presence without any vestige of sin.

Each repetition is a blow on my heart. *Hildeburg is leaving us for God!*

"Thank you, Father," Hildeburg says, her voice like a sigh on the wind. "Elfleda, come."

Tears streaming down my face, I kiss Hildeburg's cheek and take her hand. "I am here."

Mother Hildeburg lightly clasps my fingers. "Don't weep for me, Elfleda. When my soul flies to God, I will be free. Elfleda," she instructs, "love your sisters, as I have loved them. And support your brother the king."

"I will, Mother Hildeburg, I swear it."

Hildeburg closes her eyes again. Her chest barely moves, and I think it's the end. Then her eyes open. "Sisters," she says, her voice soft and raspy. "Come closer." With tears and sobs, everyone gathers tightly around the bed and leans forward to catch Hildeburg's last words. "Serve God and each other," she says. "Don't quarrel among yourselves about who shall be first. Listen to your new abbess, Elfleda, the beloved child who came to me as an infant and grew up among you. And remember, nothing will ever separate you from God's love."

I release Hildeburg's hand so she may give her last blessing. "God be with you, in your going out and your coming in, forever."

Hildeburg closes her eyes again. Mesmerized, we watch her chest slowly rise and fall until she slips away. Loud weeping fills the chamber. I throw myself over Hildeburg's body, as if I can warm her back to life. When we have no more tears, the sisters and I wash her body and prepare it for burial.

We keep vigil throughout the night. The next day, we move Hildeburg's coffin to the church. Word spreads quickly. Everyone at the abbey—lay and cleric, monk and nun—comes to the church. My mother and I accompany Mother Abbess's coffin into the crypt and place it by her uncle King Edwin's remains, as she requested. When we leave the crypt, I feel the full weight of my responsibilities and understand why Mother Abbess withdrew to her hermitage at Hackness.

Ermenburg, Queen of Northumbria

Wilfrid returns to Northumbria with Pope Agatho's decision to overturn the actions Archbishop Theodore and King Egfrid took when they divided York into four dioceses. Wilfrid insists on presenting the pope's decree in person, so my husband summons him to a royal council at Bamburg.

The king escorts me to his audience chamber and seats me near his side. Everyone drops to one knee when we pass. When all is ready, the seneschal admits Wilfrid. I don't think of him as a bishop, because he left his diocese. The seneschal doesn't allow Wilfrid's retinue of priests and monks to enter. The pope's decree is a matter between Wilfrid and the king.

Wilfrid's shoulders stoop a bit now. He uses a staff—though whether from need or for effect, I can't say. Wilfrid stops below the dais and bows to the king, ignoring me completely.

"Your Majesty, I have Pope Agatho's decree. He exonerates me from all charges and restores me as Bishop of York."

"Am I a priest, to obey the pope?" My husband speaks quietly, but with an unmistakable hint of venom.

Wilfrid flushes. "Your Majesty, the pope is God's representative on earth."

The king reaches for a beaker of ale, takes a long draw, and wipes his mouth with the back of his hand. "The pope has nothing to do with me." He shrugs. "Archbishop Theodore appoints bishops. What do you want from me?"

"You took my land," Wilfrid charges. "I want you to restore it."

Egfrid glares at Wilfrid. "You forget your position," he sneers. "All the land in Northumbria belongs to the king." He drinks more ale. "Have you forgotten that *I'm* the king? Bishops and popes may do as they please, but, as king, I own every grain of soil in Northumbria. I give land to those who serve me well and confiscate it from those who do not."

"Your Majesty," Wilfrid says in a placating tone. "I'm your most faithful servant. Only God holds a higher place in my heart."

Egfrid laughs bitterly. "Let's recount your service to my family: you encouraged my brother to rebel against my father; you supported my lawful wife's effort to avoid her marital duties; you gather resources that rival my own; until Archbishop Theodore stepped in, you controlled the Northumbrian church; and now, you wave a papal decree in my face."

As the king makes his points, his anger grows.

"Your Majesty…"

"I will hear no more. I order you confined to the prison here until I decide what to do with you. Perhaps your stay will teach you humility. My seneschal will escort you."

The hall is deathly quiet. I silently exult when the seneschal reaches for Wilfrid's arm. Wilfrid shakes him off and walks ahead of him. Several men surround the two as they leave the hall.

Egfrid rises, presents me his arm, and escorts me out of the room.

"I'm going hunting," he says, and strides away.

A few weeks later, we embark on a royal progress to the north. Egfrid wants to be seen on the northern borders, because the Picts are troublesome and need to know the area isn't neglected. Shortly before we leave, I feel ill, but say nothing. By the time we reach Egfrid's aunt's abbey at Coldingham, I'm feverish, but I put it down to my fear of facing Abbess Ebbe. She told my husband he was harsh not to release Etheldreda. She accused him of thwarting God's will. I think she disapproves of my marriage, because I haven't given Egfrid a living child.

By the time we arrive in the abbey courtyard, my fever makes me helpless. Ebbe puts me to bed and assigns sisters to watch over me. Egfrid stays by my side day and night. The entire abbey prays for my recovery. But I don't improve.

On what I'm told is the fifth morning, Abbess Ebbe comes into the chamber and sits near my head. "I'm sorry, Ermenburg, there's nothing I can do for you." Ebbe gently wipes a cool cloth across my forehead. "This illness is God's punishment on your husband."

Egfrid covers my hand with kisses and tears. "Abbess Ebbe," he begs, "tell me how to make things right. Ermen was the love of my youth."

Was?

"Egfrid, you put God's holy man into your prison," Ebbe replies without emotion.

"Wilfrid?" My husband drops my hand. "Wilfrid was never anyone's man but his own. He defies me, undermines me, and betrays my family. I won't allow him to roam Northumbria, plotting to increase his power."

"Egfrid, I don't deny Wilfrid can be forceful, but he lifts up the church. On his way to Rome, he brought the Frisians to God. When he arrived back in England, he converted the East Saxons. Wilfrid is God's warrior. Who are you to punish him?"

I feel Egfrid touch my hand again. He lifts my palm to his face and places it on his cheek.

"If you wish your wife to recover," Ebbe says, "release Wilfrid from prison."

Egfrid sends for a scribe. He frees Wilfrid but banishes him from Northumbria.

My fever breaks the next morning—though it is several weeks before I can travel. Egfrid leaves me with his aunt and continues his progress through the north.

Anno Domini 683 – The Year Elfleda, Abbess of Streoneshalh, Meets Cuthbert, Abbot of Lindisfarne, on Coquet Island

Elfleda, Abbess of Streoneshalh

The monks row the boat as close to the shore as possible, then pull the small vessel onto the sand at Coquet Island. Angry birds shriek at me. *Plop.* Several birds make deposits on my habit. *Ah, well, I suppose it is their island.* I heard Abbot Cuthbert had banished the birds from Inner Farne. Perhaps they moved here.

Inside the shelter, Abbot Cuthbert sits on a wooden bench, wearing his usual tunic of unfinished wool with a cowl wound around his neck. I kneel for his blessing. "Thank you for meeting with me."

Cuthbert gives me a smile both tired and gentle. "How could I refuse the Abbess of Streoneshalh? Your aunt was ever my friend and teacher." Cuthbert's face closes. "You come on your brother's business."

"Archbishop Theodore called a synod at Twyford to discuss the diocese at Hexham."

"And your brother wants me to attend."

"Yes, Abbot, he does. As does Archbishop Theodore. The synod needs your wisdom. You know Bishop Tunberht keeps in contact with Wilfrid. Egfrid wants him expelled from Hexham."

"Dear Elfleda, I won't be part of Egfrid's feud with Wilfrid or others in his way. He attacks innocents in Ireland without cause. He destroys churches and monasteries. I love the king, but I won't support his feuds."

"Nor I. Every day I beg God to clear his mind, but the king can be stubborn." I shrug. "Will God punish Egfrid for his injustice? Will his reign be cut short?"

Cuthbert takes my hand. "You know the scriptures. How can you speak about the length of one man's life which lasts no longer than a spider's web when a chamber is cleaned? Life is short for a man with only a year to live."

A great sorrow wells within me, bubbling up into uncontrollable sobs. Cuthbert touches my shoulder and then leaves me to wail my grief for my brother, Abbess Hildeburg, and my own inadequacies. Though Cuthbert named no time, I think Egfrid will meet his fate in Ireland.

"I can't bear to think of Egfrid gone."

"At some point, we're all gone from this world," Cuthbert says to console me. "It's in God's hands. Pray for comfort, and it will be yours."

"What will happen, Abbot Cuthbert? Egfrid has no sons, no brothers, no nephews, no one to become king after him. Shall we be taken over by Mercia?"

Cuthbert lifts my chin. "There is another to rule. A man you will love as much as you love your brother Egfrid."

"Another brother? Who?"

"How many islands are in the ocean? As many as stars in the sky? If God creates islands and stars, he creates heirs for Northumbria. Like father, like son. If Ermenburg is your brother's love, who was your father's? Think, Elfleda."

"King Oswy's first wife had a son, but he died after the Great Synod at Streoneshalh." I shake my head. "There's no one."

"Once there was an Irish princess. A woman called Fin. She knew Oswy while he lived on Iona."

"Iona? Who could he know at such a young age?"

"I have just told you. My cousin lives at Iona still. He is a scholar, a humble man with no aspirations to kingship. God has chosen him to rule. Watch, and you will see."

I swallow.

"And what of you?" I ask. "Will you attend the synod?"

"I have no wish to leave Inner Farne again. God calls me to be a bishop, but I'm in no hurry. It's time for us to leave Coquet while the tide is in our favor."

I kneel for Cuthbert's blessing. He lifts me up and kisses me on both cheeks.

"Farewell for the moment." Cuthbert picks up his staff. "We'll see each other again."

The slap of oars in the sea blends with the tide as we drift south to Streoneshalh. I ponder my new brother, the scholar. When the time comes, will he be fit to rule?

Archbishop Theodore calls the synod at Twyford by the River Alne near Wessex to accommodate Wilfrid, who lives under King Ethelwealh's protection.

Wilfrid's banishment from Northumbria isn't enough for my brother. King Egfrid wants every trace of Wilfrid removed from the kingdom, including Bishop Tunberht. The result is a foregone conclusion. The synod elects Cuthbert as the new Bishop of Hexham.

Archbishop Theodore informs Abbot Cuthbert of his new post. But Cuthbert ignores his letters, as well as those of my brother the king. Even Bishop Eata of Lindisfarne can't elicit a response from Cuthbert's cell on Inner Farne. At length, we travel to Inner Farne. Bishop Eata of Lindisfarne, Bishop Trumwine of Abercorn, King Egfrid, the monks from Lindisfarne—all of us there on our knees with tears in our eyes, begging Cuthbert to accept God's call.

Cuthbert emerges and embraces each of us. With tears streaming down his cheeks, he accepts his burden, asking only that Bishop Eata take the see at Hexham so he doesn't have to leave Lindisfarne.

☙❧

Anno Domini 685 – The Year King Egfrid of Northumbria Dies at the Battle of Dun Nechtain

Elfleda, Abbess of Streoneshalh

Cuthbert's consecration at York on Easter rivals Wilfrid's ceremonies in its grandeur. Archbishop Theodore presides, assisted by the six bishops of Northumbria. King Egfrid attends. Participants wear their finest silk robes. The altar gleams with golden vessels. Billows of incense sweeten the highest rafters. Cuthbert dresses in a simple tunic and stole. I watch Archbishop Theodore place the bishop's mitre on Cuthbert's head, sure it will never be worn again.

☙❧

Ermenburg, Queen of Northumbria

"Egfrid, think. You don't have to fight the Picts. You can threaten them and demand a bribe. I beg you, listen to Bishop Cuthbert. You don't have to fight everyone like a madman. Things worked out in the truce against Mercia."

"Only because I defeated them first. It cost me my brother."

"Elfwin was rash. You yourself said so. And we've had no trouble from Mercia since."

"Ermen, if I allow the Picts to persist in their raids and stop paying tribute, the Mercians will join in the attack. I must act now, if I'm to save the lands my father gained."

"For whom? You have no heir. Already your chiefs gather allies to fight for your throne."

Egfrid flushes. "It's clear I'll have no son from you."

"But you could from another. Spread your seed wherever you will and raise your sons to manhood."

"I must do both. You know this. I cannot allow this disrespect to continue. The Picts grow stronger every day. Bridei consolidated the tribes. They will push south unless I destroy them. Go to your sister at Carlisle, Ermen. If anything should happen, you'll be safe at her monastery."

I lay my head on Egfrid's breast. Fighting is part of being a king, but this feels different. My husband carries an anger that can't be quenched. He invaded Ireland for no reason at all and was almost killed. Now he fixates on the Picts—the painted people even the Romans left alone.

"Send me with your blessing," he says.

"I bless and pray for you daily, as I have since the first time I saw you."

He kisses me. "Do you believe I'll win?"

I nod. "You always have."

"Then it shall be so again. I promise the days of fighting will be over when I return."

I hand him his sword with its carved hilt and his helmet with its protective dragon. "Go, and may God protect you."

Egfrid writes me from Bishop Trumwine's monastery at Abercorn.

"Bishop Trumwine rides with me. God will protect us."

And then, nothing.

The novice escorts me to the refectory. Bishop Cuthbert is there, leaning on his staff as if he will walk out at any moment. I kneel for his blessing.

"Shall I send for the abbess?" I ask.

"No, Your Majesty. Shall we sit?" Cuthbert looks at me with a sad expression. "God sent me a vision."

"About the Picts?"

"The war is over."

"And my husband, the king?" I ask, though I know the answer already.

"He is dead, Your Majesty, and the army destroyed."

My heart stops. "How?"

Cuthbert shakes his head. "You must leave this place and come to Carlisle until the truth is known. Your subjects need you now."

Elfleda, Abbess of Streoneshalh

White clouds scurry across blue sky. I turn my attention to the procession about to enter the stone church on Lindisfarne. Monks enter silently and take their places for my brother's funeral. Bishop Trumwine and I walk together down the aisle, followed by Bishop Cuthbert. In honor of King Egfrid, he dresses formally, including his bishop's mitre—but the occasion has none of the solemnity or grandeur of King Oswy's service at Streoneshalh, when Bishop Wilfrid proclaimed Oswy's virtues and overlooked his failings. Bishop Cuthbert's soft voice hardly carries beyond the altar, as if there is nothing worth noting about my brother.

The queen isn't present. As soon as Egfrid's death was confirmed, Cuthbert sent her to her sister's monastery near Carlisle and personally bestowed the veil upon her. Being a queen isn't the best preparation for the religious life, but even my mother had a better disposition for contemplation than Ermenburg does. Queen Ermenburg rejoiced in her station, never appearing without a diadem. I judge harshly. Perhaps she grieved at my brother's death and went willingly away from the world. Nevertheless, she should be here today to say a public farewell.

I bring my attention back to the service. I shouldn't make my responses by rote, but there's so much to think about. Did Cuthbert send for my unknown brother? Will the chiefs accept him? Or will Northumbria break apart like wheat chaff floating in the wind?

"Gloria Patri," we sing together, *"et Filio, et Spiritu Sancto, Sicut erat in principio, et nunc, et semper, et in saecula saeculorum. Amen."*

Cuthbert makes the sign of the cross to conclude my brother's last public appearance. I follow the bishops into the niche hastily carved into the side of the church. I don't know why Egfrid chose to lie at Lindisfarne instead of our mausoleum at Streoneshalh. Is it in defiance of his father's efforts to create a family shrine? Did he feel unworthy to lie with the men who built Northumbria? Only God knows.

Cuthbert's chamber is as austere as the man himself, bare walls with chinks between the timber planks, an empty fire pit at the room's center, a table, benches. The only concession to his station is the glass beakers of wine for Bishop Trumwine and me.

"There are matters to discuss," Cuthbert begins. "Abbess Elfleda, you wonder why your brother lies on Lindisfarne. I can't tell you the reason, only that it was his request."

"Why didn't he tell me his wishes?" I demand.

"I cannot delve into the depths of a man's soul," Cuthbert responds.

"I don't understand. Egfrid was his father's son, ever jealous of his position. He wanted a royal funeral."

"Elfleda, you must trust me. Egfrid *chose* to be on Lindisfarne."

"Abbess Elfleda," Bishop Trumwine interrupts, "I conveyed the king's message to Cuthbert. When King Egfrid arrived at Abercorn, it was as if he had a premonition that something was wrong. I heard his confession. The king said that after subduing the Picts, he would make a pilgrimage to Lindisfarne. And he asked…I'm sorry to say this, because I know it hurts you, but King Egfrid made me swear that I would bring his bones here if he could not come himself. I'm sorry."

I shake my head and smooth my tunic.

"I understand," I say, though I don't. "Do you know what happened in the battle? Did someone betray the king?"

"There was no betrayal, only trickery. I traveled with the army when it left Abercorn. The king planned to attack the enemy stronghold at Dunnottar. We advanced north of the Valley of Strathmore, laying waste to any farms or villages we encountered. The king was ruthless in his determination to wipe out any chance of further rebellion."

Bishop Trumwine pours more wine into his beaker.

"We spotted an enemy war band and followed it into the mountains. Every time we drew near enough to fight, instead of standing to meet us in open battle, the band withdrew so that we had to pursue it further into the mountains. Eventually, it disappeared behind the cleft of Dunnichen Hill. Unsuspecting, we crested the hill and saw the Pict army. It was a sea of men, banging their shields, jumping up and down, hurling curses at us. They paint themselves blue. Did you know that? It was a terrifying sight, as if we were gazing into hell.

"We were too near the loch. If we tried to turn back, we'd fall into a swamp. And, of course, King Egfrid would never retreat before an enemy. He rallied his army and charged the Picts. Our men rode into an uphill charge to break the Pict lines. God seemed to be with us. The Picts fell back. We pursued.

"It was a trick. When there was no escape, the Picts turned, held their lines, and repulsed our charge. All was chaos. The blue devils were everywhere. Egfrid called a retreat, but our men had no chance. It was a rout. The Picts surrounded the king, killed him, and cut our army to pieces. It was pure carnage."

Tears pour down Trumwine's cheeks.

"A few men escaped. We waited until the Picts left the battlefield and buried our dead. We gathered King Egfrid into a shroud and brought him here, as you know. On the way, we stopped at Abercorn to rescue the monks. I don't know what will happen to them. There are too many."

Bishop Trumwine begins to sob, and I realize my folly.

"Cuthbert, I beg your forgiveness. My concern for my brother was really pride. I see that now. At Lindisfarne, his soul can be at peace."

I embrace Bishop Trumwine. "Will you join us at Streoneshalh? I need an experienced churchman to give me his advice and preside over the monks. Will you share your life with us?"

Bishop Trumwine looks up. "Cuthbert?"

"You could not be in a better place. Have no worry for your monks. We have many monasteries they can join."

"Cuthbert," I say, "I have another question. What of the queen?"

"She grieves for her husband more deeply than any I've ever seen. She may never return to her right mind, but she is safe. Shall we leave her in peace?"

Chapter 12

Anno Domini 687 –
The Year Bishop Cuthbert Dies at Inner Farne

Elfleda, Abbess of Streoneshalh

Cuthbert must have sent for his cousin, Aldfrid, as soon as he knew King Egfrid was dead. When the new king arrives from Iona, not one chief disputes Aldfrid's right to rule. For who could dispute such a holy man?

I personally visit the guest house to be sure all is in order for King Aldfrid's visit to Streoneshalh. When he arrives, Bishop Trumwine and I go into the courtyard to greet him. He dismounts awkwardly, as if he isn't comfortable on horseback. Trumwine and I bow, but he takes each of our hands in turn and bids us stand.

"I am here as a friend and brother. There can be no majesty between us," he says. "Dear sister, how special to meet you at long last. I hope you will share stories of my father with me while I'm here."

I study his rugged face.

"You have his look around your eyes," I say. "It's the way you squint against the sun."

Aldfrid laughs.

"Come inside," I say. "People have gawked long enough."

We enter my receiving room and sit on wide stools around the table.

"I don't have many stories of my father. He gave me to the church when I was an infant. Abbess Hildeburg raised me. My mother made frequent visits to get away from court. I gather my father was a difficult person, but there's no doubt he was a great warrior king and a man of God. Did you know he was planning a pilgrimage to Rome when God took him?"

Aldfrid grimaces. "So I heard. I also know he betrayed the people who kept him safe, when he declared the Roman church superior to the Columban."

"Surely you won't bring that issue back," Trumwine interrupts. "It would be too much for people to bear."

"And what of this Wilfrid?" the king asks. "Shall I bring him back from Wessex as Archbishop Theodore requests?"

"I too have a request from the archbishop. I'm a mere abbess in the Roman church. It's not my place to refuse Theodore's appeal. Besides, Jesus himself enjoined us to forgive our enemies. As a man from Iona, you know this is true."

"Yes, Jesus was very clear. Nevertheless, the monks of Iona sheltered me. I have no love for the man who persuaded my father to turn his back on their faith."

"You don't have to love Wilfrid to forgive him. And you must admit, Wilfrid only voiced what my father wanted to hear. Surely you know the decision was made before the synod convened. Oswy needed political support only Rome could give. And Wilfrid, as we all know, is politically astute."

"Dear sister, are you saying Wilfrid isn't responsible for his actions?"

"My lord, Abbess Elfleda, the issue of forgiveness isn't the point," Trumwine interjects. "If we allow Wilfrid to return, we reduce divisions within England. Wilfrid shelters in Wessex, giving their king an excuse to oppose us. Archbishop Theodore recognizes that if Wilfrid returns to Northumbria and regains his position as bishop, it will reduce conflicts among our kingdoms— and perhaps assist you in finding a bride from Wessex." Trumwine winks at my brother.

Aldfrid signals the servant for more wine. He swirls the liquid around the beaker.

"Very well." He stands. "I will accept Wilfrid's return. I'll even restore him as Bishop of York. But if he gets up to his old tricks, I'll cast him out again."

I smile with relief. "Spoken like a true Christian king, Aldfrid. A man who forgives but doesn't forget."

Cuthbert teaches me the value of silence for reflection, an atmosphere seldom present at Streoneshalh or Heretu. Both monasteries are hives of activity, from the scriptorium to the farms and weaving rooms. So I establish a small monastery at Osingadum as a retreat where I can reflect on God's goodness without the noise of visitors and workers.

To my delight, Cuthbert consecrates the new stone church. After the dedication, we celebrate in the refectory. While the feast progresses, Cuthbert sits looking distractedly into the distance. He doesn't touch his food. I notice his hand trembles, and I realize he must be exhausted. Cuthbert seeks only silence for prayer and meditation but knows people need to see him, so he travels constantly to teach and baptize. No task is too small for him, including my new church.

Cuthbert drops his knife to the floor. I signal for a servant. The lad picks up the knife, wipes it on his tunic, and sets it next to Cuthbert's place.

"That was clumsy of me. I'm glad I didn't drop my plate."

We laugh.

"Your thoughts seem far away from us," I venture.

"No, it's nothing. Just a glimpse into the future. I saw a soul pass from your community at Streoneshalh on its way to heaven."

"No one was in the infirmary when I left. What happened?"

"The person wasn't ill. I'm sure a messenger will arrive tomorrow. You'll have to tell me who it was. I will pray for him."

"You must eat now," I say. "You don't nourish your body as you do your soul."

Cuthbert chuckles again. "I cannot be eating all day long. You must allow me a little rest."

"Waga has a message for you," the little novice tells me the next morning.

I invite Waga into my chamber and offer him a beaker of ale, which he declines.

"I bring sad news, Mother Abbess. One of the monks, a man called Hathwald, fell from the tree by the monks' church. He was restoring a bird's nest when the branch cracked. Hathwald hit the ground at an odd angle and broke his neck. I'm sorry, my lady."

I place my hand over my heart and say a silent prayer for Hathwald's repose. *The soul Cuthbert saw last night—was it Hathwald's?* "Has the prior conducted Hathwald's funeral?"

"It's happened by now. The prior said he would do it after midmorning prayers." Waga bows and turns to leave, but I've got one more question.

"Wait," I say. Waga pauses, turning to face me. "Do you know what time Hathwald fell?"

"Just as the monks came out of Vespers, my lady."

"Yes. Thank you."

Just after Vespers. About the time Cuthbert saw a soul flying to heaven.

Anno Domini 687 – The Year Bishop Cuthbert Dies at Inner Farne

Elfleda, Abbess of Streoneshalh

After Christmas, Cuthbert pleads illness and relinquishes the bishop's mitre. He returns to Inner Farne and dies before Easter. Freezing wind whips across Lindisfarne, and I long for my warm chamber at Streoneshalh—or even

Heretu, which is closer. Cuthbert told me he hoped to be buried on Inner Farne, where he was at peace. That won't do, of course. Not just because Cuthbert was a great and gentle man who deserves a shrine, but because those who revere him will make a pilgrimage to pay their respects. It would be impossible for them to reach Inner Farne.

I follow the monks away from Cuthbert's grave. The rain falls like sleet. Cuthbert's death is the second crack in my heart. The first and deeper crack was when God called Mother Hildeburg to heaven. I wonder how many cracks my heart can bear before it breaks entirely. I may be the last person left in Northumbria to cherish Columban ways. The rain washes away my silent tears. Cuthbert and Hildeburg sit with Jesus in heaven, but I must prepare for the coming struggles on earth.

It's only a matter of time before Wilfrid will assert himself as Bishop of Lindisfarne. I'm surprised he isn't here already. I spend the night in the abbey guesthouse. The next morning, I bid the prior farewell and return home.

To my surprise, King Aldfrid and Archbishop Theodore appoint Bishop Eadberht to Lindisfarne. Wilfrid is unjustifiably angry, and the compromise Theodore arranged between King Aldfrid, King Ethelred of Mercia, and me begins to unravel.

The king paces around my chamber.

"Wilfrid won't be satisfied until he controls all the churches in Northumbria," he says. "He'll force everyone to follow the Roman rite. I won't allow it."

And he doesn't. The king kicks Wilfrid out of York and pushes him into Mercia, saying it's time for Ethelred to uphold his part of the agreement. I'm glad to see Bishop Bosa back at York. When he was Abbess Hildeburg's student, he was kind to me and helped me with my letters.

My mind wanders to Egfrid's first wife, Etheldreda. My mother was furious that Etheldreda wouldn't lie with my brother and give him an heir. If she had, Aldfrid wouldn't be king. I think Aldfrid is a good king, better than an untried youth would be. Etheldreda's vow caused much trouble, but she won in the end. People call her a saint and make pilgrimages to her grave, trampling over the cemetery to throw themselves upon her plot. Until now.

A letter from Wilfrid informs me that Abbess Seaxburg decided to build her sister a shrine and deposit her bones there. The thought makes me shiver. If Etheldreda said she wanted to be in the cemetery, her sister should respect her wishes. Wilfrid describes the event. He doesn't say if it was rain or shine, or if the tide was in. I picture a rainy day, because there was a campaign tent over Etheldreda's grave.

The cover must have been quite large. Wilfrid wrote that monks stood on one side of the grave and nuns on the other. *Where did he stand?* I wonder. Probably next to Abbess Seaxburg. I imagine them watching workmen dig into the damp soil. First the sod, then the next layer and the next until they hit a solid surface and smooth the dirt off Etheldreda's timber coffin. The workmen lift it from the ground and doff their caps. There are prayers before the men pry open the lid.

Seaxburg rushes forward to see her sister and shouts, *"Glory to God!"* At which point, everyone falls to their knees. After sixteen years in the ground, Etheldreda looks better than when she died, because the wound the doctor gave her when he lanced her boil is gone.

I'm sure God can perform such miracles, especially for someone like Etheldreda who dedicated herself to his service. Miraculous healings take place by her grave almost every day. But ... *I sigh*. Was Etheldreda really so pure as that? Or am I unable to see with the eyes of faith?

Anno Domini 702 – The Year the Council of Austerfield Rules Against Bishop Wilfrid

Elfleda, Abbess of Streoneshalh

I shiver, pull on my plain tunic, and twist my gray hair into its cap. If I'm going to be cold, I'd rather be home by the sea than at King Aldfrid's inland villa near Austerfield. I didn't seek an invitation to this meeting of churchmen, but Berhtwald, the new Archbishop of Canterbury, insists that every bishop, abbot, and abbess attend to discuss the pope's response to Bishop Wilfrid's latest complaint. Wilfrid wants his offices and lands in Northumbria restored. That will never happen. But we go through the motions of considering the pope's ruling on the matter. If the bishops vote in his favor, they will lose their seats—and King Aldfrid won't allow Wilfrid back into Northumbria.

We convene in the King's Hall. Thankfully, a fire burns brightly in the center. Archbishop Berhtwald sits on the dais, with King Aldfrid to his right. I have a seat with the other monastic leaders. Bishop Wilfrid is the last to arrive, flanked by abbots from his monasteries in Mercia.

Archbishop Berhtwald opens the session. "Bishop Wilfrid, we have your complaint and Pope John's response before us. The issues you raise have festered for a long time. Archbishop Theodore, my predecessor, spent many hours prayerfully considering how to bring you into unity with the kings of Northumbria—both the previous king, Egfrid, and the present king, Aldfrid.

"The controversies have been ecclesiastical, political, and personal. They harm us all. Kings and bishops must work together for the unity and harmony of England. We must solve our problems ourselves—without calling the pope's attention to our misunderstandings—and we cannot put the work of the church aside to settle personal squabbles."

Wilfrid looks straight ahead to the wall behind the opposite benches. He doesn't look at the archbishop, who is visibly annoyed.

Berhtwald raises his voice. "Bishop Wilfrid, before we begin our deliberations, I must ask whether you will adhere to those decrees made by my predecessor, Archbishop Theodore."

Wilfrid leaps to his feet and turns to face his interrogator. His face is red with anger.

"How dare you ask such a question when the Archbishops of Canterbury and kings of Northumbria have resisted apostolic authority for twenty-two years! Pope Agatho, of blessed memory, ruled that I should be restored as Bishop of York with the diocese as it was before Archbishop Theodore broke it up. Instead, King Egfrid expelled me from Northumbria more than once. How can you suggest that Archbishop Theodore's decisions shall stand and the rulings of Pope Agatho, Pope Benedict, and Pope Sergius shall be ignored?

"As God is my witness, I shall never accept any ruling made by Archbishop Theodore. I shall only submit to a policy that agrees with the laws of the church and is consistent with papal rulings."

Archbishop Berhtwald draws himself up to his full height and looks down on Wilfrid from the dais. Each man is dressed in full vestments. Each wears a mitre of office. Wilfrid appears exhausted by his adamant argument. Berhtwald raises his hands for silence and makes the sign of the cross. The hall grows quiet.

"Bishop Wilfrid, we are aware of the papal rulings, and I tell you now that Pope Agatho's decision cannot apply to the present structure of our church. Those lands and offices will never be restored to you. However, King Aldfrid and I agree it would be wrong to expel a bishop who has served the church for over forty years.

"If you accept Archbishop Theodore's rulings, we grant you your monastery and its properties at Ripon. Given all that has happened, this is a very generous offer. In exchange for your lands at Ripon, you will remain in the monastic precinct, and you may not perform any ecclesiastical offices."

The archbishop turns his back on Wilfrid and resumes his seat next to Aldfrid. Wilfrid looks momentarily speechless. His face goes deathly pale, then flushes red.

"H-how," he sputters, "can you justify your decision? It was I who persuaded King Oswy to give up Columban practices and follow Rome. I fixed the date of Easter to that of the church at Rome. I introduced the Benedictine Rule into English monasteries. I brought antiphonal chanting from Rome. No king nor archbishop, but *I*, Wilfrid, made the church what it is today.

"I will never accept your decree. I shall appeal to Pope John and see you both stripped of all offices."

I shudder at Wilfrid's defiance. If King Aldfrid hadn't promised Wilfrid safe conduct, I'm sure he would throw him in prison. The king and archbishop stand together.

"Wilfrid," the king's voice rings out, "your arrogance and defiance destroy your appeal. You have no loyalty to England or its church. Twice you've gone to Rome in attempts to cause a rift between the Holy See and England. We do not accept any ruling from Rome. In this, I agree with my brother King Egfrid. The pope may rule as he likes; it is up to him to enforce it."

Aldfrid turns to Archbishop Berhtwald. "Wilfrid must submit to your ruling. If he continues his divisive ways, my entire army is at your disposal."

"It won't come to that, Your Majesty," Berhtwald assures the king. "Wilfrid, you are dismissed from this company until you come to your senses."

Archbishop Berhtwald turns his attention to the rest of the assembly. "There being no further business before us, this synod is adjourned. Go in peace."

Wilfrid gathers his abbots and strides out of the hall, while the rest of us sit in a stunned stupor. After a few minutes, Archbishop Berhtwald leads the bishops away. I follow them to Aldfrid's church, where we all participate in the office of Compline. The words, usually so comforting, are ashes in my mouth.

❦

Anno Domini 705 – The Year King Aldfrid Dies

December
Elfleda, Abbess of Streoneshalh

I'm too old to travel on winter roads, but King Aldfrid summons me, so I leave Streoneshalh at first light. The messenger said the king is sick unto death. When we reach the king's villa at Driffield, my escort announces me. Immediately, servants guide me to the king's chamber.

Torches light the room. They and the fire make the air thick with smoke. I stand a moment, waiting for my eyes to adjust. The king lies in a bed covered in furs. A priest administers Communion and makes the sign of the cross. We pass at the doorway.

There's a stool next to the bed. I hold Aldfrid's hand and pray for his recovery.

"I won't recover." He speaks so softly, I have to lean over to hear him.

"You can't know that, Your Majesty. No illness defeats God."

Aldfrid makes a weak smile. "I was wrong to oppose Bishop Wilfrid. You must help me make it right. Did you know that when he reached Kent, he sent messengers to me?"

"I heard rumors." *I didn't think they were true.*

"I'm sure you did. Not much happens without you knowing about it. I told the messengers I would give Wilfrid an audience. What do you think?"

I take an involuntary breath and cough. "I-I'm surprised," I stutter.

"So were my bishops." The king smiles. "The bishops reminded me of all the trouble Wilfrid caused, and that his motive hadn't changed. He still wants Pope Agatho's decree to go through. And I thought then that there was no point in meeting Wilfrid, since I couldn't grant what he wished. But now…"

I stroke the king's brow. "Rest, Your Majesty."

"Elfleda, only you and I are here. Can we put my majesty to the side and talk as two friends? I need your help. I've decided we must obey the pope and restore Wilfrid."

"You can't do that," I gasp. "The entire kingdom will be up in arms."

"Wilfrid is an old man, and I'm gravely ill. We'll both be dead before anything changes. Promise you will bear witness to my last words. I decree that Wilfrid be forgiven and that the papal directives be followed. I don't want Wilfrid on my conscience when I greet God."

If Aldfrid forgives Wilfrid, I have to do the same. I don't want to forgive Wilfrid. He destroyed the Columban church. He hurt my brothers and Abbess Hildeburg.

"Is it such a hard promise for you to make, Elfleda? How many times did Jesus say we should forgive? Once? Twice?"

I swallow. "Jesus said we should forgive up to seventy times seven."

"You must agree Wilfrid hasn't wounded us so many times as that." Aldfrid tries to smile.

"No, not that many."

"Then testify that my last words are to forgive Wilfrid and obey the pope."

I squeeze Aldfrid's hand. "Very well. I promise."

The king drifts into sleep. Servants replenish the torches and bank the fire.

When he wakes, Aldfrid allows me to feed him some porridge. I wipe his chin and ask if he will name an heir.

"My son is too young to hold the kingdom. Perhaps I'll name Bishop Wilfrid as Osred's guardian. Who better than the man who wants to control Northumbria?"

For a moment, I think the king's mind wanders, but then I see his plan. If Wilfrid's holdings are restored, he'll be strong enough to protect Osred's claim to the throne.

"You are a wise king, Aldfrid."

He smiles. "Wait here a little while, and I'll be a dead one."

⚭

Anno Domini 706 – The Year King Osred of Northumbria Allows Bishop Wilfrid to Return

An empty throne is a prize worth taking. For a time, it seems a warrior named Eadwulf will be the king. Aldfrid's thanes flee north with eight-year-old Prince Osred. Eadwulf follows them to the fortress at Bamburg, loses the battle, and flees.

Osred is crowned king, with Bertfrid—the thane closest to King Aldfrid—as his regent. In the summer, Archbishop Berhtwald calls a synod near the River Nidd in order to receive Pope John's latest judgment on Wilfrid's complaints against Northumbria. Once again, Bishops Bosa of York, John of Hexham, and Eadfrid of Lindisfarne appear. I too make the journey. King Osred is present, accompanied by his regent, Bertfrid. All proceeds as if the interlude with Eadwulf never happened.

Archbishop Berhtwald opens the meeting with a concord of peace. He says he and Bishop Wilfrid received two letters from the pope. The clerk begins reading the letters, which are written in Latin. Before he finishes, Bertfrid requests translations. The archbishop raises his eyebrows.

"There's no reason to translate the letters in their entirety. The general sense is that the apostolic authority of binding and loosing was first given to St. Peter and thence to subsequent popes. And, in this instance, Pope John and three popes before him ruled that the bishops of Northumbria should be reconciled to Bishop Wilfrid. Will that suffice?"

"Thank you, my lord archbishop. It is always better when all parties understand what is at stake." Bertfrid bows and returns to his seat.

"The stakes are the same as they were in Austerfield," the archbishop explains. "Pope John writes that we may decide the matter ourselves by giving up Northumbrian possessions as Pope Agatho ruled, or we may refer the entire matter to Rome.

"It must be noted that anyone who doesn't accept the decision made by this council shall be excommunicated. I think that should clarify matters."

Bishops Bosa, John, and Eadfrid each stand to say the same thing: that no one can nullify the decisions of their predecessors, as most recently confirmed at Austerfield. They refuse to budge on this.

I say a quick prayer and stand to speak.

"Abbess Elfleda, have you something to add to the discussion?" the archbishop asks.

"As some of you know, I was with King Aldfrid a few days before he died. It was the late king's wish to reconcile with Bishop Wilfrid. The king said that if he lived, he would obey Pope Agatho's decree, and if he died, he hoped that for the peace of his soul, his successor would carry out his deathbed wish. I promised to tell you his wishes, as I have now done."

Before the assembly digests my message, Bertfrid rises.

"My lord archbishop, it is my belief that God himself wants this assembly to reconcile with Bishop Wilfrid."

"On what evidence?"

"When Eadwulf seized the throne, I knew he would seek out Osred to kill him. My thanes and I fled to Bamburg with the rightful king. Eadwulf's men outnumbered us. We took shelter in the clefts of rocks but didn't expect to escape." Bertfrid glances at the king. "Through it all, Osred behaved with the bravery one expects of a king."

King Osred smiles broadly but doesn't speak.

"My thanes and I," Bertfrid continues, "held our own council and decided that if God gave us victory, we would support Wilfrid as the man best suited to bring us together. After we made our vow, our fortunes changed, and it was Eadwulf fleeing for his life."

Bertfrid looks directly at each bishop before declaring, "We will keep the vow we made at Bamburg. King Osred supports Bishop Wilfrid's suit. That is all I have to say."

I wait for Wilfrid to press his advantage, but he says nothing. For the first time, the king and his advisors support his suit. My promise to Aldfrid binds me to Wilfrid. Only the bishops hold out, but they can't win the day. Archbishop Berhtwald and I meet with the bishops, and together we hammer out a compromise. The bishops keep their holdings. Wilfrid keeps his status as a bishop. King Osred grants Wilfrid the monasteries he founded at Ripon and Hexham.

As Aldfrid said, Wilfrid is an old man. He accepts the compromise, and the sixty-year struggle between Wilfrid and the kings of Northumbria is over.

It's strangely quiet as we drift through fall into winter. There are no wars or cattle raids, no friction between bishops and kings, no pestilence. At Christmas, Bishop Trumwine celebrates the church service with everyone from our abbey at Streoneshalh in attendance. Sweet-smelling incense curls around us, overcoming the natural odors of daily life. After receiving the host, we share the kiss of peace and walk through cold mists to the refectory where what was once called a Yule log provides light and warmth. Boughs of evergreens decorate the tables in readiness for the coming feast. Glassware glitters in the torchlight. The scop plucks his harp and begins a song Cadmon wrote: *Now we must praise the heaven-kingdom's guardian…*"

The scop is a novice monk with an almost unbearably sweet voice. In my mind, I'm six years old again, listening to the cowherd's song. Mother Abbess Hildeburg had said Cadmon was blessed by God so he could share the Gospel in the people's own tongue.

I remember saying I'd like to do the same thing as Cadmon.

"My child, you have a different purpose," Abbess Hildeburg had replied. "Your destiny is to speak to kings. Your grandmother, Ethelberga, brought King Edwin into God's kingdom. Your mother Enfleda's example justified King Oswy's plan to unify the Northumbrian church. There will come a time when God will send you to comfort a king."

"When will I do that?"

Mother Abbess had kissed my forehead then. "I don't know, child. But when the day comes, you will be ready."

"Abbess Elfleda," Trumwine says, "you seem far away from us."

"I'm just remembering something Abbess Hildeburg told me when I was a child. She said I would comfort a king."

"You did more than that," Trumwine responds. "Your testimony at Nidd ended friction within the Northumbrian church. There will always be disagreements, but the loser won't run away to Rome for reinforcements."

Trumwine chuckles. "Bishop Wilfrid knew Abbess Hildeburg was his greatest enemy, but he never expected you would be his advocate. The abbess would be proud of you." He tips his glass beaker toward me. "As Jesus said, '*Blessed are the peacemakers*.'"

Author's Note

Bishop Wilfrid died at his monastery at Oundle, possibly from a stroke, in AD 709. The monks from the monastery at Ripon interred his body in the cathedral church. Abbess Elfleda died in AD 714 at the age of fifty-nine.

King Osred died in AD 716 at the age of nineteen. He was not well-regarded. St. Boniface characterized him as a worthless youth. An early ninth century poem describes Osred as an irreligious young man who treated his nobles as enemies and compelled many of them to take refuge in monasteries.

Vikings began their attacks on England in the late eighth century. Their first attack was on the monastery at Lindisfarne in AD 793. An anonymous writer in the *Anglo-Saxon Chronicle* testified, *"In this year [AD 793], terrible portents appeared over Northumbria and miserably frightened the inhabitants: these were exceptional flashes of lightning, and fiery dragons were seen flying in the air. A great famine followed these signs; and a little after that in the same year on 8 January the harrying of the heathen miserably destroyed God's church in Lindisfarne by rapine and slaughter."*

While it is unlikely that dragons flew through the air, the rest of the entry is considered accurate.

The Vikings continued pushing south and in AD 867 they captured Northumbria, made their capital city at York, and changed the city's name to Jorvik. The Vikings also changed the name Streoneshalh to Whitby, the name in use today.

❧

The Anglo-Saxon history of Northumbria is largely one of warring tribes fighting for dominance of both Northumbria and England. Northumbria was composed of two kingdoms: Deira and Bernicia.

Bernicia was the northernmost kingdom, stretching from the Firth of Forth to the River Tees. The line of Bernician kings begins with Ida, who ruled from AD 547 until his death in AD 559. Aethelric, one of Ida's sons, became the fourth king of Bernicia from AD 568 until his death in AD 572. Aethelric's son, Aethelfrid, became King of Bernicia in AD 593. In AD 604, Aethelfrid took over Deira, the kingdom to the immediate south, to establish the Kingdom of Northumbria. Aethelfrid married Princess Acha of Deira to legitimize his control.

Aelle (r. AD 560–588) is the first known king of Deira. In addition to Princess Acha, Aelle's children included an unknown prince, usually thought to be Hereric, and a son named Edwin. When Aethelfrid took over Deira, Edwin fled first to Mercia, where he married Princess Cwenburg, and then further south to East Anglia. When King Redwald refused to deliver Edwin to King Aethelfrid, the latter made good on his threat to meet Redwald in battle. The result was victory for Redwald at the River Idle in AD 616. Redwald placed Edwin on the Northumbrian throne as a sub-king in AD 617. King Aethelfrid's sons, Oswald and Oswy, fled to Iona. King Redwald died in AD 624.

After the deaths of Redwald and Edwin's first wife, Cwenburg, King Edwin married Princess Ethelberga of Kent to further secure an alliance between Northumbria and Kent. At this point, Edwin was functionally the Bretwalda (overlord) of England. However, in AD 632, Penda of Mercia and Cadwallon of Gwynedd joined forces. They defeated Edwin at the Battle of Hatfield Chase in AD 633. Edwin's family fled to Kent, and Aethelfrid's sons, Oswald and Oswy, returned to Northumbria.

In AD 634, Oswald defeated Cadwallon and became King of Northumbria. Oswald ruled until AD 642, when Penda of Mercia defeated him at the

Battle of Maserfield. Oswald's brother, Oswy, became king, first of Bernicia and eventually of a united Northumbria. King Oswy married King Edwin's daughter, Enfleda, in AD 624 as a way to secure political support.

Abbess Hildeburg's father was Hereric, King Edwin's brother. When Aethelfrid took over Deira, Hereric also went into exile. He took shelter with King Ceretic of Elmet and died by poisoning. His wife, Breguswid, and two daughters, Hereswid and Hildeburg, survived. When Edwin became king, he brought his nephew's family back to Northumbria.

I became aware of Abbess Hildeburg in 1985, the first time I visited Whitby Abbey in Whitby, England. The site contains the visible ruins of the eleventh-century Benedictine Abbey founded by Reinfrid and abandoned during the sixteenth century when King Henry VIII dissolved the monasteries.

In recent years, Abbess Hildeburg has become a popular subject of women's history, despite the fact that very little is known about her. Like many women in history, she was present but not visible. As I worked with the source materials, I decided that the best way to tell Hildeburg's story was in the context of her contemporaries. In this story, Hildeburg is not the primary figure but belongs to a network of women living in a difficult time.

Saxon Heroines: A Northumbrian Novel is a work of historical fiction based on available source material, which is extremely sparse. The Anglo-Saxons themselves were largely illiterate in the seventh century. I consulted numerous primary and secondary sources during my research, but when I began to write, I relied most heavily on Bede's *The Ecclesiastical History of the English People* and the *Anglo-Saxon Chronicle*.

The best source on the period is Bede's *The Ecclesiastical History of the English People*, completed in AD 731. It is the first written account of Anglo-Saxon Britain; however, Bede's primary interest was the history of the Christian church in England. The women he included were all relevant to the church. Queen Ethelberga of Kent, for example, influenced King Edwin's decision to accept baptism. And Abbess Hildeburg presided over the Abbey at Streoneshalh in AD 664, when King Oswy's synod decided the church would follow the Roman rite. Abbess Elfleda associated with Bishop Cuthbert and King Aldfrid.

Bede (c. AD 672–735) was born on lands owned by the monasteries at Monkwearmouth-Jarrow. He entered Monkwearmouth at the age of seven and died at Jarrow. Bede's tomb is in the Galilee Chapel of Durham Cathedral.

I also referred to the *Anglo-Saxon Chronicle*, probably compiled during the reign of King Alfred of Wessex as a source of information on the origins of the West Saxons. Many of the *Chronicles* were initially compiled as oral history. The earliest manuscript used in the *Chronicle* is the *Parker/Winchester Chronicle*, compiled by a single scribe up to the year AD 861.

Questions and Topics For Discussion

1. Who were your favorite characters? Why?

2. What did you think about Queen Ethelberga? How much control did she have over her own life?

3. What did you think of Bishop Paulinus? How much influence did he have on King Edwin's decision to convert?

4. King Edwin made a huge decision when he converted to the Christian church. Why would he do such a thing? Do you think he believed the reason he survived an attempted assassination was because he wore the tunic Pope Boniface sent him?

5. After King Edwin died, his family fled to Kent. What impact did this experience have on Princess Enfleda and Princess Hildeburg?

6. Do you agree with Ethelberga's decision to pressure her daughter Enfleda into a marriage with King Oswy of Northumbria?

7. Why did King Oswy want Princess Hildeburg to return to Northumbria?

8. Why did Princess Hildeburg accept Aidan's offer to return to Northumbria and become an abbess? Do you think she made the right decision?

9. Do you think Queen Enfleda was happy with her marriage? Why was she pleased when her husband gave her daughter, Princess Elfleda, to the church?

10. What do you think of Bishop Wilfrid? How would you compare him to Bishop Paulinus?

11. Why did Wilfrid have so many conflicts with Northumbrian kings? Do you agree with Wilfrid's position of trying to regain his diocese, or with the actions of the other bishops and the various kings?

12. What did you think of Etheldreda of East Anglia? How would you compare her efforts to control her own life to those of Queen Ethelberga? Which woman is more appealing to you as a person?

13. In the marital conflict between Queen Etheldreda and King Egfrid did you find one character more sympathetic than the other?

14. What did you think of King Oswy? Was he a "good" king?

15. Do you think Oswy's concern about whether the Columban or the Roman rite was correct was motivated more by political concerns or by religious scruples?

16. What do you think was the main difference between the Columban and Roman rites? Was it an issue of style? Did they differ in their fundamental beliefs?

17. In the debate between Bishop Wilfrid and Abbot Colman, who had the more persuasive argument?

18. Queen Ermenburg is a minor character. The record says little about her, except that she was King Egfrid's second wife and that she despised Bishop Wilfrid. I created a long-term relationship between Queen Ermenburg and King Egfrid. What do you think about her role in the story?

19. Abbess Elfleda spent most of her life at Streoneshalh. Her relationships with churchmen and kings made her an important person in Northumbria. What sort of individual do you think Elfleda was?

20. What sort of person was Bishop Cuthbert?

21. What did you think of King Aldfrid? Why was he so angry with Bishop Wilfrid?

22. Did Bishop Wilfrid get what he wanted? Did anyone?

23. In the final pages, Abbess Elfleda remembers a conversation with Abbess Hildeburg many years before. Abbess Hildeburg credited Queen Ethelberga with King Edwin's conversion and Queen Enfleda with King Oswy's decision to follow the Roman rite. Do you agree? How much influence did these queens actually have?

24. Bishop Trumwine calls Abbess Elfleda a "peacemaker." Do you agree?

25. Which woman was best able to exercise personal agency: Queen Ethelberga, Queen Enfleda, Abbess Hildeburg, Queen Etheldreda, or Abbess Elfleda? Why?

Timeline

616

- King Aethelfrid dies.

617

- King Edwin takes the throne of Northumbria.

624

- King Edwin of Northumbria and Princess Ethelberga of Kent marry.

625

- Archbishop Justus of Canterbury consecrates Paulinus as Bishop of Northumbria.
- Easter – King Edwin survives an assassination attempt.
- Easter – Princess Enfleda is born.
- June 6 – Bishop Paulinus baptizes Princess Enfleda and her household.

626

- King Edwin of Northumbria is victorious over King Cwichelm of Wessex in the Battle of Win Hill and Lose Hill.
- Yule – Coifi destroys Woden's temple at Goodmanham.

627

- Easter – King Edwin, with his family and thanes, is baptized in York.

633

- King Edwin is killed in the Battle of Hatfield Chase.
- Archbishop Paulinus and King Edwin's family flee to Kent.

634

- King Oswald takes the throne of Northumbria and sends for a missionary from Iona.
- Dowager Queen Ethelberga founds Lyminge Abbey.
- Dowager Queen Ethelberga sends Prince Wuscfrea and Prince Yffi to Frankland (year is approximate).
- Archbishop Paulinus becomes Archbishop of Rochester.

635

- Aidan arrives in Northumbria and establishes the Columban church.
- King Oswald defeats Penda of Mercia at the Battle of Heavenfield.

638

- Prince Oswy marries Princess Rieinmelt of North Rheged. Prince Oswy may have been sub-king of the region.

640

- With Abbot Aidan's sponsorship, Abbess Hieu establishes a double monastery at Heretu (Hartlepool).

641

- August 5 – Penda of Mercia kills King Oswald at the Battle of Maserfield.
- August 5 – Prince Oswy becomes King of Northumbria.

643

- King Oswy marries King Edwin's daughter, Princess Enfleda.

645

- Prince Egfrid, son of Queen Enfleda and King Oswy, is born.

647

- Princess Hildeburg takes instruction from Abbot Aidan at Hieu's monastery on the River Wear.
- Queen Enfleda sponsors Wilfrid's entry to Lindisfarne monastery.

649

- Princess Hildeburg becomes Abbess of Heretu.

650

- Penda of Mercia attacks the Northumbrian fortress at Bamburg.
- King Oswy claims Deira.
- August 31 – Abbot Aidan dies.
- Bishop Finan of Lindisfarne baptizes Prince Peada of Mercia before his marriage to Princess Alchfled of Northumbria.

652

- Queen Enfleda sponsors Wilfrid's first pilgrimage to Rome.

654

- King Oswy makes a vow that if he is victorious against Penda of Mercia, he will give his infant daughter, Princess Elfleda, to the church, and will also give ten hides of land for monasteries.

655

- King Penda of Mercia attacks Northumbria.
- November 15 – King Oswy kills Penda at the Battle of Winwaed.
- Prince Peada becomes sub-king of Mercia.
- King Oswy becomes Bretwalda of England.

656

- Easter – King Peada is murdered, allegedly by his wife, King Oswy's daughter Alchfled.

657

- Abbess Hildeburg founds a new double monastery at Streoneshalh (Whitby).

658

- Wilfrid returns to England.

659

- Princess Osthryth, daughter of King Oswy and Queen Enfleda, is born.

660

- Prince Alhfrith, sub-king of Deira, becomes friends with Wilfrid and rejects the Columban rite in favor of the Roman rite.
- Prince Alhfrith, sub-king of Deira, grants Wilfrid the monastery at Ripon.

- Prince Egfrid marries Princess Etheldreda of East Anglia.

664

- The Great Synod is held at Streoneshalh (Whitby).
- Wilfrid is appointed Archbishop of York and travels to Frankland for his consecration.
- Prince Alhfrith leads a revolt against King Oswy and is defeated.
- Prince Egfrid becomes sub-king of Deira.

668

- March 26 – Pope Vitalian consecrates Theodore as Archbishop of Canterbury.

669

- Archbishop Theodore arrives in England.
- Wilfrid returns to Northumbria and acquires monasteries and estates.
- Queen Etheldreda grants Wilfrid land for a monastery at Hexham from her dower lands.

670

- February 15 – King Oswy dies.
- Prince Egfrid becomes king.
- King Egfrid names his brother, Prince Elfwin, sub-king of Deira.

672

- Wilfrid dedicates his rebuilt monastery at Ripon.
- September 26 – Archbishop Theodore presides over a synod at Hertford where Pope Agatho's decision is read.

673

- King Egfrid divorces Queen Etheldreda.
- Queen Etheldreda founds the monastery at Ely.
- Bishop Wilfrid is expelled from York. He goes to Rome to appeal to Pope Agatho.

674

- King Egfrid of Northumbria takes Lindsey from Mercia.

675

- King Wulfhere of Mercia dies fighting King Egfrid. His brother, Prince Ethelred, becomes King of Mercia.

676

- Cuthbert, Abbot of Lindisfarne, moves to Inner Farne to live as a hermit.

677

- King Egfrid has married Ermenburg (date unknown).
- King Egfrid and Bishop Wilfrid quarrel. Bishop Wilfrid is imprisoned and then expelled from Northumbria. He appeals to Pope Agatho.

679

- King Ethelred of Mercia marries Princess Osthryth of Northumbria.
- King Ethelred of Mercia defeats King Egfrid of Northumbria in battle. Prince Elfwin is killed.
- Pope Agatho convenes a council that rules in favor of Bishop Wilfrid's petition.
- September 17 – A synod is held at Hatfield.

680

- Abbess Hildeburg of Streoneshalh (Whitby) dies.
- Princess Elfleda and Dowager Queen Enfleda become co-abbesses at Streoneshalh (Whitby).
- Bishop Wilfrid returns from Rome. King Egfrid doesn't comply with the pope's decision to restore Bishop Wilfrid's ecclesiastical lands and office.

c. 683

- Abbess Elfleda meets Abbot Cuthbert on Coquet Island.

684

- Abbot Cuthbert accepts an appointment as Bishop of Hexham.

685

- March 26, Easter – Bishop Cuthbert is consecrated at York. Bishop Cuthbert exchanges bishoprics with Bishop Eata: Cuthbert becomes Bishop of Lindisfarne and Eata is Bishop of Hexham.
- May 20 – King Egfrid is killed at the Battle of Dun Nechtain in Scotland.
- Queen Ermenburg enters a monastery near Carlisle.
- December 14 – Aldfrid becomes King of Northumbria.

686

- Bishop Wilfrid and Archbishop Theodore reconcile.
- Bishop Wilfrid returns to Northumbria.
- Bishop Cuthbert resigns and departs for Inner Farne.

687

- Bishop Cuthbert dies at Inner Farne and is buried on Lindisfarne.

690

- Archbishop Theodore dies.
- Berhtwald becomes Archbishop of Canterbury.

692

- Bishop Wilfrid and King Aldfrid quarrel. Bishop Wilfrid is banished again and immediately leaves to make his appeal in Rome.

697

- Prince Osred, son of King Aldfrid, is born.
- Mercian nobles murder Queen Osthryth, daughter of King Oswy and Queen Enfleda of Northumbria.

702

- King Aldfrid convenes the Council at Austerfield. The Council upholds Bishop Wilfrid's expulsion. Bishop Wilfrid departs to appeal to the pope.

705

- King Aldfrid of Northumbria summons Abbess Elfleda and conveys his wish to forgive Wilfrid.
- December 14 – King Aldfrid dies at Driffield.
- Prince Osred becomes King of Northumbria.

706

- The Council at Nidd allows Bishop Wilfrid to return to Northumbria.
- King Osred grants monasteries at Ripon and Hexham to Bishop Wilfrid.

709

- Bishop Wilfrid dies at Oundle and is buried at Ripon Abbey.

714

- Abbess Elfleda dies.

716

- King Osred is killed in battle, possibly fighting the Picts.

793

- Vikings attack Lindisfarne.

867

- Vikings control Northumbria.

Glossary Of Names

Acha of Deira–King Aelle's daughter. Married King Aethelfrid of Bernicia, joining Deira and Bernicia, which together became Northumbria.

Aelle–(d. AD 588) Ruled Deira from AD 560 until his death in AD 588.

Aethelfrid–(d. AD 616) Ruled Bernicia c. AD 593–616. In AD 604 he also ruled neighboring Deira, possibly through his marriage to Acha.

Aethelric of Bernicia–(d. AD 572) Fourth ruler of Bernicia (AD 568–572). Father of Aethelfrid, the first king to also rule Deira.

Agilbert–(d.c. AD 675) Present at AD 664 synod held at Streoneshalh representing the Roman party. Retired to Gaul where he consecrated Wilfrid as Bishop of York in AD 664.

Aidan–(d. AD 651) Columban missionary to Northumbria. Abbot of Lindisfarne.

Aethelric of East Anglia–(c. AD 606 to c. 647) Hereswid's husband. Father of King Ealdwulf of East Anglia.

Alchfled–Daughter of King Oswy and his first wife Rieinmelt. Married Peada of Mercia. One child, Koneswid of Mercia.

Aldfrid–(d. AD 705) King of Northumbria AD 685–705. Illegitimate son of King Oswy and Fin of Ireland.

Alhfrith–(AD 630–c. 664) Son of King Oswy and his first wife Rieinmelt. Sub-king of Deira (AD 655–664). Led the Roman party at AD 664 synod at Streoneshalh.

Bertha–(c. AD 565–c. 601) Daughter of Merovingian King Charibert. Queen of Kent. Mother of Ethelberga, Queen of Northumbria, and King Eadbald of Kent.

Breguswid–Wife of King Edwin's brother Hereric. Mother of Hereswid and Hildeburg.

Cadmon–(fl.c. AD 660–684) First Anglo-Saxon poet. Monk at Streoneshalh.

Cadwallon–(d. AD 634) King of Gwynedd AD 625–634. Killed King Edwin of Northumbria at Battle of Hatfield Chase in AD 633.

Cedd–(c. AD 620–664) Bishop of Essex. Led missionaries to Mercia in AD 653. Supported Columban side at AD 664 synod at Streoneshalh.

Coifi–(fl.c. AD 627) Woden's high priest at King Edwin's court. Destroyed shrine at Goodmanham.

Colman–(c. AD 605–675) Bishop of Lindisfarne (AD 661–664). Supported Columban side at synod of AD 664.

Cuthburh of Wessex–(d. AD 718) Sister of King Ine of Wessex. Spouse of King Aldfrid of Northumbria. Founder and Abbess of Wimborne Minster.

Cwenburg of Mercia–First wife of King Edwin of Northumbria. Mother of Prince Osfrid and Prince Eadfrid.

Cwichelm–(d. AD 636) Co-King of Wessex. Involved in assassination attempt on King Edwin's life.

Cyneburg–Wife of Alhfrith, sub-king of Deira. Daughter of Penda of Mercia.

Cynegils–Co-King of Wessex c. AD 611–642. Involved in assassination attempt on King Edwin's life.

Cuthbert–(AD 634–687) Bishop of Lindisfarne AD 684–687.

Dagobert–(c. AD 603–639) Last Merovingian King of Frankland (AD 629–634).

Eadbald–(d. AD 640) King of Kent AD 616–640. Brother of Queen Ethelberga of Northumbria.

Eadfrid–Son of King Edwin of Northumbria and Queen Cwenburg.

Ealdwulf–(AD 640–713) King of East Anglia (AD 662–713). Son of Hereswid and Aethelric of East Anglia.

Ebbe–(AD 615–683) Sister of King Oswald and King Oswy of Northumbria. Abbess of Coldingham Monastery.

Edwin–(AD 585–633) King of Northumbria (AD 616–633). Father of Queen Enfleda of Northumbria. Uncle of Abbess Hildeburg of Streoneshalh and Queen Hereswid of East Anglia. Brother of Prince Hereric.

Egfrid–(c. AD 645–685) King of Northumbria (AD 670–685). Son of King Oswy and Queen Enfleda. Husband of Etheldreda of East Anglia (1) and Ermenburg (2).

Elfleda–(AD 654–713) Daughter of King Oswy and Queen Enfleda. Raised by Abbess Hildeburg. Abbess of Streoneshalh (AD 680–713).

Elfwin–(AD 661–678) Sub-King of Deira. Son of King Oswy and Queen Enfleda.

Emma–(d. AD 642) Queen of Kent. Wife of King Eadbald of Kent.

Enfleda (AD 626–fl.c. 685) Queen of Northumbria. Daughter of King Edwin and Queen Ethelberga. Wife of King Oswy. Mother of King Egfrid of Northumbria, Abbess Elfleda, Queen Osthryth of Mercia, and Elfwin, sub-king of Deira.

Eorpwald–King of East Anglia c. AD 624. Assassinated c. AD 627.

Eostre–Goddess of spring.

Ermenburg–Second wife of King Egfrid of Northumbria.

Eorcenberht–(d. AD 664) King of Kent AD 640–664. Queen Ethelberga's nephew. Queen Enfleda's cousin.

Ethelberga–(AD 601–647) Second wife of King Edwin of Northumbria. Mother of Queen Enfleda of Northumbria. Founder and Abbess of Lyminge.

Ethelbert–(c. AD 550–616) King of Kent AD 589–616. Married Bertha of Merovingia (Frankland). Father of Ethelberga, Queen of Northumbria, and King Eadbald of Kent.

Etheldreda–(c. AD 636–679) First wife of King Egfrid. Divorced AD 672. Founded double monastery at Ely.

Ethelred–(d. AD 704) King of Mercia AD 675–704. Husband of Queen Osthryth. Son of King Penda of Mercia.

Ethelthryd–(No Date. Died in Infancy.) Daughter of King Edwin and Queen Ethelberga of Northumbria.

Eumer – (d. AD 625) Assassin sent by King Cwichelm of Wessex to kill King Edwin.

Fin of Ireland–Had a relationship with King Oswy while he lived on Iona. Mother of King Aldfrid.

Freya–Goddess of love and fertility, among other attributes.

Hereric (d. AD 613)–Brother of King Edwin of Northumbria. Husband of Breguswid. Father of Hereswid and Abbess Hildeburg.

Hereswid–(b. AD 612) Niece of King Edwin of Northumbria. Daughter of Hereric and Breguswid. Sister of Abbess Hildeburg. Married Aethelric of East Anglia. Mother of King Ealdwulf of East Anglia.

Hieu–Founded double monastery at Heretu (Hartlepool). Abbess Hildeburg trained at her daughter monastery on the River Wear.

Hildeburg–(AD 614–680) Niece of King Edwin of Northumbria. Daughter of Hereric and Breguswid. Sister of Hereswid. Abbess at Streoneshalh AD 648–680.

Ida–(d. AD 559) First king of Bernicia (r. AD 547–559).

Lilla–(d. AD 625) King Edwin's thane. Died blocking Eumer's attempt to assassinate King Edwin.

Osfrid–(d. AD 633) Son of King Edwin and Queen Cwenburg. Killed at Battle of Hatfield Chase.

Osred–(AD 697–716) King of Northumbria. Son of King Aldfrid.

Osthryth–(b. AD 659) Daughter of King Oswy and Queen Enfleda of Northumbria. Married Ethelred of Mercia in 679.

Oswald–(AD 604–642) King of Northumbria AD 634–642. Brother of King Oswy. Killed at Battle of Maserfield.

Oswy–(AD 612–670) King of Northumbria AD 642–670. Brother of King Oswald. Husband of Queen Rieinmelt (1) and Queen Enfleda (2). Father of King Aldfrid, Prince Alhfrith, Princess Alhflaed, King Egfrid, Abbess Elfleda, Princess Osthryth, and Prince Elfwin.

Paulinus–(d. AD 644) Roman priest who accompanied Queen Ethelberga to King Edwin's court. Baptized King Edwin at York on Easter, 627.

Peada–(d. AD 656) Son of King Penda of Mercia. Sub-king of Mercia. Married King Oswy's daughter Alhflaed.

Penda–(d. AD 655) King of Mercia AD 633–655. Defeated King Edwin in Battle of Hatfield Chase and King Oswald in Battle Maserfield. Killed by King Oswy in Battle of the Winwaed.

Redwald–(d. AD 624) King of East Anglia AD 599–624. Protected King Edwin and appointed him sub-king of Northumbria.

Rhun–(c. AD 524–?) King of Rheged.

Rieinmelt–(d.c. AD 630) Princess of Rheged. Wife of King Oswy of Northumbria. Mother of Alhfrith and Alhflaed.

Seaxburg–(d. AD 699) Queen of Kent AD 640–664. Abbess of Ely AD 679–699. Sister of Queen Etheldreda of Northumbria.

Theodore of Tarsus–(AD 602–690) Archbishop of Canterbury AD 668–690.

Wilfrid–(AD 633–709) Bishop of York. Supported Roman perspective at synod of AD 664. Frequently clashed with kings of Northumbria.

Woden–God of war

Wuscfrea–(b. AD 629) Son of King Edwin and Queen Ethelberga. Queen Ethelberga sent Prince Wuscfrea and his older brother's son Yffi to King Dagobert in Frankland for protection.

Yffi–Grandson of King Edwin and Queen Cwenburg. Son of Prince Osfrid. Queen Ethelberga sent Yffi and Prince Wuscfrea to King Dagobert in Frankland for protection.

Key to dating abbreviations:

b. "born"

c. refers to *circa*, "about"

d. "died"

d.c "died about"

fl. refers to flourish, a date when the person is known to have been alive

r. "ruled"

Glossary Of Terms

Agrimony – An herb, the leaves and seeds of which Anglo-Saxons used for healing wounds.

Bretwalda – Anglo-Saxon term for rulers who became overlords of most or all of the Anglo-Saxon kingdoms.

Elf-shot – People believed the mysterious onset of an unknown disease was caused by elves shooting arrows called elf-shot into the afflicted people or animals

Giefstol – Anglo-Saxon word for "gift stool," a stool from which a lord distributed wealth as a reward to his followers.

Hide – The Anglo-Saxon term for family. One hide of land was sufficient to support a family. A hide was about 60–120 acres of land, contingent on the quality of the land.

Maythen – Anglo-Saxon name for chamomile.

Pyle – A man who sat at a lord's feet in the hall. His duty was to challenge any claims made by a guest. It would be ungracious for the lord to challenge a guest.

Reeve – General term for a man in charge of royal estates. The reeve managed the estate and farm, administered justice, presided at the popular court, and collected fines.

Scop – Poet. Scops traveled to mead halls to recite or sing poems.

Seneschal – The steward in a great house who oversaw domestic arrangements.

Solstice – The longest day in summer or the shortest in winter.

Somonath – A season coinciding with the month of February, when special
    cakes were placed in the fields before plowing to ensure a plentiful harvest.

Torc – Large, stiff neck ring made of metal, most often gold, either a single
    piece or strands twisted together. Identified the wearer as someone of
    high status.

Valhalla – The Hall of the Fallen where Woden received worthy dead warriors.

Wergeld – The compensation paid to the kindred of a man killed or injured
    in order to prevent a blood feud or war. The price was adjusted according
    to the rank of the injured party.

Witan – A council that advised the king.

Glossary Of Places

Bamburg – Town on the northeast coast of England, seventy-six miles south of Edinburgh. Bamburg was the primary fortress of Northumbrian kings and one of two seats of government. The other was at Yeavering, further inland.

Bernicia – Anglo-Saxon kingdom established in the sixth century with boundaries from the Firth of Forth in the north to the River Tees. The area encompasses modern Northumberland, Durham, Berwickshire, and East Lothian.

Canterbury – Cathedral city located in Kent. Canterbury Cathedral was founded in AD 597 when Pope Gregory the Great sent Augustine to convert King Ethelbert of Kent to Christianity.

Carlisle – Capital of the British kingdom of Rheged. It became part of Northumbria when Princess Rieinmelt of Rheged married Prince Oswy of Northumbria.

Catterick – Village located west of the River Swale in Yorkshire. Site where Bishop Paulinus performed a number of baptisms. Site of the Battle of Catterick in AD 598.

Coldingham – Village in the Scottish Border area. Site of the double monastery founded by Abbess Ebbe.

Coquet Island – An island of about fifteen acres located off the Northumbrian coast. Abbess Elfleda met with Abbot Cuthbert here.

Deira – Anglo-Saxon kingdom. Its area extended from the River Humber in the south to the River Tees in the north. It merged with Bernicia to form the Kingdom of Northumbria.

Driffield – Site of the Anglo-Saxon villa where King Aldfrid died in AD 705.

Dunnichen – Village located north of the Firth of Forth and close to Dunnichen Hill, where the Battle of Dun Nechtain occurred in AD 685. King Egfrid of Northumbria died in the battle.

East Anglia – Anglo-Saxon kingdom established in the seventh century. It included the modern counties of Norfolk, Suffolk, and part of Cambridgeshire, and also the Isle of Ely after Princess Etheldreda married Prince Tondberht.

Ely – The Isle of Ely in East Anglia is fourteen miles northeast of Cambridge. Etheldreda founded Ely Abbey there in AD 673.

Essex – The Kingdom of Essex is south of East Anglia.

Farne Islands – Islands off the eastern coast of Northumberland to the east of Lindisfarne. Both Abbot Aidan and Abbot Cuthbert sought seclusion on Inner Farne.

Goodmanham – Village in East Riding, Yorkshire. Site of Woden's high shrine until AD 627 when Coifi destroyed the temple.

Gwynedd – County in northwest Wales. In AD 633, Cadwallon of Gwynedd and Penda of Mercia conquered Northumbria at the Battle of Hatfield Chase.

Hatfield Chase – Area near the town of Doncaster in northern England. King Edwin was killed at the Battle of Hatfield Chase in AD 633.

Heretu (Hartlepool) – An abbey founded by Abbot Aidan in the seventh century. It was administered first by Abbess Hieu and then by Abbess Hildeburg, AD 649 – 657.

Hexham – Town located south of the River Tyne. Bishop Wilfrid founded Hexham Abbey in AD 674.

Kent – County in southeast England. One of the first areas settled by Anglo-Saxons. In AD 597, St. Augustine converted King Ethelbert to Christianity here.

Lindisfarne – A tidal island off the northeast coast of England, also known as Holy Island. Abbot Aidan established the center of Columban Christianity here.

Lindsey – A district lying between Northumbria and Mercia.

Lyminge – Village in Kent on the southeast coast. Site of Lyminge Abbey founded by Dowager Queen Ethelberga of Northumbria.

Mercia – The Kingdom of Mercia was directly south of Northumbria and centered on the valley of the River Trent in an area known known as the Midlands. Between AD 600 and AD 900, Mercia dominated England south of the River Humber.

Northumbria – The Kingdom of Northumbria was composed of Bernicia and Deira with their boundary at the River Tees, and other conquered areas such as Rheged and Lindsey. At its greatest extent, Northumbria reached from the Firth of Forth in the north to the River Humber, the Peak District, and the River Mersey in the south.

Picts – Tribes north of Northumbria.

Reculver – Village in northeastern Kent.

Rheged – The area of modern Cumbria where Carlisle is located. Rheged came under Northumbrian control before AD 730, probably due to the marriage of Prince Oswy of Northumbria and Princess Rieinmelt of Rheged.

Ripon – City that is the site of Ripon Abbey founded by Bishop Wilfrid in AD 658.

River Humber Estuary – Tidal estuary on the east coast of Northern England. It served as the southern border of Northumbria.

River Thames Estuary – Tidal estuary where the River Thames meets the North Sea.

Rochester – Town in Kent, about thirty miles from London. The Diocese of Rochester is the second oldest in England, after Canterbury.

Sancton – Village in East Riding, Yorkshire; the site of one of the Northumbrian kings' villas.

Streoneshalh (Whitby) – Settlement on the North Yorkshire Coast overlooking the North Sea. The word "Streoneshalh" refers to a fort or tower from a previous Roman settlement on the site. The Vikings renamed the site *Hwitebi*. That name became Whitby, the name still in use today.

Sussex – Kingdom southeast of Kent.

Wessex – One of the earliest Anglo-Saxon kingdoms.

Yeavering – Hamlet in Northumberland on the River Glen near the Cheviot Hills. It was the site of a large seventh-century Anglo-Saxon settlement and the second of two seats of Anglo-Saxon government. The other center was at Bamburg on the coast.

York – Trading center located at the confluence of the rivers Ouse and Foss. Romans founded the city in AD 71. After King Edwin was baptized at York in AD 627, it became the ecclesiastical center of Northern England.

About The Author

Sandra Wagner-Wright holds the doctoral degree in history and taught women's history at the University of Hawai`i for over twenty years. She lives in Hilo, Hawai`i. *Saxon Heroines: A Northumbrian Novel* is her third work of historical fiction.

SANDRA'S BOOKS

Historical Fiction
Two Coins: A Biographical Novel
Rama's Labyrinth: A Biographical Novel

Nonfiction
The Structure of the Missionary Call to the Sandwich Islands 1796-1830:
Sojourners Among Strangers

History of the Macadamia Nut Industry in Hawai`i:
From Bush Nut to Gourmet's Delight

For Beer and the Bible:
One Hundred Years at the Lutheran Church of Honolulu

Edited Journal
Ships, Furs, and Sandalwood:
A Yankee Trader in Hawai`i 1823-1825

CONNECT WITH SANDRA

Website: www.sandrawagnerwright.com
Facebook: facebook.com/SandraWagner-Wright/
Twitter: https://twitter.com/SandraWWright
Pinterest: pinterest.com/sandrawagnerwri
Goodreads: goodreads.com/sandrawagnerwright

* * *